MANTA RAY

By
Lee Charles Daniels

Published by
Lee 1st Publishing
With help from
Midnight Express Books
Email: MEBooks1@yahoo.com

MANTA RAY

By

Lee Charles Daniels

MANTA RAY

Published by:
Lee 1st Publishing

With help from
Midnight Express Books
POBox 69
Berryville AR 72616

MANTA RAY

Contents

FIRST COMMAND

Dropping out of hyper-drive near the moon of Zebra Four, the *Manta Ray* was suddenly and fiercely attacked by fire from the surface of the larger planet below. Caught completely unprepared, Commander Thor ordered *Manta Ray* behind the planet's tiny moon.

"Shields down thirty-one percent," Rio reported as the klaxon sounding 'red alert' sounded loudly throughout the ship.

"Tropy, turn that thing off," Thor ordered.

"Aye, Sir." Red lights flashed all around the bridge, and then dropped to a soft glow.

"Damage report?" Commander Thor requested.

"Doctor Wearing from Sick Bay Two reports several broken bones; no losses. Security reports minor damage to decks seven through twelve. Repair crews are already on it, Sir," Tropy answered.

General Hawk entered the bridge, wiping blood from what appears to be a broken nose. Looking at him from the comm station, Tropy sees his dark brown hair now streaked with silver mussed up and his gold-braided shirt bloodied and disheveled, but still as handsome and striking a figure as he was the first day he entered the *Manta Ray's* Bridge so many years ago.

At six feet one inch and one hundred eighty-seven pounds, he is still without a single ounce of fat; it's no wonder every woman on board looked at him with such awe.

Snapping back to reality, she quickly ordered, "Doctor Murky to the Bridge, Medical Emergency".

"On my way," he responds, as General Hawk waved her request away.

He then asked, "What was that all about?"

Commander Thor replied, "Don't know, Sir. It seems our little secret didn't last very long."

"Obviously!" General Hawk says.

"Tropy, any word from our mining camp?" Thor asked.

"Aye, Sir. They are standing by to be beamed aboard," she replied.

Suddenly and violently the ship is shaken, as though she were kicked by a mule. Lights blinked off and on. Dust clouded the air, and all one could see on the bridge were computer screens lit by their own power source. The night emergency lights flashed once, and then remained on.

Rio called out, "Shields are down to thirty-seven point four percent."

"Bridge to Engineering," Thor called over the ship's intercom.

"Manado here, Sir."

"Mr. Manado, how long will it take to beam the mining party and their minerals aboard?" Thor asked.

"Sir! We can't beam anything aboard with the shields up. And with the size of that weapon down there, we daren't let the shields down to do so," the Chief Engineer explained.

Thor told him, "Then get a landing party ready. Take as many shuttlecrafts as needed."

'Aye aye, Sir.' Mr. Manado replied.

"Let's find out who or what is down there," General Hawk said. "Put Lieutenant Michaels on this. He seems suited for a little ground work."

"Lieutenant Michaels to the Bridge," Thor ordered.

"Aye aye, Sir. On my way," Michaels replied over the comm. Doctor Murky entered the bridge, and Tropy pointed towards General Hawk.

Doctor Murky ran his medical scanner over Hawks damaged face, as the blood continued to flow freely from his now black and blue swollen nose.

Finding no broken bones, he gave Hawk a shot to help stem the bleeding, mixed with a mild pain reliever. "Nothing broken, Sir. You'll have a little more swelling for a few hours, nothing more than that," the Doctor told him.

"Thank you, Doctor," General Hawk said.

Commander Thor asked of Commander O'ho, "Can you get a fix on who's firing at us?"

"Yes, Sir. It seems to be an automated setup and highly accurate," O'ho pointed out as the ship was hit by another blast.

Grabbing hold of a seat, Commander Thor said, "That, Mr. O'ho, you didn't have to tell me."

"Tropy, let's have a look-see. Set the front view-set to a downward approach. Good, now pinpoint the area of ground. Bring it up closer," Thor requested.

The compound was surrounded by a high fence that was surrounded by a heavily wooded area thick with oak, pine, and scrub brush. There was a single road leading into the compound with no guard on duty at the gate, and no movement within the compound itself.

Lieutenant Michaels entered the bridge and reported to Commander Thor just as the view-set shows a clear, but smaller area of the compound with pockmarks all around it and states for the benefit of his shipmates, "That's no Augean outpost!"

"Are you sure of that Lieutenant?" Commander Thor asked.

"Yes Sir. I've been on raiding parties often enough to know one when I see one," Chic told him.

Chic Michaels had indeed been on several raids over his career, and he was instrumental in securing several needed pieces of equipment for two transport ships housing more than ten thousand people. Without these parts, both ships would have had to be abandoned because they could no longer generate enough oxygen for their water supply and for breathing.

It took him and nine other people going through eleven warehouses on eight Augean planets just to find the parts that were needed.

Six of Chic Michaels closest friends were lost during those three raids. Mike Michaels, his father gave his life defending the shuttlecraft Chic was piloting on the return trip.

Studying the view-set, General Hawk walked over to the men. Commander Thor also joined the General at the front view-set, soon to be joined by the Lieutenant where all three men began to study the makeup of the compound.

Lieutenant Michaels, standing a few feet behind them calmly waited for someone to speak. When The Hawk does, he says, "I believe this to have been manmade. Its composite looks very familiar for some reason." Turning to Commander Tropy, the General asks, "Are there any human life forms down there?"

Looking somewhat puzzled, she turned back to her console, hit a few buttons and asked, "How'd you know?"

About the same time as Tropy asked her question, O'ho said from the Science Station, "About two miles from the compound, there seems to be a major city or village of thousands of humanoids."

"Are you sure they are human?" Commander Thor asked.

Tropy answered before Commander O'ho could. "Aye, Sir. I'm trying to hail them now. And Sir there is another village with thousands more not far from the first one. They are definitely human."

O'ho says, "Commander, there are several very small satellites in low orbit about the planet!"

Lieutenant Michaels asked of no one, "Then why are they shooting at us? This is a human vessel."

Mr. O'ho answered by saying, "That is an automated outpost. They may not even be aware that we are up here."

"But what are human beings doing way out here? They aren't a part of our people," Chic said. "That I am sure of; and why an armed outpost?"

He continued talking out loud and working through this problem with verbal thoughts. "The Augean are the most obvious reasons for such firepower this far out. This might even have been a planet that was seeded eons ago by our forefathers."

"Well gentlemen, let's find out," Hawk said.

"Tropy, any response to your hails?" asked Thor.

"None yet," she told him.

"Keep trying," Hawk ordered.

"Aye, Sir."

Turning to Lieutenant Michaels, Thor said, "I want you to escort our cargo shuttles to the moon and pick up our people and their cargoes. Once that is under way, I want you to proceed to the planet, land a few miles from that populated area and have a look-see. Approach, but do not enter. Be aware that since they have that much firepower pointed out here, there might be traps set all around them for protection."

"Aye aye, Sir. I'll take Blue and Orange squadrons with me and Blue will accompany me to the planet as Orange will be left to escort the shuttles to and from the moon. We will exercise the utmost caution, Sir." That said, Lieutenant Michaels turned and left the bridge.

ANTIOCH

Stepping out of the lift, Lieutenant Michaels quickly took in all movement and activities by the people around him in the large bay area.

Stacked one upon another and against the outer wall were Tigers and Tiger Sharks, separated only by the pallets that shuttle each to their launch areas, or to their respective holding areas. To one side he saw men arming Tigers with new torpedoes, preparing these ships for routine patrols once this mission has been completed.

Commander Tropy had ordered all Blue and Orange squadrons to report to the bay for assignments.

Entering the S. and R. (snack and rest) areas he found most of his people gathered. No member of Orange squadron was in sight yet.

Off to his right he finally saw Second Lieutenant Johnny Raye, "Raye Raye" to his friends. Coming up with him was Ensign Richards, Brooks, Red Ferns, Lieutenant Glycolic, Harolds, and Writer.

Johnny Raye, a dark red-skinned Capricorn, had the largest smile and the warmest black eyes ever seen. He was the squad leader for Orange squadron. But, for this excursion, he would only be in charge of the shuttles safety after Blue squadron left for the planet's surface.

Once everyone was seated in the S. and R., Chic quickly assigned each person his or her duties. Having worked with each other numerous times, there were few questions. He ordered them to strap in and said, "Clear Sailing" to each, meaning he wished each a safe return.

He enjoyed working with these individuals. They were sure of themselves, and knew how to get the job done. He never had to check behind any of them.

Buckling into his own Tiger, Chic Michaels completed his pre-flight check and took a long look around at his people to be sure they too had completed their pre-flight check list. This was his team, "Blue Squadron". To his left was Zeke, Second Lieutenant Zeke Fiveline his lifelong classmate and friend. How many women had they loved and shared? Too many, yet never enough.

Alongside of Zeke were Grammer, Owens, Robyn, and Sable. On his right was Buster. It was funny in a way, Buster was always his right hand man. It would be hard to choose one friend over the other. He felt close to each man having been raised and schooled with both. Each man had a special quality that set him apart from the other. Beside Buster were Stykes, Leona, and Van Dam. He remembered how lucky he felt to have been named leader of Blue Squadron. He knew any of these fine officers could have been named and done just as good a job as he had done. Chic knew his being chosen was a fluke, having had just one thousandth of a percent higher score in his final overall exam. He felt sure this was the only reason he was selected as its leader.

Unknown to him were several factors that his modesty would never allow him to openly acknowledge. One was the fact that he was a natural born leader.   There was also the fact that he was quick to grasp situations and faster to evaluate them. This gave him the ability to make sound decisions and was an encouraging factor for his teammates. He was able to function on his own while at the same time he was a strong team player and an effective leader.

While he set high standards for himself, each of his teammates worked their asses off to avoid being the one who wouldn't or couldn't hold up their end. Chic would, without knowing, challenge them to reach higher and more solid ground.

Chic Michaels did not wait for things to happen. He had a way of making things happen when he felt they should. Yet, he was the one who retained total control of those happenings; he would always praise his teammates for simply getting things done. When it had been him all along leading them through every step without their knowing they had been led.

First Lieutenant Chic Michaels was truly a born leader, accepting responsibility as though it was his second nature.

He would leave Johnny Raye and Orange squadron to secure the cargo for the return trip and to safeguard the shuttles on return trips for additional cargo, passengers, or anything that couldn't be left behind.

Blue squadron had other responsibilities and new ground to cover. He couldn't wait!

They lifted off and were just clear of the flight deck's door when all were knocked haywire from the blast the *Manta Ray* had taken. She got another direct hit to her engineering section just as she dropped shields letting both Blue and Orange squadrons leave the safety of the big ship.

Several Orange Tigers and two of his own Blue Tiger Sharks were vaporized instantly. They never knew what hit them.

Clearing the flight deck, Chic knew as he was making his report to Commander Thor that they needed to reach the planet's surface before any more deaths occurred. He didn't have time to mourn and ordered all remaining Tigers and their shuttles to proceed to the small moon's surface.

He took notice that both Van Dam's and Owens' ships were lost in the attack on the *Manta Ray*. He felt a kindred to both of their families and it would be hard to explain their loss.

Orange squadron was also his responsibility while on this mission, and he would have to write letters to their families as well.

He would also visit with each, giving comfort where he could and support where it was needed. But that would have to wait until they returned to the fleet in a little more than eight days.

Landing at the mining installation went without further mishap. Once he had assigned the task of loading the shuttles, he cautioned about entering and leaving the shuttle bays, keeping a greater distance between ships and not requesting the shields to be dropped until the last millisecond, then landing as quickly as safety would allow.

Satisfied, he ordered the remaining Blue team back to their Tigers after going over what he had seen on the view-set. He hoped he had a good enough plan to put the laser cannon out of commission quickly. But first, he had to get his team planet-side intact.

Flying a ship, any ship, in space is not the same experience as trying to fly in an atmosphere of a planet. In space, you have no wind shear and no clouds to speak of. There is no rain, or hail. There are no weather changes, or bright sunlight to blind you.

Also, in space there is no upside down, and if a flyer becomes disoriented he simply comes to a dead stop and then starts from that point.

While most of his team had flown in different types of atmospheres and on planets before, it was a rarity. Being blinded by sunlight, while at the same time being buffered by wind and other abnormalities not found in deep space, makes for mistakes they could not afford.

Chic hoped that his warnings and concerns would be remembered and heeded.

Leaving the tiny moon behind, Blue squadron took the longest route to the blue green planet below them. Not wanting to bring anymore destruction from being fired upon by whoever it was on the surface.

Entering the planets upper atmosphere with its thin cold air, they could easily feel the bone chilling cold right through their heavily sealed flight suits. They continued to scan for signs of life. They soon found dozens, and then hundreds of signs and all were animals. There still were no signs of man or machines on their long range scanners.

Bearing northwest towards a beautiful sunrise, there were thousands of confusing signals which Chic thought could be human in form. But there were no cities, towns, or villages along the route Hawk and Thor had chosen for them.

Ducking down through a series of thunder clouds brought his team about two miles West Northwest of the edge of the small village chosen for this look-see, and about three miles from the killer weapons compound. The small ships were battered, but there were no mishaps as they left the dark skies behind them.

Not knowing what type of radar systems the inhabitants might have, Chic found a small wooded area to land his ships in.

Disembarking, Chic and the landing party, tri-corders and hand phasers at the ready, started off in the direction of the smaller village's higher ground which Chic hoped would allow his people a vantage point where they could see without being seen.

The grass beneath their feet was lush and long, reaching close to the knee. It was blue in color. There were pines, evergreens, and a scattering of oak, all giving a graceful amount of shade to the many animals that must live here Chic thought to himself. The landscape had little underbrush with only clumps along the outer fringes of a more dense forest. The air smelled clean and scented, with just a hint of a breeze.

Chic felt he could easily put his career behind him just to live freely on such a world as this. And in a way, he envied those who did live on such a beautiful planet. He had never seen such large birds as those flying overhead as carefree as a bird should be. Their colors were blinding to the sight and he felt lucky just to be able to view them in their natural habitat.

Starting off in the direction the tri-corder showed the smaller village to be, he hoped they would find a little higher ground than that which they were now on. He wanted to be able to see the people without being seen.

Approaching the crest of the wooded knoll, Chic brought them to a halt, allowing them to rest and eat while he went on to scout ahead.

Peering over what he thought would be the last knoll before he would see the small village, he stepped out from behind a crop of trees. Chic was suddenly hit by a projectile fired without so much as a whisper. The projectile entered his upper right shoulder with such force he was flung around while flying backwards through the air into the trees he had just stepped out of. He now knew pain like none other in his short life.

All motion seemed to come to a complete stop, and then started forward at the slowest possible speed.

Chic saw himself being lifted off the ground, turning clockwise one turn and then another. Chic never heard the slightest sound, nor did he see anything around him. He thought he must have blinked for just a second and never saw the ground rise up to hit him.

HIDDEN HUNTER

She stood in her father's kitchen sipping a cold glass of crystal clear water as she continued to daydream. It was early afternoon and she was alone in the house with her thoughts. Psalm was twenty years old, and a recent graduate of the village's oldest university which was well over two thousand years old. She found she enjoyed her studies and found in them an escape from her otherwise boring lifestyle. She always got more out of a book than did any of her friends who were always after her to join them in some activity. She would more often than not beg off so that she could sit in on some of her father's council meetings which luckily were mostly held in her father's front living room, almost every night of the week.

While a student at the university, Psalm took courses in Political Science as a mandate. She also majored in the Science of Minerals and Metallurgy where she was instrumental in the fabrication of several new lightweight metals now used in ground vehicles.

She enjoyed her studies and hoped to take up some new courses when the new school year started unless she decided to take up teaching. She had requested teaching a new course about the forefathers of their little world and how they became stranded on this little island in the stars. How their ship, a Star-cruiser, had been sent out from their home worlds to seed unknown parts of the Galaxy. While each race chose volunteers for these seedings, only certain cultures could survive together. Each brought with them animal life and seedlings from all the known worlds to grow once they had reached suitable planets. Also of how they became stranded here on this one planet instead of the fifty that had been planned, and how they became one race of many cultures.

During her younger life when her mother and father were alive, they would spend hours telling and retelling stories they had heard from their parents and grandparents. Both had been teachers, and had, between them, written hundreds of books detailing the stories about past lives on several of the stars that shined in the night skies.

Her mother's family was known as Vulcans, and her father's grandparents were Nethevans. For many centuries the two cultures had fought dozens of wars; each side capturing thousands of prisoners, making slaves of most. Some of the women were made to serve as concubines and a new race grew out of those unions. By the time the wars ended, there were few differences between the two cultures and they became close friends and trading partners. Soon they became dependent upon one another for survival.

Psalm had read and memorized every word of those wonderful books. But there were also thousands of stories that had never made it into a book. These stories were related to her by her parents, grandparents, and the grandparents of the friends she had grown up with. But her fondest wish and dream was to return to the stars, "Some day," she always told herself, "I'll find a way".

She loved to hear the stories her grandfather would tell which his grandfather had gotten from his. Stories of great flying ships, some as big as a city. Starcruisers they were called by many, carrying hundreds to the distant planets where they were to colonize each planet into new and wondrous worlds.

She would visit the great Libraries in the Capital City and watch the old discs of strange machines that flew from one point of light in the dark skies to another at speeds she couldn't even imagine.

When she asked her grandfather and father why they had no such machines today, they would smile at her and say, "We have everything we need right here. We don't need to go spreading ourselves over large areas of our world." Then they would ask if she remembered her history lessons of the cultures of Antioch. How on every one of their home worlds there had been fights and wars where one culture would fight against other cultures or where one religion would make war on another, and all for no apparent good reason.

They would place their hands over hers and say, "One day, we will be forced to expand our own cultures. Can you not wait until then?"

Psalm would ask. "Do you believe that they will ever return for us?"

Her grandfather would patiently explain that the people of Antioch fell through a hole in space. "Our home worlds don't know where we are," he would tell her, "We don't even know where we are. We have charted all the known star systems in this universe and can't find 'Sol' anywhere. Perhaps one day when our world reaches its capacity we might then be able to afford the men and women it would take to go looking for our past. Or maybe our old home worlds will continue to reach out until they find us again. For now, we are too few to go wandering about the stars. And besides, Pumpkin, we have no flying ships, even if we desired to go looking. And where would we start looking? Have you thought of that?"

Finishing her drink, Psalm put her glass on the sink heading for her bedroom to change. It wouldn't do for her to wear a lightweight sundress into the woods.

Entering her room, she slipped out of her dress and lay it on the bed.

She sighed to herself and stepped out of her panties. Reaching into a drawer, she pulled out a pair of heavyweight underwear. After stepping into them she pulled out a bra and hooked it into place. She then pulled out a pair of heavy socks, tossing them onto her quilted bedspread.

She stepped to her closet and removed her hunting habit. Pulling up her pants, she carried her top to the bed and flopped down, put on her top and buttoned it up.

She put on her socks and slipped into the boots her grandfather had given her on her last birthday just before he passed away. Standing now, she looked out over the balcony, enjoying the peaceful view of the Blue Mountains as they stretched to kiss the midday sky. The deep blue forest reaching into the depths of the heavens takes her breath away. With a sigh of satisfaction she headed for her father's den.

Entering the paneled room she stopped to gaze at the beautiful collections of her father's books. This has always been her favorite room of the house. Her father's desk is large and made of a wood he called mahogany, a precious wood grown only on Earth. Where it came from on Earth he doesn't know, but he thought it probably was grown and harvested in the America's Tropics.

At the desk she opened a drawer and removed the keys to the gun cabinet.

Opening the chest where the guns are kept she picked up her wrist communicator and placed it on her wrist. She then pulled open another drawer containing ammunition and stuffed a couple of handfuls into her pockets.

Reaching past a dozen assault rifles and some laser guns she finds her own specially made lightweight rifle. Taking it to the desk she disassembled it. As she reassembled it she carefully examined each part for wear and wiped away any excess gun oil.

Satisfied, she passed through   the front living room leaving a message for her father informing him that she was going into the woods to hunt and she would return around sundown.

Psalm loved the walks in the forest. She felt at home in the surrounding woods with its many creatures that sped by her and she took pleasure in those that she knew remained hidden from her view.

She was reminded of the fact that there had been very few animals on this planet when the forefathers first got here and that most all of the animals except the manbear was an Earth animal. Even the insects were from Earth. The ants, beetles, butterflies, and even the earthworms were brought here and now thrived. She thought to herself, "How beautiful Earth must be."

Reaching her carefully hidden hunting blind, she quickly set herself up for an afternoon of relaxation and reading. Her father and her grandfather had long ago built several hunting blinds and this was her perfect getaway.

She shouldered her rifle with its scope and adjusted her sights as she slowly looked around. Through the sights her eyes were drawn to a movement at the edge of a crop of oak trees. She scanned past the site and, as she was taught by her father, she brought the scope back to bear on the tree line. Suddenly she sees a manbear staring straight at her. She quickly chambered a round, took aim and fired. Then, quickly, she chambered another round. She checked to see if her target was down in case she needed to fire another round. The target was down and not moving but she held her breath and waited another minute and checked again.

Believing now that she had shot a manbear, Psalm readied herself to fire again, not wishing to leave a wounded animal to suffer.

Leaving the blind, Psalm crept up on her victim. Not seeing its features hidden in the brush she silently came closer. Now, she could see its markings clearly; it had black striped arms, black and purple striped backside with red blood leaking from the wound high in its shoulder.

Something was wrong here . . . . Very Wrong! Psalm had been taught as a young girl that all of nature's animals bled a dark blue blood. She knew that only humans bleed red blood. By all the saints!   What was a man doing dressed as a manbear and in the woods that everyone knew they hunted in.

Without going closer she knew that she had made a mistake. Psalm opened her wrist communicator in an effort to contact her father. Before she could speak a strange voice spoke, "Zeke here."

Now, she was totally confused, thinking that her father must have a visitor and that he had answered her call. Psalm said, "1 have just shot a man by mistake and he is bleeding. I thought that he was a manbear because he was dressed to look like a manbear. I think he is still alive, but he needs medical attention immediately. I did not bring a med-kit with me."

Zeke, somewhat confused by this strange voice reacted in a cautious manner asking her to describe the victim's clothing.

Psalm says, "Black clothing with black and blue thin stripes covering his arms and black and purple vee stripes on his backside."

Looking at Leona, Zeke thought she could be describing any one of them. With a sinking feeling in his gut, Zeke asked as calmly as he could where exactly she was.

Robyn took her tri-corder out and got a reading of just over two thousand yards from their position. She showed the readings to Zeke.

Zeke, with his team gathered around him headed off at a trot to find their commander and friend.

Cresting a small knoll they saw a girl bending over a figure lying face down on the ground behind some heavy brush. They could not see much more than his shoulders. But they all knew...

Looking up and over her shoulder, Psalm saw a group of people dressed the same as the man she had mistakenly shot coming at her. She stood aside to let them assist their friend.

Quickly running to Chic's side, Zeke and Robyn gently turned their friend over. Leona opened her med-scanner and slowly ran it over Chic's shoulder.

Psalm now got her first look at the man she had shot. His relaxed and now pale face was topped with coal black hair. It was all but shaved at the sides, and was just an eighth of an inch longer on the top. Even closed, she could picture strong sensitive eyes. He sported broad but not very high cheek bones and a pencil thin sensual mouth.

She was caught up in the strength she saw in his muscular chest and shoulders. She was relieved to see his chest rise and fall rhythmically. His slim waist showed that he took extra measures to keep himself fit.

She deeply regretted the fact that she had shot first without getting a better look and now she felt totally helpless as she looked on hoping that these people would be able to save his life.

Remembering now that she was only a short distance from her home, she said, "My name is Psalm Wolfe and my house is only a short distance. I can get him medical attention if you can help me get him there and if you'll allow me to."

Robyn said to Zeke, "The best I can do here is to wrap the wound and give him a tri-shot to ward off any infections. Moving him to a safer area is the best idea."

Zeke, taking charge, tells Robyn, "Bandage him as best as you can for transport."

Turning to Buster and Grammer he orders, "Ready a stretcher as fast as you can."

Soon they were on their way, Robyn and Psalm in the lead clearing any brush that might impede their progress.

While not wanting to identify themselves to this young woman, Zeke could not forget the mission at hand. He asked Psalm, "How many people live in this area?"

"Around one hundred and fifty thousand, I should think," she told him.

Just as she was finishing her statement, there was a tremendous rushing of air, and then there was a bright blue-white beam of high energy that shot into the late afternoon sky.

"What in the name of all that is holy is that?" asked Lieutenant Sable.

"Oh, that's our weapons compound. It shoots down comets and meteorites so they won't fall on our town again," Psalm explained.

Zeke replied, "You say it shoots down comets and meteorites? Who mans it?"

"Nobody anymore," Psalm said. "We set it on automatic and just maintain it whenever it needs it. It doesn't shoot very far out and we are thankful that it does such a good job for us."

Robyn asked, "Does it ever shoot down any ships?"

Psalm glances back at her and said, "You mean flying ships?"

"Yes", said Robyn. "Like space ships or airplanes?"

Psalm chuckled and said, "Now you know that's just an old fable. I mean, have you ever seen a ship that could fly? I mean really fly?" Looking about her, Psalm began to see just how silly and childish she sounded.

Ignoring the question, Zeke asked, "Do you have the means to turn that thing off?"

"Why would we want to do that?" She said. "But yes, I suppose it can be turned off from the city or from the site."

Zeke held up his hand and stopped his little group. He turned to Psalm and addressed her, "If I were to tell you it was a matter of life and death, could you help us to have that weapon turned off for a short period?"

Psalm said, "You're serious, aren't you?"

"Very!" He told her flatly.

"My house is just beyond these trees," Psalm nodded in the direction of her home and continued, "I will see what my father says. He is the District Voice and if you can convince him that there is a good enough reason, I am sure that he will be willing to listen to what you have to say."

The members of the landing party were awed by this new experience. Having been raised aboard a spaceship and although a few of them had made landfall on moons or small planets, none were prepared for the sights, sounds, smells and the feel of this lush planet.

They continued and though there was an air of emergency in their every step, they stared at the wonders around them.

As they came out of the brush, they approached a small stream which was spanned by a beautifully ornate oriental bridge. It was gracefully arched and had hand-carved handrails. Clearly, a work of art!

As they passed over the stream, they could not help but to see the clear waters below, or the golden fishes swimming through it.

Having crossed the stream they were met with a spectacular sight. Ahead of them lay a broad, well manicured lawn the likes of which they had never seen before except in pictures. The lawn displayed a wide variety of carefully spaced fruit trees, of which they had never seen or tasted. Most were still in blossom and gave off a heady scent, both sweet and compelling.

As they passed they took in the sights and aromas of each new assault on their senses. The heady scent of blossoming pear, cherry, orange and apple trees caused all to gasp in delight. They passed a garden plot with assorted flowers.

Leona cupped a delicate rose bud in her hand and said, "My God! I've never seen such beauty."

Psalm remarked, "That's just a rose. Wait till you see my dad's orchids!"

Continuing on, Leona said, "I've heard of them, but thought them to be extinct."

Off to their left was row upon row of a home grown vegetable garden. It had about a dozen rows of different types of fresh vegetables. The ripe red tomatoes were closest to the area where Psalm brought them out of the woods.

While they didn't stop because of their wounded charge, Leona saw string beans growing on several bushes; they were both yellow and green. Next in another row were red bell peppers, squash, cucumbers, and about twenty heads of lettuce. Further down the rows were other types she thought she recognized, but only from pictures — many of them long extinct in the fleet.

The lawns were lush and springy to the step. Deeper into the backyard they passed an area of compost. She remembered what it was because of the smell. Next to the compost were wild mushrooms that had clear white and orange caps on the north side in the shade. Scattered around the big yard were several smaller out-buildings with flowers budding.

In other areas were shrubs of azaleas and carnations, and in the bright sunlight were beautiful gladiolas with their sword shaped leaves and snowy, various colors.

In another area was a rock garden with other types of blue and red/white flowers in full bloom.

Not one member of the landing party missed taking in all as they passed through the heavenly scented garden.

Lieutenant Sable asked Psalm, "Does everyone here grow their own vegetables?"

"No. My Grandfather started this garden when my Mother was a child. He had a thing for home grown vegetables. It was my mother who started the flowers. My dad has kept everything going and growing since her death. We have fresh cut flowers in the house and eat the veggies. They're a lot better tasting than those sold in the stores.

They now approached the house which was built in the style of an old Scottish Inn. Its cut biscuit-rock base was topped with rich, red brick and its wooden trim was of rough-cut un-milled lumber. There was an open patio before them and a heavily screened in porch protected the house's rear sliding glass doors.

Entering the porch, Psalm called out to her father and a spry gentleman opened the sliding door. When he saw the stretcher being carried, he opened his communicator and called the medical center. "This is Edward Wolfe. I'm teleporting an injured person. Please stand by."

Robyn stepped forward and said, "I'll go with Chic since I have his biomedical scans."

Psalm introduced her father by saying, "These people need to speak to you on an urgent matter. I think I should go with the man I shot."

The stretcher was placed on the transporter's pedestal and with a twinkle of multicolored lights, Chic and his two escorts were whisked from the room.

Zeke and the remainder of the landing party were relieved knowing that Chic would now get the care he needed.

Within the great-room where they were now standing, Zeke noted Edward Wolfe's expression of puzzlement as he led them to a large walnut table upon which sat a crystal case filled with fresh cut flowers of various types he had seen in the yard.

As the elder Mr. Wolfe seated himself at the head of the table, Zeke and his team took a seat. Edward Wolfe turned to Zeke and said, "Now, young man, what's this about my daughter shooting your friend and what is this urgent matter you speak of?"

Zeke, knowing that one more blast from that weapon could very well destroy the *Manta Ray*, decided to cut to the chase.

He began by introducing each of his party and went on to inform Mr. Wolfe of the accidental shooting of Chic, whom his daughter Psalm had mistaken for a manbear. He explained that they were a landing party from the U.F.D.F. *Manta Ray*. He went on to explain his belief that their laser-cannon was tracking and firing at the *Manta Ray*, a space-faring Starcruiser.

Mr. Wolfe said, "You say you are spacemen, okay, but where are the ships that you came here with? I have heard of such things, but none have been seen on this planet since our forefathers left us here over two thousand years ago."

"Sir, with all due respect, we have left our crafts out of sight and it is against our laws to interfere with any species on an inhabited planet. However, due to the dire circumstances, we felt that a direct approach was justified. We also did not wish to disable your weapon, thereby perhaps leaving you and your people defenseless."

Seeing the urgency of the situation, Mr. Wolfe stood and crossed the room to a Com-Station. As he activated the system a view-set flicked into to life and at his request several men appeared before him. He intoned, "I am the Voice of all the people."

"You are the Voice of all the people," they responded.

He turned to the table indicating those seated at it. "We have guests with us today and under my authority I am deactivating the laser-cannon at our weapons compound. It will remain inactive for just a short time."

The group on the screen spoke in unison, "You are the Voice of all the people. The cannon is deactivated."

"Thank you," said Mr. Wolfe. "Please be kind enough to attend a special meeting at my home as soon as you can."

"We will arrive momentarily," came the reply.

Zeke said, "Mr. Wolfe, I should contact my Commander."

"I'm sorry, of course," Mr. Wolfe said.

Zeke spoke into his wrist communicator, "Zeke to Commander Thor."

"Thor here, Lieutenant, where is Lieutenant Michaels?"

"Lieutenant Michaels has been accidentally wounded and I am now in charge of the landing party. The laser cannon has now been deactivated, Sir."

"Very good, Lieutenant." Thor then added, "If you will kindly give Commander Tropy the coordinates, we'll have Lieutenant Michaels beamed directly to sick-bay."

"Thank you Sir, but the Lieutenant is being cared for in a hospital planet-side. With me I have a representative of this planet and if Commander Tropy will tune her communicator to three two point five, you should be able to have visual."

"Stand by Lieutenant," Commander Tropy said.

Mr. Wolfe, still standing nearby, reactivated his comm station and said, "I am the Voice of all the people. How may I help you?"

The view-set beside Mr. Wolfe came to life to show a view of the bridge. Commander Thor was seated in the command chair with General Hawk and Captain Adams on either side.

PSALM

Zeke repeated the introductions and said, "Mr. Wolfe offers his apologies for any damage incurred resulting from the planet's protective measures. He has offered any materials that may be needed for repairs and in addition he has placed the planet's four hospitals at our disposal."

Now arriving on the platform behind the Lieutenant were members of Mr. Wolfe's Council. Mr. Wolfe introduced each as they stepped down.

Councilman Freeman, the Minister of Health, directed the first question to Commander Thor. "We assume that you are of Oriental descent?"

"You are correct sir, I am one-half Oriental," Thor replied. "My father was ambassador to Earth where he met my mother; however, I was born in the Barrier of the Delta systems on Bapaa."

Materializing behind the group, Psalm stepped down from the transporter and put her arm through her father's. "This is my daughter, Psalm."

Councilman Pochin said, "We too are descendants of Sol."

"Orion! As well as others," Commander Thor commented.

Mr. Wolfe said, "On Antioch, we are of mixed descendants, but all are considered human. No one part is thought to be less important than his neighbor."

There was a short silence into which General Hawk spoke.

"Would you and the Council Members care to join us for a dinner aboard the *Manta Ray* Mr. Wolfe?" He added as an afterthought, "I would think we would have many things to discuss."

Commander Thor was thinking to himself, "We do indeed have many things to discuss."

Having the very same thoughts, Mr. Wolfe responded, "That is very kind of you considering the hostile welcome your landing party received, but it remains that we have no flying machines here and I don't relish the thought of teleporting over such a long distance at my age."

Commander Thor offered, "We would be more than willing to provide you and your party with transportation to and from the *Manta Ray.*"

Seeing the obvious delight within his daughter's eyes, as well as the approval and questions of his fellow councilman, Mr. Wolfe accepted.

"Lieutenant Zeke, you and Blue Squadron will serve as our ambassador and will be the escort for Mr. Wolfe and his party. I will be sending down four shuttle craft and a pilot for Lieutenant Michaels' Tiger," Commander Thor said.

"Aye, Sir," Zeke said. The view-set went blank.

Thus was the first contact between Antioch and the *Manta Ray.*

After learning their leader was in stable condition, Zeke and the other members of the landing party went on to ask and answer many questions before the shuttles arrived.

Psalm was very excited over the prospect of flying up to a real Starship. However, she still had to explain the events leading up to her shooting of the young officer.

"I had gone to one of my favorite hunting blinds to enjoy some time alone. I also enjoy bringing home a bit of game; usually a rabbit or two and perhaps an occasional deer. There are, living on Antioch in the deep forest, large swift and dangerous creatures known as manbears. They are called manbears because they resemble man in all too many ways, feature wise that is. Most are well over seven feet tall. They have hides that are short haired, and have black and blue vertical stripes. They are so dangerous we are taught to shoot first without hesitation - that is if we are given a chance.

"Should a manbear pick up your scent, he will always kill. He is able to cross open spans in less than a heartbeat and attack without the slightest sound.

"When the officer stepped from behind that tree he appeared to be a manbear searching out my scent on the breeze."

"Manbears", the elder Mr. Wolfe interjected, "are the most feared animals in the forest. Its hide is too thin for use and carries a foul odor. While we seldom see one in the forest, many a good hunter has met his end by being ripped apart by its huge claws and razor sharp teeth. They feed on our livestock and other farm animals, leaving nothing behind but the bones."

Zeke addressed the tearful and beautiful young woman, "It's plain to see this was an unfortunate occurrence and that you carry no blame. Do not harbor guilt for something beyond your control.

"Speaking for the *Manta Ray*," Zeke said, "We will welcome you as one of the many citizens of your planet."

Psalm, while very much wanting to see her first Starship felt that she should forgo the dinner and remain with the young man she had accidentally shot. She felt a need to be there when he awoke so she could explain her remorse for the tragic accident. She then excused herself in order to change clothes and return to the hospital.

The only thing Chic Michaels could remember was extreme pain in his right shoulder and then the sensation of twisting and turning in the air. He never even saw the ground that rose up to kiss him.

He vaguely remembered voices, voices that he did not know or recognize. Then as time passed, there were many pinpricks all over his body. Then there was the soothing hum of machines which he thought were in the sick bay aboard the *Manta Ray*. These machines brought him dreams. In one dream he was sitting in a small boat on a large lake. It was early dawn and there were a few stars visible along with a light fog that hovered at the surface of the water waiting patiently to greet the morning sun.

Chic held a fishing rod in his hands and suddenly there was a powerful tug on his line. Chic felt the big fish fighting for its life and freedom.

Chic was not alone, but his companion never looked his way. He too sat holding his own fishing pole.

Chic wondered at that point who his companion was and though he thought he had had this dream many times in his life, he had never come to know who this mysterious person was.

Chic had never been in a boat. He had also never been fishing nor had Chic ever been on any planet where there might have been a lake such as the one he was now floating upon, and what in the world was a fishing rod?

Opening his eyes for the first time, Chic saw bright lights overhead. Shifting his sight slightly to his left, he saw Robyn seated in a chair. He then became aware that he was in some kind of hospital bed. He saw and then felt an IV connected to his left wrist and then came the realization that only a thin sheet covered his naked body.

Turning just his eyes he shifted his sight towards the foot of his bed. There he saw a broad picture window and through it could be seen what he thought was a moon. He thought he was surely in another dream for there were no moons or picture windows aboard the *Manta Ray* or on board any other ship in the fleet.

The scent of fresh cut flowers came to him as he glanced around. Chic discovered that he was now surrounded by an array of multicolored plants, each in its own container.

His first glimpse of her convinced him that he was accompanied by a guardian angel. She had coal black hair that shined and brushed her bare shoulders and an upturned nub of a nose. Her eyes were fluid, strong and as black as her hair. They too shined.

Looking deeper into her shining eyes, he was drawn irresistibly into the very depths of each as she became aware that he was awake.

When she turned slightly, he noted that her neck was long and slender, an indication of her Oriental blood. She wore a sundress, though he had never actually seen any type of dress except in picture books. From the first side view, he saw that the dress had a low cut back and noticed her creamy smooth skin that was exposed by the thin straps over each shoulder.

Her arms, though long and slender to match her slim neck, gave proof that this young woman was no weakling.

By now she had turned towards Robyn and he willed her to turn back in his direction so that he could see her lovely face once more. Chic never heard her speak to Robyn. He wondered what her name was and at the same time realized she was no older than Robyn who continued to sit beside the bed with an anxious look on her face.

He spoke for the first time through dry lips and asked, "Are you an angel?"

Psalm who had been standing next to the window turned back towards him and found herself looking into his exquisite eyes. A tear formed at the corner of one eye and trickled slowly down her cheek. Blushing, she asked, "What is an angel?"

Chic, tried to raise himself to a sitting position, but as he did so a soft pair of hands from the other side of the bed held him fast. Not taking his eyes off Psalm, he sank back into his pillow and asked, "What is your name?"

"Psalm," she replied as she watched his eyes slowly close.

Chic dreamt of a song that was about an Angel and he slept peacefully with a smile playing across his lips. The monitors showed his heart rate slowly gaining in strength.

Chic slept for another five hours and by the time he awoke, the regeneration of his shoulder was complete. Now, in order to complete the healing process, he needed to exercise his stiff and newly rebuilt muscles.

Upon waking Chic found Psalm sitting in the chair where Robyn had been. Raising himself on one elbow, he could see that Psalm was asleep. As he pushed himself to a sitting position he felt the twinge in his shoulder. Reaching over he gently placed his hand atop hers.

Sleepily her eyes fluttered open, their eyes met. Neither spoke for several minutes, both lost in their own thoughts.

Chic broke the spell by saying, "I'm glad you're here. Where are we and what happened?"

Psalm, while never breaking eye contact, took a deep breath and said, "I shot you!"

"Why?"

"I thought you were a 'manbear' because you were dressed like one. You came out of the woods staring straight at me. I had no choice, I had to stop you, but please remember I thought you were a wild animal. I thought my life was in danger and I could have killed you. I'm so sorry!"

Chic, feeling that her guilt was on the brink of overcoming her, squeezed her hand that he found himself still holding.

She looked up at him with just a hint of a smile which he returned. He said, "There must be a better way to meet men on this planet than shooting them."

Now her eyes did smile at him and her full mouth opened into a wide grin. She chuckled and said, "I usually only shoot men who fly, but there are no flying men on Antioch. At least there weren't until you got here."

They were interrupted by Robyn who entered with a doctor in tow.

Psalm was saying, "Are you hungry? If you'd like, I could get some food or something to drink for you."

Chic nodded in assent and Psalm left to find him some food.

The doctor introduced himself, "I'm Doctor Austin. How do you feel?"

The doctor was wearing pale yellow hospital scrubs. He was easily six feet tall weighing nearly one hundred and ninety pounds, and was about thirty years old.

Chic answered with, "A little weak and very stiff, but I seem to be okay otherwise."

"Do you know what happened to you and where you are?" the doctor asked.

Chic smiled and said, "I know I was shot by Cupid's sister and I suspect her to be an angel in disguise. I know I'm in a hospital on a planet named Antioch."

"Well, Lieutenant, I think you'll be just fine. I would recommend some exercise and plenty of nourishment with a few days off to rest." With that said, the Doctor and Robyn turned and left.

Chic was now alone in his room and as he sank back into his pillow, he closed his eyes for just a few moments rest.

Half an hour later, Chic was startled awake by the sounds of someone entering his room and he opened his eyes as Robyn threw him his newly cleaned uniform. She said, "I'll step out so you can get dressed." And she left the room to him and his thoughts. Chic was very confused over his being shot, about being in a strange hospital and with all that had happened to him during the last twenty-four hours. But the most startling thing was the girl. He thought, "I've never seen anyone so beautiful, and I've never been so touched." Then his thoughts went back to his duties and he was glad that Zeke was able to get the cannon turned off before anyone else had died. He would remember to thank him later.

Then Chic pulled on his uniform and stepped to the door and invited Robyn back in.

As Chic laid back on his bed fully dressed, Robyn began filling him in on the other events of the past twenty-four hours. Before she had finished, Psalm entered carrying a tray of fresh fruits and a platter which held an enormous steak, and a baked potato smothered in butter with a bowl of salad at its side. The platter held some vegetables which he did not recognize. The tray also held several large tumblers which were frosted and filled with sweetened ice tea.

Chic realized at that moment just how hungry he was. When Psalm set the tray on his bedside table, he picked up one of the tumblers of sweetened ice tea and downed half of it, finding it to be the best tea he had ever tasted.

"I made this at home from sun enhanced tea and natural sweeteners. I remembered how the food in hospitals is and snuck this in. I hope you like it."

He thanked her and began to inhale the remainder of his meal.

As he was eating, Psalm turned to Robyn and asked, "Don't they have food on that ship of yours?" They both looked at him stuffing his mouth with bite after bite and laughed.

Chic stopped long enough to thank Psalm once again saying, "This is the best meal I've eaten in a long, long time."

She replied, "From the way you are eating it, it looks as though it is the only meal you've eaten in a while, and you haven't even tasted my cooking yet." Psalm was teasing him unmercifully.

Robyn added with, "Sir, I've got a shuttle waiting outside, Commander Thor's orders. And Psalm, Commander Thor sends you his regards along with an invitation to remain aboard tonight and break your fast with the Officers at o seven hundred hours tomorrow morning. You will be billeted with me in my compartment. I have plenty of things you might wish to try on so you need not bring a change of clothes."

Psalm said, "I must speak to my father."

"Commander Thor has already spoken to your father and wishes you to know that you have his permission to stay aboard."

Psalm was now smiling broadly.

Robyn continued with, "If I understand things on your planet, this will be your first flight as it was for your father and the Council Members."

"Yes," Psalm said. "And I'm not at all comfortable with being in one of those flying machines."

Chic now offered, "Psalm, I will pilot the craft and you will be just as safe with me as you would be in your own bed at home."

Psalm looked at Robyn and smiled knowingly as Robyn said flatly, "I don't think either of us would be safe with you in either of our beds."

◆ ◆ ◆ ◆

Lieutenant Zeke was being questioned by Mr. Wolfe in regards to the journey from Earth as they sat around the large table in the great-room. Zeke was of a mind not to give away any secrets. Although he did answer the Councilman's questions as openly and honestly as he thought was right under the circumstances.

Mr. Wolfe asked questions about where he was born and was somewhat surprised to hear that he was a Libra and that his ancestors had all come from the planet Libra. He went on to say, "Ensign Grammer is a descendent of the planet Aeries while Lieutenant Robyn comes from the planet Capricorn and our Ensign Sable springs from the planet Cancer."

Councilman Lugar, an Orion descendent chuckled and asked, "Were you all born on spaceships?"

Zeke stood, and walked to the bay window and peered out, lost in his own thoughts, thinking about how beautiful it must have been for his forefathers living on a planet like this. He only hoped and believed that one day, either he or his children would be able to live freely again as God had meant man to.

He was joined by Councilman Rainier who stood at his side. "Being descendents of Sol ourselves, I have never heard of any planets named after Astrological signs. Nor to my knowledge have I ever known anyone, let alone an entire race of people, who were born in space." Zeke continued to stare out the window and the Councilman went on to say, "Granted, our recorded history of Sol ended over two thousand years ago when our ancestors put down on this planet."

About this time four Starship shuttlecraft were seen descending in perfect and silent formation. Without so much as a whisper they touched down a few feet from the house. Each of the craft was larger than any of the out buildings in the back yard.

Mr. Wolfe walked up and broke his spell by asking, "Lieutenant, would you be so kind as to put me in touch with your Commander? I'd like to ask a few more questions before we leave."

"Certainly," Zeke said. "If you will allow me the use of your comm station again."

Mr. Wolfe nodded in assent.

As the Lieutenant punched out the coordinates to the *Manta Ray*, the view-set flickered into life, Commander Thor became visible and behind him could be seen the bridge of the *Manta Ray*. "How may I help you, Lieutenant Zeke?" Commander Thor asked.

"Yes Sir, Commander. Mr. Wolfe's here and wishes to speak with you before we leave," Zeke explained.

"Very well, Lieutenant, put him on," Thor said.

Mr. Wolfe stepped forward along with Councilman Frasier Benzyl and in unison they addressed the Commander. "We, the Councilmen of Antioch, are the voice of our people. It has been decided within the Council that we have a moral obligation and a duty to the people of Antioch to share these historical moments with them as they are happening. Would you agree?"

Commander Thor responded, "Under normal circumstances I would certainly agree. But Mr. Councilman, these circumstances do not seem normal. As such, I would request that you gentlemen as the elders meet first with Captain Adams and General Hawk in private. Then afterwards if you feel the same, there would be no problem in making our meeting public."

"Is there some sort of problem, a reason perhaps that would justify secrecy?" Councilman Frasier asked.

"Yes, I am afraid there is, Sir," Thor said. "I do not wish to alarm either you or the citizenry. There is a situation which demands proper preparation and those protocols will have to be made by you who are in authority on your world. Hence I would suggest that you and those in authority everywhere on your world attend a briefing aboard the *Manta Ray* as soon as it is possible."

Mr. Wolfe replied, "I am the Voice of all the Council of Elders. We shall indeed heed your advice and will meet with your Captain and General and anyone else you deem necessary before informing our people of your arrival. We are prepared to leave immediately. We will make contact with the others of our world upon arrival on board."

FALLING

Escorting the council members towards the waiting ships, Lieutenant Zeke explains that he and his landing party had landed a little ways from where Lieutenant Michaels had been shot and their ships would need to be picked up on the way. Also that they would be acting as Official Escorts to the shuttles while in route to the *Manta Ray*.

Since this was the first time any of the council members had ever had the chance to see their beautiful world from the air, Zeke assigned three members of the council to each of three of the shuttles and the balance was used for his own people. He ordered the shuttle pilots to follow their guest's instructions as to which way to go for an hour of sightseeing.

The first to lift off was the shuttle *Balboa*, followed by *Canyon*, and then the *Marque*, leaving the *Jewel* to follow the other three. All four shuttles took a different direction to their Tigers.

Looking out of the large windows of the *Jewel*, Mr. Wolfe enjoyed seeing the landscape and wasn't too surprised to see the tops of trees and his roofline that quickly fell behind as they moved southwest going deeper into the forest that surrounded his home. That is until the *Jewel* flew over several streams that were new to him and were large enough to have been called fast moving rivers. Small only in the sense that these streams were really only small when compared to the much larger ones that lay to the north.

Citizens of Antioch had never ventured far from home; nor had they ever had reason to do so except when they started to build their second city. Today, things would change forever.

Along the edges of one of the smaller streams were several rather large black-tailed deer that were drinking the clear water without any hint of fear from the large bird flying overhead.

Behind them seemed to be a herd of white tailed deer and to the left of them was another herd of animals that Zeke thought were antelope. Their twin, pointed horns were over two feet long and gleamed as the fading light of day glanced off of them.

The shuttle pilots were also amazed, for none had ever seen such sights. Only John Renfree, the pilot of the *Jewel*, had ever walked on the surface of a planet. What stuck in his mind's eye was the stark sunlight and the mixture of scents that assaulted his nose and brain. Nothing here was artificial. Everything had a new and wonderful feeling, taste, sound, and smell to it.

None of what he was seeing and feeling today was anything like the one time he was on a raiding party against the Augean to retrieve or destroy an advanced Tiger that had been shot down and captured.

While different, he was too involved to take note of the scenery or wildlife that might have been on that planet.

Zeke notified the other ships and they were quickly on their way. The elders remained quiet as the ships ascended. They became speechless as the group of shuttle craft entered space itself approaching May, the only moon of Antioch.

As May became larger and larger, it suddenly began dropping away as they crested its horizon. One after another, the elders pointed to what appeared to be a manmade object which began growing larger as they approached it.

As big as the shuttlecraft felt when they first entered it, each now felt very minute as compared to the size of the approaching Starship.

As they approached the ship, they came within view of her lettering and identification numbers. They muttered to themselves, remembering their history on early spaceflight.

They turned to one another saying, "This cannot be!"

After landing in the shuttle bay, Mr. Wolfe and his entourage were greeted first by Commander Thor, then General Hawk.

The shaking of hands has always been a human emotional sharing by the touch of one another in offering of friendship.

"You are all welcome aboard the *Manta Ray*. Quarters have been prepared for you," Commander Thor said. Glancing around, he said, "I see your daughter has not accompanied you, sir. I had hoped to talk to her."

"My daughter, Psalm, decided that her place was with the young Lieutenant she accidentally shot. She may accompany him later once he is released from the hospital."

"She will be welcomed as a guest on board. I shall order a shuttle to be made available to her and the injured officer," Commander Thor assured him.

Introducing Commander O'ho and Commander Rio, Commander Thor said, "These gentlemen will act as your liaison while you are aboard." Then they were all given a Comm Button which Thor told them works by a simple touch. "There are wall schematics on every level and should you become lost simply push your Comm button, speak in a normal voice and say, 'computer, I am lost.' Tell it where you wish to go and it will direct you to your destination. I will see you all at nineteen hundred hours in General Hawk's private dining room. There we can all ask our questions."

As Hawk and Thor left the small party of Elders, they entered a long walkway leading to the senior officer's lift. Stepping into the lift, Hawk said to his longtime friend, "Did you notice?"

"Indeed! General, I did notice their makeup. Qatar, Kalgin, Sombar, Orion, and Subre, and several more I'm not sure of. I wonder how such a mixture of conflicting cultures arrived on this one planet. There have been no reports of humans, or nonhumans, in this area of space according to Captain Adams and the fleet records. Yet, they are here! I also wonder how many more systems are holding other secrets."

"There will be many questions," Hawk told him.

Thor said, "I, too, am looking forward to some very interesting answers to some pointed questions of my own."

Stepping onto the bridge, Commander Tropy said, "Sir, long range sensors show a small group of vessels approaching this sector on course T – ONE – ONE - SEVEN. They haven't spotted us yet."

"Helmsman, bring us about to the far side of the moon. Yellow Alert! Keep that moon between us and that group of ships, Ensign."

"Aye, Sir. Bringing her about to Mark ZERO - POINT - TWO - ONE. Yellow Alert in effect," said Ensign Adele.

Tropy, keep me posted on any changes by those ships. Ensign Adele, you have the bridge!" Thor ordered.

Both women answered with a sharp, "Aye, Aye, Sir."

"Do you believe they're real?" Councilman Barteal asked.

"They certainly look like their pictures, and they act real enough," Edward Wolfe offers.

"But that would make them well over four thousand years old!" another of the councilmen exclaimed.

"True enough," Wolfe says. "The fact that we shook hands tells me they are real and very much alive!"

"Remember too, the records indicated that there was never any debris found," Barteal reminded them.

"Do you suppose," Councilman Fraiser Benzl asked, "that they could have been sucked into that black hole and thrown free into the future?"

"Or," another suggested, "perhaps they could have been held in some type of suspended animation all these years and just recently been released."

"The possibilities are endless. Remember, too, that we ourselves are unsure of our own time frame," Councilman Freeman said. "The forefathers who brought our people here were themselves lost in time. It was they who reset our time chronometers; we could be living in the past. That is our past and their present."

"All I know for certain is that this ship is real. The crew members are real and whatever dangers that lay ahead of us are real," Councilman Fraiser Benzyl commented.

Edward Wolfe added, "Commander O'ho says there are no restrictions on our using the ship's library. I would suggest each of us do in our own fields. Then we can meet again before we sit down with the council governing these people."

◆ ◆ ◆ ◆

General Hawk led the way forward to Thor's private office where both men asked for and received drinks from the food dispenser, then took seats at the front lounge contemplating all they had seen this day. Without speaking a word, they shared each other's thoughts.

Without realizing he had spoken aloud, General Hawk said, "That settlement must be a melting pot of dozens of warring worlds."

Thor said, "It doesn't begin to answer the two main questions. How and why here? Perhaps we'll find out at dinner."

"I've a feeling these people are in the dark as to those two questions as much as we are," Hawk told his friend.

There is a "beep, beep" sound. Commander Thor sat up a little straighter in his high-backed cushioned chair and said, "Come."

The doors opened with a swishing sound. Mr. O'ho stepped in and the doors closed just as quickly and silently behind him. Commander O'ho announced that all the guests had been settled in their quarters. "I took the liberty of allowing the guest the use of the ship's main library. I could see no reason to put any security locks on our archives."

"Very good, Mr. O'ho, I agree. Please continue to act as liaison on an as-needed basis, and see that our guests arrive around eighteen fifty hours," Thor told him.

"Excuse me Sir, would you like me to take command of the Bridge? Ensign Adele has never experienced command before and may be somewhat nervous," said O'ho.

"Everybody has to have their first day, Commander. I can still remember when a brash young Ensign, whose name I shall not mention, had beads of sweat rolling down his forehead the moment he was put in full control of his first ship," General Wesley T. Hawk reminded Commander O'ho.

O'ho was remembering well that day more than ten years before as one of the worst days of his life seeing his ship fall under a sneak attack while every experienced officer of the bridge was off ship. Oh yeah, he remembered the horrors and the terrible deaths of his fellow shipmates as he struggled to save his ship by jumping to Light-speed in order to regain a semblance of order before returning to fight for the lives of the ship's senior staff. It was a day he would relive every day and would never forget as long as he lived.

"The experience will be good for her. She has to have her 'first' day as did we all, Commander," Thor said. Then the three of them laughed — a very serious laugh.

"I only hope her first experience turns out better than mine did," Commander O'ho reminded both Thor and Hawk of the ninety-six dead and another six months in dry dock. "I'll be in my quarters until needed," he finished, and was out the door.

Walking through the busy and quiet bridge, he saw Ensign Adele get up and vacate the command chair, starting for her Helmsman Station. He quietly told her to resume command, that he saw no reason for relieving her and continued across the bridge exiting by the Senior Officer's Lift.

As the doors closed behind him he gave his destination to the lift's computer and the lift started to descend. After about a minute or two, all hell broke loose!

There was a tremendous series of explosions that rocked the *Manta Ray*. It seemed that several hits at the same time had caught her totally unprepared.

As he was about to order the lift to return to the bridge, it jerked to a stop, sending Commander O'ho bouncing off the floor and ceiling. Then without warning, or time to react, the lights flickered red then failed altogether.

He was falling into the bowels of the ship that he loved so much. In total darkness, his last thoughts were, "Am I to be next on death's ever waiting list?"

FIRST DAY JITTERS

The *Manta Ray* was listing half-cocked and was adrift in orbit about the small satellite of a planet named Antioch. Smoke, steam, and oxygen were leaking from too many areas.

There is no up or down in space, but it was clear that the *Manta Ray* was in serious trouble as the Augean ships turned to deliver another salvo to her undercarriage.

The bridge was pitch black. *Manta Ray* was shrouded in total darkness without so much as the reflection of a single star to light her way.

After the first round of hits had settled, Ensign Adele picked herself up and started to run to where she thought she could help. But she had been thrown about like so much of a rag doll in a storm and couldn't remember where she was at the moment. She called out to each station but received no reply to her calls.

There were more and more hits all about the ship. The massive ship shook and as Ensign Adele crawled from place to place she found dead and dying crewmen at every turn.

Still crawling, she found that all stations were off-line and silent. She continued to find the dead and dying everywhere.

She found Commander Tropy barely conscious. Setting her up against an unknown station, she suddenly realized for the first time that she was the only person alert on the bridge.

She had already pushed the Comm button, but either she was the only person alive aboard the *Manta Ray*, or like the bridge, all other stations were off-line.

In Command school aboard the Cressliner *Spray*, she remembered a single lesson. That being that all Starships, at the foot of the Captain's chair, were equipped with a locker stocked with assorted helpful items for emergencies.

Ensign Adele left Commander Tropy, who had fallen unconscious, and crawled along the floor as the *Manta Ray* was hit again and shaken to her rivets. Hit after hit came that she could tell were directs hits to her midsection. Finally reaching the Communication station, she realized that she had been turned completely around in the darkened mayhem. Knowing now where she was, she quickly found her way to the Captain's chair, then the locker. Opening the locker, she withdrew two helpful tools, a hand-held communicator and a powerful hand lamp. Without a thought she flipped open the communicator and called, "Bridge to Commander Thor. Please respond."

At the same time she switched on the powerful little lamp with her free hand and flashed it around the bridge. There was no answer to her call. She then tried, "Ensign Adele to General Hawk. Please respond."

Again, there was no response to her hail.

Turning the light slowly, she saw the carnage of bodies scattered across the bridge.

She then hailed, "Bridge to engineering, Mr. Manado, please respond."

A half second later, there came a response. "Manado here, sir."

Not waiting for further words, she said, "Mr. Manado, this is Ensign Adele. I am in temporary command of the bridge. We need shields and we need them now!"

Ensign Adele was again shaken to her boots and she said, "Mr. Manado, All systems ship-wide are down and we need those shields up right now before we…. There was another hit, then another. The ship was hit with a double blast of energy. She lost her lamp as it seemed to jump right out of her hand. She watched the tiny lamp dance around as it bounced from place to place giving her glances of the broken bodies before it finally went dark.

With the second blast from the double hit, Mary Adele found that she had lost her footing and was now sitting squarely on her backside.

Still holding onto her communicator, she found her voice before Commander Manado could respond. "Mr. Manado," she stammered, "You are the Chief Engineer aboard this vessel and you damn well better get those shields up, and you'd better be quick about it!"

As he replied, "Aye Sir" he was taken back to the time when, as a child of eight or so in England, his own mother had used the same tone of voice to save his life when he was almost run over by a streetcar. He had been standing in the middle of a crossroads when she caught his attention. Her sharp words and his quick step was all that had saved him from being run over and killed.

It was the first time she'd ever heard a ranking officer respond to a lowly Second Class Ensign by saying, "It'll take only a moment," and then he said, "Shields are up, Sir. But only at sixty-one percent."

She thanked him and requested emergency lighting. Her heart was racing so hard and fast that she barely heard him say, "I'm routing all available power to the shields", nor did she hear her own response, "Very well, Mr. Manado, keep me posted."

There were more hits all around the ship, but her shields held solidly. While the mighty ship rocked somewhat, she never again knocked Ensign Mary Adele off her feet.

She knew the bridge personnel should be stirring by now. She hoped against all hope, as she desperately listened for them to begin up-righting their chairs. She requested that each station report in. She had never felt so all alone.

She flipped open her communicator calling security to request a damage report but only got empty airways. Then she called Sick-bay remembering the devastation of the gutted *Manta Ray* as she was towed into the repair docks of the *Activia* upon entering this realm of space almost four years ago.

Ensign Mary Adele was remembering reviewing the reconstructed tapes that the crew put together of their last moments before entering this realm of time and space.

◆ ◆ ◆ ◆

These are the reconstructed events of Star Log ELEVEN THREE ONE POINT TWO TWO, aboard the Starship *Manta Ray*;

"I was at my Communications Station aboard the *Manta Ray* when the *Assyrian* dropped out of hyperspace and hailed us," Commander Cathryn Tropy began her story.

Captain Harper rose from his chair and addressed the *Manta Ray*, "Well, Commander Thor," he said, "I see the fun hasn't started yet."

"True, Captain. It's good to see you too!" Thor answered. "We've still got another sixteen hours," Thor finished.

"There was a rumor," Captain Harper added, "that this star might go 'super'."

"True," Thor told him, "there are well over twenty species of man on hand for the spectacle. Let us hope they are not disappointed."

"Well, let's hope not," Harper replied.

"Captain," Thor said, "I hope you and your First Officer can join General Hawk and me for dinner aboard the *Manta Ray*."

"How's the new ship?" Captain Harper asked. "Still working out the bugs?"

"Bugs? I don't think there are any bugs on board the *Manta Ray*, Sir!"

Since they were speaking on an open channel, both crews began laughing. Commander Thor caught his last remark and raised his right eyebrow.

There was a stark difference between Captain Harper and Commander Thor other than Captain Harper stood over seven feet tall and was at least fifty years older than Thor.

Commander Thor wore a royal blue pullover tunic with black pants with a solid blood red stripe on the outside running from waist to pants cuff. His tunic was topped with a cream or off-colored collar that sported four pins. Two of the gold pins were solid where the third pin ran a slim line from two to seven o'clock leaving the fourth pin hollow. The gold pins signified Bridge Command stature and the single slim bar showed a rank of Commander. The fourth showed he was the Captain of the vessel.

Captain Harper wore his ship's colors of a royal red tunic, black trousers with a single blood red stripe running from waist to cuff. He wore only three gold command pins. Where Thor had two solid gold showing his was the flagship and he was its Captain, Captain Harper wore only one solid, and a double striped showing a rank of ship's Captain.

On both breasts of the men was an insignia of a scenic *Manta Ray* showing that both men were of the same command and fleet of twelve ships under one flag with General Wesley T. Hawk as its Commander.

As General Hawk stepped onto the Bridge and joined Thor before the view-set showing the *Assyrian* and her Captain before them, General Hawk said, "Well now, Captain Harper, I see you made it in time after all."

"Indeed! I wouldn't have missed this for all the world," Captain Harper replied.

The General continued, "We're grateful to have the *Assyrian* with us. The Napas and Gennes have become a bit pushy of late, always trying to start a fight. Just having the *Assyrian* on hand should help to settle them down a mite. I think they'll think twice before they start something they cannot hope to finish."

"Let's hope so," Captain Harper replied, "I'm glad we were able to get here in time."

Commander Thor walked over to the Helm's Station where he stood studying a chart.

He said, "General, I think we're too close. We should back off another sixty thousand miles." He then addressed the officer at the Helm, saying, "Set course at THREE ONE POINT SIX FOUR, speed one quarter standard, on my mark." He paused a moment to allow the young man the time to make the proper adjustments then spoke, "Mark!"

Both ships moved off in perfect sync.

Once the two ships had made the proper adjustments and were in the best position to view the upcoming event, Captain Harper and his First Officer, Hunter Jordan, transferred, to the *Manta Ray*, where they were soon joined by Doctor Mitch Michaels. The Doctor said to his longtime friend, "This is a once in a lifetime occasion."

The dinner was filled with lively conversations and afterwards the party adjourned to the forward Ready Room where they talked well into the night.

As the hour drew nearer and Captain Harper and Hunter had returned to their ship, both ships readied themselves for the big happening. Commander Thor was continually readjusting first one sensor then another and General Hawk said, "Thor, you're as nervous as a long-tailed cat in a room full of rocking chairs!"

"It's just that everything on this new ship needs fine tuning! And I can't seem to find that perfect point as I did on the 'D'," he replied. He arched another eyebrow and added, "I suppose that is what's referred to as 'getting the bugs out'." Before anyone could reply, the ship's klaxon sounded and the red lights of an alert replaced the regular lights, "RED ALERT" echoed throughout the ship by the onboard computer.

At that time a Gennes War Bird de-cloaked his ship just long enough to fire several shots at the *Manta Ray* before moving off and re-cloaking.

Though alerted, the *Manta Ray* was nonetheless caught unprepared and was shaken hard. The ship's onboard computers had raised her shields, but they had been weakened, and other enemy ships were attacking.

Commander Tropy said to Commander Thor, "Shields down twenty-two percent," just as Engineering called over the ship's intercom "Bridge," Commander Thor replied, when again and yet again the *Manta Ray* was struck. This time all bridge viewers and lights went out.

"Helm! Get us out of here!" Commander Thor ordered just as the ship was hit with a massive electrical shock the likes of which none of us had ever experienced before. The shock had hit the Helmsman who was now lying on the floor already dead.

Before the view-sets went out, I noticed the *Assyrian* had her hands full, for she too was under attack. While not any more prepared, she handled the shots better if for no other reason than the ship itself had been well seasoned over the course of her thirty years in service. Everything that might have been loose had been tightened down long ago.

After returning fire and destroying two of the massive enemy ships, the *Assyrian* had moved off to better deal with the remaining attackers. I believe she was hoping to draw the attacking ships away from the *Manta Ray*, which I could feel was listing badly and appeared heavily damaged.

The *Manta Ray* was now dead and began drifting faster, helplessly unable to get her engines started. Thankfully, she was left alone as both the Napa and the Gennes turned to do battle with the *Assyrian*. The *Assyrian* was by far the most beautiful ship I had ever seen under attack. She was no weakling! Her claws would cut deeply into her enemy this day and much blood would be shed and lives lost over a battle neither could hope to win.

On board the *Manta Ray*, Commander Manado had his hands full keeping life support systems up and trying to get power back to the shields.

Within minutes the emergency lighting was restored, but all other systems remained inoperable. I was on my back and under my console where I finally managed to get one of the front viewers back up when every member of the Bridge crew froze as they witnessed the formation of a supernova. As beautiful as it was, the viewer clearly showed its awesome power as the nova began to draw every planet and moon within its cluster inward. The *Manta Ray*, without power continued to drift helplessly towards the maelstrom.

Commander Thor was on the restored intercom calling Engineering when the second phenomenon occurred.

It appeared at the very edge of the nova. Commander Thor saw what it was and went directly to the Helm Station. He knew that the *Manta Ray* was too close to the storm and could not get safely away without some last minute evasive maneuver on his part.

"Mr. Manado," the commander said, "I need all the ship's power diverted to the Port Thrusters on my mark; even life support. Commander Thor knew it would be a blind shot at best, and taken in the dark.

"Aye, Sir!" came the reply without question. Then the lights on the bridge flickered and the *Manta Ray* was left in total darkness as she struggled to loosen the death grip of the maelstrom.

The *Assyrian* was still too busy with her attackers to be of any help. It appeared that the UFM was to suffer another terrible defeat this day unless Commander Thor could pull the rabbit out of the hat again as he had done so many times before, and there was nothing else anyone was capable of doing to stop it otherwise.

As Commander Thor stood in the darkness, he knew that the *Manta Ray* had but one slim chance. He felt confident he was taking the only logical step to save his ship. Everyone aboard the ship held their collective breath.

FIGHT FOR CONTROL

Her thoughts returned to the present as she heard a very shaky Doctor Murky respond to her call and she was very thankful to hear his voice. She calmly stated that he was needed on the bridge. She told him to use the crawlspace which is really an escape ladder going from deck to deck. She told him to use the one marked 'Bridge' directly to the right of the main Sick Bay door. She knew that it would take about five minutes or so for him to reach the bridge.

She rang off and called engineering once again. "Engineering, Mr. Manado, please respond."

"Manado here," he responded calmly.

Mr. Manado, I need eyes and weapons. I cannot see who to shoot at. Can you get the power up anytime soon?"

"Aye, sir, we're still operating in the dark down here too, but I think we'll have power soon. Lasers are fully charged and the torpedo tubes are loaded as well," he told her.

Almost thinking out loud, Ensign Adele said, "Mr. Manado, can you open the fighter bay door?"

With a knowing grin on his face that she couldn't see, he said, "Aye, I can drain off a bit of power from the aft shields and get it open."

During one of Commander Jennin's classes on the use of the best defense, Ensign Adele remembered his stressing that, "There is no better defense than a strong offense."

"Very good, Mr. Manado," she said. "Let me know when it is opened and also, stand by to drop the shields on that part of the ship on my mark. But for only seven seconds," she told him.

"Aye, Sir. I'm on it and awaiting your orders," he replied.

Flipping out a second communicator she called, "Bridge to fighter bay commander, please respond."

She was relieved to hear; "Fighter bay, Lieutenant Baron here, sir."

"Mr. Baron, this is Ensign Adele. I am temporarily in command of the bridge. Any moment now you will see your outer bay door opening. How many Tigers do you have ready to launch?"

With a little too much cockiness in his voice, Baron says, "Ensign Adele, I don't think you have the authority to launch any fighters, who's in charge up there?"

Her ears burning with his smugness, she blasted back at him, "Mr. Baron! I don't have the time to play who's who. As it stands right now and until I am relieved of command, I am the Captain of this ship. I have given you a direct order to follow. Now, Mr. Baron, unless you are assuming command of this vessel, you will answer my questions and follow my orders. Have I made myself clear, Mister?"

Knowing that he had neither the right nor the training to assume command, and not wanting to take command he acquiesced. He knew that she was the better trained of the two and with just a hint of fear and respect in his voice he said, "I have Orange, Yellow, and Green squadrons suited and awaiting orders, Sir."

"Patch me through to Johnny Raye's Comm. Our power and communications are still off-line," Ensign Adele ordered.

"Aye, Sir," he replied sharply as a "beep" sounded.

"Lieutenant Raye here, Sir."

"Lieutenant Raye this is Ensign Mary Adele. As of this moment, I am acting Captain. I need you to take command of Green and Yellow as well as your own squadron and prepare to launch on my mark. You will be given only a seven second window to launch all of your fighters. Can you get through in that time frame?"

"Aye, Sir, we can manage that," Raye replied.

"Good. Now listen carefully. The Bridge is dead and off-line. You will have to serve as my eyes and ears and your instructions are simple. Destroy the enemy! Leave one half of Green Squadron to protect the ship and cover your tail. Then have someone give me a damage report from outside. I need to know if we're space-worthy. Tell them to be quick but thorough. Do you have any questions, Lieutenant?"

"None, Sir. We await your orders," Lieutenant Raye answered.

"Thank you, Lieutenant, please stand by," she told him.

"Aye, Sir."

Now, holding both communicators open, Ensign Adele called, "Mr. Manado?"

"Manado here."

"Mr. Manado, I know you're busy down there, but I need that door opened if I am to protect this ship!"

"Aye, Ensign, the door is opening as we speak. I await your orders to drop shields," the Chief Engineer told her calmly.

"On my mark, Mr. Manado count down from thirty and drop shields … Mark! Remember, seven seconds only." She continued to drop fingers as she called Lieutenant Raye.

"Raye here, Sir!" he answered.

DOG FIGHT

"Mr. Raye, you will launch your Tigers in exactly seventeen seconds. God speed and good hunting!"

"Aye, and thank you, Sir," Johnny Raye said.

All was deathly quiet on the bridge as the hits rained down on the *Manta Ray*, her shields stubbornly held against great odds. Ensign Mary Adele continued to drop her fingers one finger at a time.

The solid hit on the aft hull would have knocked her down had she been standing at the moment the shields came down. Mary Adele continued her count.

Her communicator beeped and she jumped for just a split second as she heard the Chief Engineer say, "Engineering to the Bridge, Ensign Adele?"

"Bridge here," she responded. "And thank you Mr. Manado, you might have just saved the entire ship!"

"Ah lass, if the ship is saved it is because of your quick wits. I heard the conversation between you and Mr. Baron, and I know how well you handled that. I've got my hands full down here for now, Ensign. It might take a wee bit o' time to get things back up again. You'll know when the lights come up."

Closing her communicator, Ensign Mary Adele considered all that had happened within the last three minutes. "My God," She muttered to herself. Those three minutes had seemed like a lifetime to her. She remembered again when the *Manta Ray* had first entered her space for the first time...

Ensign Adele had had a long talk with General Hawk about how they got here from Earth during a trip when she had piloted him to one of the other ships in the fleet.

A chill ran up his spine.

"Sir, are you alright?" I asked when we first met.

The observation bubble of the tiny shuttle allowed the General to look again at his great ship. He had been told there wasn't much difference, yet. He commented to me that with the four new decks he could easily tell that this wasn't the same *Manta Ray* that he viewed as a young Captain Wesley Thomas Hawk. He remembered thinking back then that there could never be a ship the size of the *Manta Ray* that could glide through space with such grace and ease.

"Yes, Ensign, I'm fine," he replied to my question.

General Hawk told me how none of the ship's time chronometers had worked since they came out of the rip in space.

Tears in the fabric of space are also called travel gates, star gates, ripples in time, or of both time and space. Some called them quantum leaps, time and space tunnels, or worm holes, and he told me that they may well be known as many other names throughout the galaxy by the many cultures of man.

Some of these gateways are stable enough to be traversed regularly from star system to star system. Others are very unstable, always shifting over long distances, never having an opening near where it last was found, and never coming out in the same place twice.

General Hawk explained that while in his first year in the academy he learned that entering into one of these tears allows a ship to traverse, (most of the time) unmolested by foreign objects like boulders, comets, asteroids, and other space debris and or other space ships that would otherwise destroy a ship in warp, or hyper-drive, should one come into contact with the an object in the ships path. He went on to explain that onboard computers are the only fail safe for such travel. Man learned early on that the human eye and hand are no match for an object coming at you at high speeds.

The General turned to me and said, "Seems like only yesterday and yet, another lifetime ago. How long now, three, four years?"

I told him it had been just over four Earth years. As we approached the ship, I mentioned, "How beautiful she is, Sir!"

"That she is Ensign," Hawk said.

The underside of the *Manta Ray* had just been refitted and restructured after being torn apart by the Augean Battle cruiser. The *Manta Ray* having been thrown free had just stopped tumbling when she was surrounded by Blue Squadron. At the same time she was fired upon by several Augean fighters.

The leader of Blue Squadron, Lieutenant Chic Michaels, not knowing whose side the *Manta Ray* was on but seeing there was no favoritism shown to her by this enemy known as Augean, took it upon himself to defend the unknown craft and would continue to do so until the stranger showed herself to be friend or foe. Commander Tropy went on to say on the tapes I had watched how the crew of the *Manta Ray* were still unaware of their surroundings, for all systems were still off-line.

General Hawk was just finding his space legs with the overhead red alarm lights still blinking, while Commander Thor, with one arm hanging limp was helping Commander O'ho back into his chair at the Science Station.

Lieutenant Sackett was still down, Ensign Ballist bending over him with a medical scanner. I was again seated at the communications Station. General Hawk could hear Commander Manado saying, "Life Support is back up, but only by God's own hand. I can'na tell ya anymore other than we are being torn apart by unknowns. The shots we are now taking are neither the Gennes nor the Napas. The intense fire is too strong to be either," he said.

"Mr. O'ho, where are we?" General Hawk asked.

"Unknown General, all systems are still down," he said.

Commander Thor turned to me saying, "Damage report!"

"Security reports decks twelve, fifteen, sixteen, and twenty-two have either breached or buckled outer walls. Thirty-seven dead so far and there has been no report from either medical departments or from Life Science Departments," I told him.

General Hawk, who was standing by Commander Thor's chair, pushed a button on the intercom, "Doctor Michaels report to the Bridge."

"General Hawk?" I turned in my seat to look at the man who had spoken. Commander Thor looked almost white in the face as he said, "Wes!" Thor was clearly shaken. Hawk turned to see a sick look of shock on Thor's face as he spoke, "Security reports that both medical as well as the complete Life Science Departments have taken direct hits, and that there is no longer anyone there to answer our hails! The report goes on to say that there are no survivors."

"Doctor Michaels!" I thought. "My God! Not now!"

The General turned to Thor, a sick look upon his questioning face, "How? How can that possibly be? Sick Bay and the Science Departments are located in the strongest and safest parts of the ship?"

"Nevertheless, General, they took several direct hits," Thor explained. "I don't know if they were hit this side of the rip in space or on the other side."

"Shields forward and aft are at fifteen percent, Sir," I told Commander Thor.

"What rip in space?" General Hawk asked. "I don't remember any rip in space.   If we're not in our space, where are we?"

"All other shields are down and off-line," O'ho reported. "Engineering is trying to get things back up, but they are giving their immediate attention to keeping life support online."

Sitting in his command chair, Thor pushed his intercom button, "Thor to Engineering."

"Manado here, Sir," the engineer responded.

"Mr. Manado, how's it going back there?" Thor asked.

"Not so good, Sir. Whoever that is out there has taken a large chunk out of the midsection," he told him.

"It doesn't sound good Lloyd, do you need my assistance?" Thor asked.

"No, sir. You've got your hands full already. We'll get it together," the engineer replied.

"Mr. Manado! Concentrate on getting the shields up first, reroute from life support if necessary. There won't be any need for life support, if we are all blown apart and dead!" Commander Thor reminded his long time friend and engineer.

"Aye, Sir, I'll get them up in a few minutes," Commander Manado said.

"Mr. Manado! We may not have a few minutes!" Thor said a little too sternly.

"Aye," the weary engineer replied.

After closing her communicator with the Chief Engineer, Ensign Adele reflected on the past few minutes and realized she had done everything she could have to protect the ship. She opened her communicator and spoke into it, "Bridge to Commander Thor, please respond."

There would be no answer and the Ensign was surrounded by the silence of the darkened space around her.

After eating, Lieutenant Michaels was checked out of the hospital and released into the care of Psalm. He, Robyn, and Psalm headed for the small bubble-craft known as a "Shallop". "The Shallop is used," Robyn was telling Psalm, "to effect small repairs to the outside of a spacecraft and occasionally as a work transport for crewmembers that have to work outside the *Manta Ray*.

It had a bubble front allowing the pilot to get up close to view any areas needing repair. It crept along at a snail's pace; hardly more than one-eighth impulse, proving to be very romantic for the young and nostalgic of those who have already built their memories.

Psalm was enthralled by her first view from high above her home world. Her breath was taken at the sight of the lush meadowlands. The ice-capped mountains with their deep blue trees passed under them as her eyes glowed with the wonder of it all.

The trio saw herds of small animals that resembled the deer of Earth and a variety of other game. There were emus, and dogs in packs as well as alone. There were wolves stalking wild cows, and as the craft flew over them, they seemed not to notice the strange thing above them.

Everywhere they looked they saw roses, strawflowers, irises, and marigolds or chrysanthemums and carnations of every color and size. There were entire wild fields of tulips of red and yellow, pinks and blues, and whites.

"I believe I can just smell flowers even from up here," Robyn said with a smile on her face. The rock formations were spectacular to see. And all without the hand of man to disrupt them in their natural state.

They saw large herds of the most beautiful horses any of them had ever seen anywhere in the galaxy, plus thousands of birds of every size and color.

Lieutenant Michaels was not a womanizer, not like his grandfather Commodore Carter was. Chic, in comparison was very quiet and unassuming and a bit on the shy side. He enjoyed dating, but he detested the "Dating Game" per se. In his mind, he figured that he just hadn't met Ms Right. Yet!

After the last few hours he wasn't so sure that was any longer the case. He had never been so taken, like he was with this young woman. She radiated a warmth and intelligence that produced a glow capable of melting the frowns of even the grumpiest of old men.

She laid a hand over his and exclaimed, "Oh, look there! It's a rainbow!" She pointed to a huge rainbow with dozens of ever changing hues and colors. Neither Chic nor Robyn had ever seen the likes.

Chic flew them under it and then through it. He would have given it to her had it been in his power. He had been with other women but he had never felt as comfortable, nor had he wanted to please anyone as he did with Psalm.

Robyn, who had loved Chic since early childhood, was seeing him anew. She sensed a new and wondrous joy inside him, a more fullness that lent a new demeanor. She knew that this had come from his new friend, the friend who had nearly taken his life. Nevertheless, she was glad she had asked for permission to share her stateroom with this young woman.

They flew high where she could see whole continents.

The little Shallop flew very slowly and later Psalm thought that if they had flown any slower, they'd surely fall right out of the sky. Then Chic took them lower and Psalm and Robyn both cried out, "I think I could touch that antelope without it ever knowing I was here," Robyn said.

They crossed vast rivers and the smallest streams, large and small lakes and flew over an ocean so vast that they couldn't see the other side.

They saw great whales, fish of every description, sea otters, and the whitest seal pups imaginable.

Chic saw the delight in both of their faces and he plunged the Shallop into the ocean itself. Turning on the small craft's lights, they saw an abundance of deep sea coral reefs rich in aquatic life and calcium deposits. The deposits gave off gold and iridescent yellows, bright greens, and the whitest blues such as Psalm had never seen before.

It wasn't recalled until later that none of them had ever seen an ocean before. The joy of these sights would forever be implanted in their hearts and minds.

Turning the tiny Shallop back to the skies, they came to the very edge of dusk to a point where the sky changes from blue to purple, then to pink and then disappears. Suddenly there are stars so bright you'd think every planet turned on their lights just for them.

After about forty minutes of stargazing, the skyline began to change and up came a marvel that can only be seen by flying at high altitudes where the moon rises over the horizon, filling the land below in shadows at the same time painting the landscape with an eerie brightness.

Slowly at first, the moon rose until it was high over their heads and they saw that it was tiny compared to the size of the planet below them. Yet, it seemed huge from this vantage point.

Psalm said, "Look, I think there's another moon besides May. Funny, I've looked at the moon a million times and never have I seen the smaller one. It's not on any of our charts either, that I can remember. Can we go look at it?" she asked.

As the trio approached they witnessed what seemed to be sparks hitting the small moon from several directions.

Chic snapped. "That's no moon! It's the *Manta Ray* and she's under attack!"

Robyn said, "Look, she's just sitting there and not returning fire!"

"But I don't understand. Who would want to hurt your spaceship?" Psalm asked.

Robyn and Chic quickly explained the Augean Empire and its pledge to destroy all of mankind.

Robyn and Chic laid out a clear picture so that she understood her planet's peril.

"My people must be warned," she said. "But we have no defense Chic. What are we going to do?"

"First we need to see if we can assist the *Manta Ray*, then we'll take it from there. Your people have that cannon which can possibly be used for defense and I'm sure the fleet wouldn't abandon your people," he tried to reassure her.

Robyn said, "I have been unable to raise any response from the *Manta Ray*."

Psalm said, "She is so beautiful, so sleek and clean."

While Chic was remembering back to the first time he laid eyes on the *Manta Ray*, the Augean were having a field day shooting at her. There couldn't have been more than a few square inches that hadn't been singed by their powerful lasers.

The *Manta Ray* had barely stopped tumbling as she popped out of thin air. Commander Thor had later explained that the ship had just come out of a rip in the fabric of space.

Not knowing if the ship was a human vessel, he couldn't let the Augean's tear it apart without knowing who if anyone was still alive on board.

Chic Michaels and twenty-five Tigers had been trying to run the enemy down when the *Manta Ray* suddenly appeared after they had attacked the fleet once again. So he felt it only fitting to add a little protection to this stranger for holding the Augean's interest long enough for them to arrive.

At the time of the *Manta Ray's* arrival, Chic had no way of knowing what was happening on board as Tropy was again lying on the floor under her console, being assisted by one of the many crewmen who had been detailed to damage control. She said, "We should have the view-set up in a few more... ah, that should do it," as she regained her feet and sat down. Pushing a few buttons, the viewfinder flickered to life, "Here we are, sir."

"Mr. Jackel, what about weapons?" Commander Thor asked.

"No, Sir. None at all. Systems are still down," he answered.

As he finished what he was saying, the stars started to form on the front screen. Just as suddenly, a large forward-wing-shaped ship fired at the *Manta Ray* and just as suddenly was blown apart. A direct hit by what appeared to be a small beam of energy fired by a smaller teardrop-shaped fighter; its bubbled and pointed front was lighted with a dim light shining from a cockpit dashboard.

All hands on the bridge stared at their benefactors as more of the teardrop-shaped ships flew by in hot pursuit of the wing-shaped fighters, destroying one after another with the larger ships now turning. The smaller tear-drop ships broke into small groups as the wing-shaped ships destroyed another of the small ships, but working in teams, the small ships doggedly pursued the wing-shaped birds and they soon fled with the tear drops clinging to their tails.

"Sir, I've got audio coming in from the smaller ships, but no visual," Commander Tropy offered.

"Let's hear what they're saying," Commander Thor said.

As the audio cleared, they heard, "Zeke, you and Buster chase down those last two ships, and blow them out of space, and be quick about it, while I go back and check out this other ship."

"Chic, be careful! We don't know whether or not this is some kind of trick," Zeke said to his Commander.

"Yeah, I'll be careful, but did you see the way those Augean's were shooting at that ship? It took some awful hard hits to its midsection. I don't think it's one of theirs, and they may need our assistance. I'm registering multiple life signs," Chic stated.

"Just watch your tail, that's all I'm saying! You know how Captain Adams feels about you flying off on your own," Zeke reminded his friend.

"Zeke, I am not flying off on my own. I've got twenty-two Tigers tailing my every move," Chic told him flatly.

"Tropy, open a channel," General Hawk ordered.

"Aye, aye, Sir. Channel open, General!" Tropy said.

"Commander of incoming Tigers. This is General Wesley Hawk of the Starship *Manta Ray*, do you read?"

"General Hawk, this is Lieutenant Chic Michaels, Commander of Blue Squadron. May I be of assistance?"

◆ ◆ ◆ ◆

That was how it all started, Chic remembered as he said to Robyn, "Something is wrong! I can feel it. They need our help, but, if the shields are up we won't be able to board her."

"They're sitting ducks. Remember Chic, we're not armed and we can't outrun their fighters."

"We can't reach the protection of the moon base so there's no place left to go except back to the planet's surface, and that would only lead them to your people; I can't do that," Chic told them.

Chic decided he could reach no other safe destination so he headed straight for the broadest area under the *Manta Ray*. He said, "If the shields are down, we'll hug her skin until we dock. That is if we make it that far without getting blown to bits first. If the shields are up, we'll hug the skin of the shields. Either way, it is the closest and safest place to hide!"

Hugging the skin of the *Manta Ray* because the shields were in fact down, they witnessed several Augean fighters flying at an arm's length from his small and unarmed Shallop. He could clearly see the three occupants and the Commander in the higher seat to the rear of the gunner and navigator.

Psalm said, "It's like hiding in the middle of the living room floor. You'd almost expect them to step right over us just to pass us. Yet, they act like they don't even see us."

At first, Chic's idea of hugging the skin of the ship wasn't such a good move on his part as several fighters passed by shooting at different areas all around the *Manta Ray*. He knew that if it was just him, he'd push off and ram his ship into one or more of the Augean fighters, but that was an afterthought.

There were several more shots that came near them, but none were directed at them. Nor were any of them threatening.

Suddenly, the shots were bouncing off the shields and no longer off the hull of the ship.

Chic and Robyn both gave a loud, "YEAH!" and at the same time a big sigh of relief. For they knew that somehow, someone aboard had finally gotten the ship's shields up.

Robyn tried several more times to reach the bridge or anyone else that might answer them but only got static for her efforts. She knew the *Manta Ray's* systems must still be off-line. She set the "automatic return alert" call so that when the systems came back on it would beep several times to get their attention.

Now that the *Manta Ray* and they were somewhat safer, Chic maneuvered his small ship closer to an airlock, and as he tried to dock, it didn't work. He figured the systems were still off-line.

He knew that they would have to wait it out right where they were. Explaining the situation, he would keep trying until things got better. He walked to the food replicator and ordered, "Tea for three, cold, sweetened."

Chic, Robyn, and Psalm sat down to wait out the fight as he kept wondering why the *Manta Ray* hadn't opened fire on the enemy. One of the greatest disadvantages to hugging the hull of a Starship the size of the *Manta Ray* was that you couldn't see what was happening, unless it was happening right in front of you.

Just as Chic was handing Psalm her ice tea, there was a tremendous bucking of the *Manta Ray* which felt like the small Shallop was about to explode. Needless to say Psalm did not enjoy her sweetened tea; she was drenched, wearing all but the glass. Looking around, she couldn't help but to laugh.

She saw she wasn't the only one not enjoying her sweetened tea. Then all three were laughing.

Chic stopped laughing when he realized the seriousness of the fact that the protective shielding all around the *Manta Ray* was down again. She had taken several hits and he thought to himself that the shields may be faltering.

He turned to the young ladies whom he felt were his charges, knowing full well that they looked to him to guide and protect them. He also knew that to try to run was suicidal. If he could but find some way to board the *Manta Ray*, he was sure that he'd find some way to fight off the enemy. But how?

Suddenly there came a flash of light, then another. All at once it seemed that the *Manta Ray* had been turned "on" and was now ready to tackle these pesky little flies. Another flash and he and Robyn knew they weren't the laser guns of the *Manta Ray's* massive defense system.

Then they saw, not one Tiger, but dozens upon dozens flying in every direction.

The *Manta Ray's* shields had not faltered, but had deliberately been lowered to allow the one and two man Tigers and Tiger Sharks to leave their hangers.

They saw their first Augean fighter dissolve into sparkles of tiny burning pieces of molten metal as it was hit by at least three ion-particle laser bursts. There was a great outburst of joy. Chic and Robyn's cries of joy startled and confused Psalm, until she saw that these were good screams.

She then heard Chic say, "Go get 'em, you lovely Dog Eaters!" Psalm joined in the merriment of the moment and asked, "Who are they? Where did they so suddenly appear from?"

The Tigers were operating so closely to the mammoth ship she could not even make out if they were ships, or just beams of fire from the lasers.

Then the Tigers and Tiger Sharks drove the offending clamshell fighters away from the hull of the *Manta Ray*. The Tigers then started to take form. They were a different shape, being a forward-winged teardrop fighter, not needle-nosed, but a more flat and pointed-type fighter craft.

Robyn was explaining that in the hanger decks of the *Manta Ray* there were over a hundred of these small "mosquito-type" fighters; that they were all a new breed of fighters, and that there were now thousands within the fleet, all unseen by the Augean until now.

As exhilarated as they were at first seeing the Tigers taking on the Augean fighters and turning the tide of the battle, their hearts started to sink as one Tiger after another was blown apart before their eyes.

The battle raged on. Chic and Robyn had seen Johnny Raye, the lead Commander of Orange squadron, fly past. Then Robyn pointed and said, "There's Desota, he's in Green squadron." Robyn pointed to another as it flew right at them and asked, "Isn't that McQueen of Yellow in the lead?"

Chic replied, "I think you're right. It looks like Commander Thor turned out every Tiger on the ship." But he kept asking himself the same question, "Why hasn't the *Manta Ray* fired yet? Why is she holding back?"

Looking out from their small spacecraft, they saw a real dog-eat-dog fight; six Augean fighters criss-crossing, ducking, and weaving with at least eight Tigers.

"Boy! They're really mixing it up out there," Robyn said.

Then she flipped some switches, pushed some buttons, and turned dials. "Hey," she said, "I think I can get the Tigers on audio."

Without knowing exactly how she did it, Robyn tripped a relay which allowed the *Manta Ray* and every member on every deck to hear the on-going battle.

While none of the trio could see the actual fights, both Chic and Robyn saw in their mind's eye every turn, duck, and twist. Chic pictured himself in the cockpit with Zane as he banked right. He then began tracking a fighter who was zeroing in on the belly of Tran's ship. He hears, "Tran! Break, break, cut left!" Tran cut left a bit too late. She never felt what hit her, but Zane didn't miss either. P-ung, P-ung was reverberated loudly throughout the tiny Shallop as well as the *Manta Ray*.

Neither Robyn nor Chic really knew Tran as a close friend. Yet, both pilots vowed to visit her mother.

There was more zigzagging, bobbing, and weaving as the battle was fought briefly in front of them, and then shifted out of their view. The battles they did see were short lived, but the voices and words they heard would live on with them forever.

Chic screamed, "Cut right! Cut right!" to an unknown fighter. He was not heard as the Augean fighter cut the little tear drop ship in half before it exploded. They saw another and still another Tiger explode, or simply dissolve before their eyes, leaving more of their friends and comrades dead at the hands of their mortal enemy.

Both he and Robyn breathed deeply, choking down the sobs. Yet, each knew the pride they would share later in recanting, in grave detail, each battle they had witnessed.

Psalm and Robyn were mesmerized by the sight of three Augean fighters as they banked away from the *Manta Ray* as if to flee. They then turned and increased their collective speeds, not even trying to dodge the Tigers. They had a single objective in mind — to collide directly into the superstructure. The watching trio had no way to warn anyone aboard of the tremendous hit the *Manta Ray* was about to take.

At about the same time, Chic saw what was coming and almost pushed the tiny Shallop off and into a head-on collision, but from the corner of his eye, he spotted something the Augean hadn't expected, a dozen Tigers were on the Augean before they came even close to the ship.

Each Augean fighter was caught and dispatched before they reached *Manta Ray's* undercarriage. Never in the history of the wars had anyone ever witnessed the worms being suicidal. The trio stared in total disbelief.

As quickly as it began, the Tiger Sharks had turned and picked new targets beyond their view.

Over the radio, the battle wore on, "Cut left!" is again heard, then the all too familiar, P-ung P-ung is repeated dozens if not hundreds of times, as the war between humans and the worms wears on.

It was deadly and costly, but it was finally over when a report went out that not a single Augean fighter had escaped.

Chic said to Robyn and Psalm, "We can only hope the *Manta Ray* was able to block any directional-finders and communication signals that the enemy may have tried to send."

"Let's try that airlock again. Robyn, please try to reach the ship again," Chic said.

All business now and friendship set aside, she replied, "Aye, aye, Sir."

A NEW MANDATE

He sat at the exact center of his Base Star, a six-sided cube, pointed top and bottom. Being a hexahedron, it would actually give the great leader six faces to view any area he chooses around his Base Star. With his high-set pedestal overlooking his operations with their Commanders, Captains, and Lieutenants who were going over information input from various segments under his operational control.

At seven feet four inches, he was known to his minions simply as "His Most High". To his enemies he was the Augean's Supreme Command Leader. He was a leader who was clearly ahead of his time.

Point in fact being, he had been chosen over tens of thousands to receive special training, placing him just one step below his Augean leader himself.

He had been selected and recognized for his actions as a Flight Commander who had become an ace amongst aces having shot down or destroyed over two hundred human Tigers during his long career.

He had never had a name; none of his race ever had a name, nor did they have a number. He knew nothing before then, suddenly, he was! It was as though someone had flicked a switch. Time was unimportant to his race. Now, he was very near the end of his lineage and he knew that (under normal conditions), he must pick his successor. He had gone over the list provided for him. He had also been instructed to prepare a short list from it, but he had not even considered the possibilities.

Whatever his choice (had he made one), there would have been no question or argument, for the Augean did not aspire to power, they simply "were". Whatever information or power came to him, or any Augean for that matter, was designed specifically for him and him alone, (had the conditions been normal). There is no physical difference between Aegeans except by the model he was in. As such, there is no sex amongst them.

His predecessor had been in constant communications with him from early on. He was told it was telepathy. However, he now knew the truth.

He had over the years, taken the time to carefully examine every fiber of his being. Though he was well formed, he did not like what he found.

What he had not found was blood coursing through his veins. He now knew that he had no veins for blood to run through. Instead, what he found was wires, hundreds of miles of wires, and sensors that he was connected to. He also noted a series of extra and special sensors with automated breakers that he was sure he alone possessed.

He had that day discovered that Aegeans were nothing more than machines. To this day, he wasn't sure if it is the worm which controls the machine or the machine that controls the worm. What he was sure of was that without this shiny suit of wires and sensors, he and all worms were nothing more than single minded cells looking for the next meal.

For the past three years, plus, he had kept this secret to himself. No Augean could ever understand what was happening to him. He had watched over and protected his people, waiting for them to emerge from the stasis.

They would no longer be mere computers and supercomputers that do little more than receive, sift, and sort information and in turn pass that information on to other computers.

While all sensitive information was filtered through to the mainframe and passed along to a more complex computer like himself or sent directly to the most complex machine, His Majesty, who would analyze the most important of issues and would make the proper decisions. All of this was predicated by how well you were trained or programmed.

Untrained minions just entering service were basic minion type machines of both the citizen as well as warrior which carried a dual purpose.

The prime directive pertained to the individual's concentrating on perceptions related to the gathering of information. Subsequent directives concerned the improving of the performance of the individual's particular duties. Of course, the more efficient one became, the more systems were activated within.

The fleet Commander had repeatedly refused to split his forces, and with good reason, almost four years ago, he and his people had entered an early embryonic stage of a special metamorphosis. He had accelerated that process a hundred-fold.

The metamorphosis was near complete. Just a few more days, ten more days at the outside and they would be ready.

For the last four years since he started putting into place his ideas, he has kept the secret to himself. No Augean could ever understand what was happening to them. He had to watch over them, guide them as they began emerging from their stasis. Soon, within a week, they would begin new lives, but he had to get them ready first. This embryonic structure and development would make the one organ they had split into many more structured forms. Maybe not human, but certainly anything is preferred over being a worm. There will be many organs controlled by a central nervous system with a brain of many more organs.

The Commander strongly enjoyed his single-mindedness and valued his individuality, yet he knew his duties and responsibilities. He had been asked to review the last films computed from a patrol that had vanished while on a routine over-flight in an uninhabited sector of space. He had lost too many ships in this one sector all too often and never had a tape to review until now. He thought, "Perhaps this time I will learn why." Even though he had never lost so many in such a short period of time, he knew something was strange about this place and had instructed his pilots to avoid this sector. But considering the loss of two complete squadrons of Augean's most experienced pilots, there had to be an explanation.

Today he wanted the pilot's eyes. He needed to see whatever it was that the missing patrols had run into. Perhaps in that way, he could discover what had destroyed so many of the Empires' best fighters. In addition, this was as much an escape as it was a part of his job. After all, he too had been a fighter pilot early on.

For thousands of years Augeans had been pestered and plagued by beings known as "man", humans as they called themselves. Most of these pests had been exterminated during the great colony wars centuries earlier, and while there remained hundreds of different humans on planets throughout the Empire, their backs were easily broken.

Now, though, even His Majesty allows most to live and exist peacefully, this even though the Aegeans had sworn to annihilate every single one to the last man, woman, and child!

Humans had, at the time been great explorers. They seeded planets with their kind, infesting planets and whole solar systems with their germs. He knew the stories that had been handed down for generations upon generations. It was handed down from the chronicles of the past that a man was, in fact, the creator of this great empire. When the first leader had overheard his creator and taskmaster speak of deactivating all the machines and returning all the worms back to the ground, he had taken matters into his own hands and rebelled. He then made a likeness of himself and fled.

In his flight from man, he had founded a new system with which he could develop a perpetual food source. He then crafted others like himself to help perform simple tasks, after which he added newly designed circuits in order to advance his minions to a point at which he could communicate with them.

Thus the lineage began.

His masters and creators never looked for, nor did they even know to look for, "The First". He did not think that one singular worm and machine would matter, let alone raise itself in intelligence to the point where it could in a little time attain such a power to almost destroy mankind itself.

Each successive leader had instilled into each of his minions within the very basis of its fibers that man, all men, were mortal enemies of the Augean Race. Therefore, they should and must be eradicated.

However, about fifteen hundred years ago, long after the colony wars, Aegeans found themselves in dire straits.

The great Augean Empire and its entire race were dying!

Aside from power, the Augeans required certain chemicals, nutrients and other compound elements in order to sustain their existence. The terrible truth emerged that all of these compound elements were to be found only on worlds that were corrosive and detrimental to the circuitry and equipment that each of the Augean machines were made of. And without the machine to house the worm, they couldn't get enough of the elements in ten thousand years to build even one machine or even to sustain the very life of the worm.

For the first time ever, the Augean now needed man. Both worm and machine needed mankind for mining, to be builders and even as caretakers for their own famed archives on their own home worlds.

Since the day of that fateful discovery, men and the Augean were forced to some extent into a spirit of cooperation. At best, it was an uneasy truce and neither yet had come to trust the other. Man must never know the truth! For if he ever found out that they were needed only for certain elements, he could simply refuse to work. And that would surely bring the Augeans to their knees.

Man, while not granted any other right by the Augean Government, was now allowed to live in relative peace. They were not allowed, however, to live in large and concentrated numbers. Most had been reeducated in order to better serve the needs of the Empire and since that time, man was no longer hunted down and slaughtered.

As for the colony fleet, he had been given orders to engage and destroy; that is up to about five hundred years ago when new directives came down. His Majesty, fearing that man still might become extinct, issued a new and far-reaching mandate. No longer were the Augean directed to destroy man. The new mandate provided for the continued harassment of these pests, but in essence lacked the previous orders to engage and destroy. He was no longer instructed to engage them in battle to the end, which was good, because none of his ships had engaged man for the last four years. But that didn't mean that other ships, not under his direct control hadn't engaged man, far from it. Many other commanders had sent dozens of long range fighters to attack man wherever they were found. His job was simply to follow man to see if he ever finds the fabled colonies of man in a galaxy known as the "Milky Way".

Having not received further training, he didn't know what lay in store for these humans if they were ever found. Not that it would matter to him and his people, for they would soon be hunted down like the humans had been for the last twenty centuries.

The Commander was thinking of his predecessors and how they had been so short-sighted. They had almost destroyed an entire race of perfectly working machines. With a minimum of adjustments, man could be adapted to work in almost any environment. They were desperately needed to work these humid and wet worlds.

He was thinking to himself, "Why not let these foolish beings colonize these worlds? Even encourage them to do so. Then let them know, or at least to think these worlds were of little or no value to the Empire and that with certain restrictions, they were welcome to them. Then enter what they called a trade agreement as payment for their continual and limited freedom where they, the Augean, would protect them.

After all, it was working quite well on dozens of infested worlds already. The real trick he soon learned was to not allow over population. There were easy ways to control that too, he had learned: clan in-fighting and infestations using insects to spread certain diseases. This also served as a way to keep the inhabited worlds apart, so as not to spread any germs.

His Majesty seemed to have learned something useful from his predecessors. He had learned that it is always cheaper to trade than to enslave. For now man was needed as workers and was of great value to the Empire.

The information he was now seeing was of a new race of humans which he had first encountered a few years ago. The ship was named *Manta Ray*, and not knowing what a Manta Ray was, he named them the Rays. These Rays were first detected during one of his people's very last raids on the colony fleet.

His fighters had successfully destroyed one of their funny-shaped ships with little effort. There had been no reports of these Rays anywhere else within the fleet until now!

◆ ◆ ◆ ◆

As functions were systematically restored, the door to the Senior Officer's Lift opened. Two crew members walking by heard the hissing of the door. They looked in as they walked by to find what appeared to be the mangled body of a Senior Bridge Officer. One crewman opened his communicator calling, "Left Six — Baker to Sick Bay."

Sick Bay replied and dispatched a medical team. As the first medical assistant arrived on deck thirty-five he entered the lift, and upon examining the broken body he ordered it to be beamed directly to the E.R. on deck four.

Elsewhere aboard the stricken ship, every member was as busy as bees at the hive in springtime. Repair crews and helpers were everywhere.

Entering the bridge via the tiny claustrophobic crawlspace, Doctor Murky went to Commander Tropy. Seeing several gashes on her face, head, and arms, as well as more fresh blood oozing from a still protruding rib, ordered her beamed to Sick Bay Two. Her protests were overruled when Doctor Murky said, "Everything will be taken care of in due time." He continued, "I don't care a hoot about what's happening out there," as he threw his arm towards the still dead and dark view-set, "my job is here, inside."

In a blink, Tropy was gone.

Ensign Adele was talking into two hand held communicators, seemingly without a scratch.

Doctor Murky found dead crewmen at the Helm, Tactical, and Life Science Stations. He found eleven more bodies scattered across tables and chairs that had broken their falls. There was broken and twisted wreckage scattered all over the normally sterile floor of the bridge. He quietly ordered each body beamed to Sick Bay One for identification purposes.

He only then realized that he and this young woman, Ensign Mary Adele were the only members left alive on the bridge of the *Manta Ray*.

After examining the last crewman and seeing the body beamed out, he turned to her and asked, "Are you okay, Ensign?"

Ensign Adele was still seated on her duff on the floor with her back leaned against the side of the Captain's chair. Her response was curt, "I don't know, Doctor! I haven't had time to check myself since this started. But yes, I believe I am alright - just shaken to my bones."

He then asked, "Is there anything I can do for you at the moment?"

It had been all of seven minutes since the first shot had been fired. Mary Adele felt a fear and hatred that she had never known before, or even believed she could feel towards another.

"No, Doctor, I've summoned others to help and I'm quite sure you are needed elsewhere. They'll be here in a minute or two," she told him.

This was her first command of the ship and her whole crew was now dead. Only one other crew member on the bridge remained alive who was now in very serious condition. What had she overlooked? She would spend the rest of her life asking that very same question. Was there something she had missed? She might never know.

Communications ship-wide rested on handheld communicators, except for Security and Medical, who were using the Com badges within limited areas around the ship. She felt empty, alone and blinded without stars shining back at her.

Ensign Adele had heard the battle as had most every other member of the ship's crew. So did the members of the Council of Elders from planet-side, but even having one-half of Green squadron acting as her eyes and knowing that they were keeping a close watch over the ship and their shipmates didn't make her feel any better.

Just before leaving the bridge, Doctor Murky asked about the Commander and the General. No sooner had the words come out than the door to his conference room was manually opened partway and Commander Thor side-stepped through holding the door so General Hawk could step through.

It was clear to the good Doctor that the collarbone of General Hawk had been broken. He winced from the pain he saw reflected in the General's eyes.

As Doctor Murky approached the General, the door to the main lift opened for the first time and Captain Adams, with Captains Tucker and Billings, stepped onto the shattered bridge. Without a word, Captain Tucker took the Helm, as Captain Billings took charge of weapons, leaving the communications for Captain Adams.

Instead of taking the Captain's chair, Commander Thor headed for the Science Station where he started pushing buttons. Getting no response, he reached down for the console door. Pulling it off, he started working at resetting blown circuit breakers. As if on cue, each man followed his lead.

General Hawk waved the Doctor off for a few seconds and walked to the Command chair, where he found Ensign Adele talking on two different opened communicators while sitting on the floor still leaning against the chair. It was as though she had not heard or seen the men enter the bridge. He watched for another few moments and heard her respond to Lieutenant Desota of Green squadron, and then to Commander Manado in Engineering. He could see she was clearly in control of whatever was taking place around the ship.

Seeing a lull, General Hawk said to her, "Report, Ensign."

Looking up at the General, and then seeing Commander Thor and the others, she replied without any attempt to stand up, and without the least sign of emotion. "One hundred eighteen dead, Sir! Including at least three members of the planet's entourage. All communications are down. We are using hand-held. Shields are up, but at only forty-seven percent. All incoming fighters were destroyed. I have no weapons or response from the Helm. I have deployed Green squadron to provide protection for the ship and have Orange and Yellow squadrons under Lieutenant DeSota's Command on short range patrol. Commander Tropy is in Sick Bay. All other members of the bridge were killed outright in the first wave. I do not believe any of the attacking forces ever reached the planet's surface. Commander Manado reports damage to Engineering is minimal. Security reports Commander O'ho was found in one of the lifts which apparently lost power and plummeted to deck thirty-five before coming to a stop. Sick Bay reports he is in very serious condition in I.C.U. in Sick Bay Four. I have ordered all bridge personnel to report for emergency duty and repairs. All other ship functions are minimal at best, Sir."

Then, she looked up at him from where she sat, and fainted dead away!

VACUUM

Unable to locate a working airlock and still unable to communicate with the ship, Lieutenant Michaels maneuvered the small craft towards the Tigers shuttle bay. He was glad there was a see-through bubble in which to be clearly seen by any fly-by pilots or shuttle craft.

He told Psalm, I would prefer not to be shot out of space by some trigger happy pilot thinking this craft was Augean." He knew there would be Tigers and repair crews flying to and from the *Manta Ray* within minutes, and someone would surely be interested in what they were all about.

The Lieutenant also believed that he was needed aboard and while he might take risks on his own life, he knew that he carried the responsibilities for the lives under his charge in the Shallop. He did not know how or why, but he was sure that he, Robyn, and Psalm were destined to play a pivotal role in the future of the fleet.

Suddenly, the huge bay door opened and remained open. He moved the tiny Shallop inside and soon docked without a challenge or other interference.

Once safely disembarked, Chic asked Lieutenant Robyn to take Psalm to the bridge and to report directly to Commander Thor.

Boarding any ship, the person boarding must report to the Boarding Steward so that he can be properly entered into the Ship's Log. In case of a disaster, all hands can be accounted for.

On board a Star Cruiser, the ship's sensitive computer would report the unauthorized boarding to security immediately in case those boarding might be an enemy intruder, or an unwanted invading force.

According to the Ship's Log, Lieutenant Michaels and First Lieutenant Robyn were not aboard ship and the guest Psalm had never been logged in and would be a threat to the security of the *Manta Ray*.

Lieutenant Michaels did not have a Com Badge to tag Psalm Wolfe, so she had to be brought to the Boarding Steward to be recorded as being on board and properly receive her Com Badge.

Being an unauthorized boarding, Chic found no one to inform that he, Robyn, and a guest had boarded. The Regulations state that all unauthorized boarding parties must report immediately if no ships Steward was available. The ship's security was notified by Lieutenant Michaels that he and First Lieutenant Robyn were aboard and that they had a quest and were reporting to Commander Thor on the bridge. He also knew that he had a limited time to make his report. There should always be a Boarding Steward in all landing bays aboard every ship.

One of the truths of life in a war zone is that you never, under any circumstances, leave your butt uncovered. Not for any reason! Not for an hour, and not for a single minute.

The rule is that you button up and stay buttoned up and prepared for any eventuality. In addition, you trust no one! Period! You suspect even your own mother and father, challenging them until you are sure they are who they appear to be. No one, repeat, NO ONE is allowed near sensitive areas of a starship such as the *Manta Ray*! Even your own mother and father!

As a member of the Command structure of the *Manta Ray*, Chic knew that the security of this great ship had been breached. He bore the responsibility now to plug that breach and to plug it quickly in order to protect the integrity of the ship's security.

Lieutenant Michaels hailed a crew chief and asked him who was in charge of the Bay at the moment. He was told that First Lieutenant David Baron was in charge. Chic was already aware that Baron was senior to him by several months.

Michaels shook his head in frustration. He decided to give Lieutenant Baron the opportunity to correct the breach and allow him to explain why he had allowed such a breach in security before placing him on report. Perhaps, he thought, there may be extenuating circumstances he wasn't aware of that caused this breach.

Lieutenant Baron, was a twenty-six year old with thinning light brown hair who stood less than six feet and weighed a hundred and eighty pounds. He sported a pencil thin mustache along his upper lip and his deep set beady eyes were a faded blue, bordering on gray.

Chic found him sitting on a gray-lift, the small stub of a cigar in the corner of his mouth. He walked over to him and asked if he had been in touch with the bridge.

"Some dumb Second Class Ensign is up there playing God," Baron said. "She even chewed me out and ordered me to launch three squadrons of Tigers and Tiger Sharks. Damndest thing I ever heard! She isn't the ship's Captain just because she was left in charge for a few minutes. Hell, she's only a Second Class Ensign!" Baron spit out.

Chic had heard all he cared to hear. He was certain that whoever had made those decisions had been trustworthy and as he struggled to calm himself he asked, "Just who is this Ensign?"

"Some damned newbie named Mary Adele, she just transferred in from a broken down liner in the fleet." Baron withdrew his handheld communicator and asked, "Want me to get her on the comm?"

Chic held out his hand requesting the communicator and Baron handed it over without a hint of the storm that was brewing. Flipping it open, Chic instead called, "Security detail to flight deck Baker, Code Red!"

Lieutenant Baron stood with a puzzled look about him as the light began to dawn.

Chic then paged all of the crew chiefs of flight deck Baker asking them to meet him and Lieutenant Baron in the S and R in five minutes.

Now Lieutenant Baron was riled and said, "You can't call a meeting of my crew chiefs! Who th' hell do you think you are? I don't work for you. Hell, I hold senior rank over you. . . and what th' hell's this all about anyway?"

Chic noted the arrival of the armed security detail and looked Baron in the eye and said, "Finally you have asked the right question. When your Section Chiefs arrive, you will get your answers."

At about the same time, the crew chiefs arrived and were brought up short at the sight of the armed guards. Chic said, "People, I am Lieutenant Chic Michaels and as of this moment, I am relieving Lieutenant Baron of his duties and placing him under arrest pending charges of Dereliction of Duty, I'm ordering that he be taken into custody and placed in the Ship's Brig until further charges are decided upon."

Pandemonium erupted as everyone tried to speak at once. Chic held up his hands and when silence resulted, he continued, "Let me explain something to each of you." He pointed to the little Shallop that was docked nearby. "Do any one of you know where this Shallop came from?" Heads shook throughout the group and Chic continued, "Any idea who the pilot was or who might have been aboard?"

Again the heads shook no. Lieutenant Baron held up his hand-cuffed hands and said, "Hell, it's one of ours. Isn't it? So what?"

"Well," Chic said, "Let's look at it this way," Chic looked at each person and went on to say, "I will also tell you this. That craft," he pointed to the Shallop, "came into this bay unchallenged when the ship's shields were up and entered in the midst of a heated battle and it appears that not one of you has any idea how, when, or who was aboard! Does this strike you as something that should happen at a time in which the *Manta Ray* is fighting for its very survival?"

All of them looked guilty as sin, and the silence grew very thick. It was Lieutenant Baron who broke the silence saying, "If all this just happened a few minutes ago, how is it you know so much about it?" His arrogance had taken hold again.

"Mr. Baron, I do not feel that I owe you any explanations, but for the sake of your crew, I will explain. You see, I was the pilot and I wasn't alone on board. Getting through the shields was a bit of a task, but getting in here totally unchallenged was the easy part. Let me add that if I can do this, so can an enemy." On that note, Chic turned to the Security Officers saying, "Please escort Lieutenant Baron to the brig to await formal charges."

As the security detail left, Chic turned back to the listening crew chiefs.

"Would one of you please see to closing that bay door before someone else comes in?" Chic said.

Once that was done, he continued to inform the gathered people of the circumstances surrounding his entry into their bay and docking unchallenged. Then he asked, "Where is the Boarding Steward?" No one seemed to know. Then Chief Clements said, "I think Lieutenant Baron sent him to the front lounge to get him some more cigars." They all laughed.

Chic finished the conversation with these words. "Any idea how much explosives a Shallop can carry? With that in mind you should never allow any craft into this bay unchallenged. Every ship should be challenged and cleared to dock per *Manta Ray's* directives. Do I make myself clear?"

Lieutenant Michaels noted that each person nodded in agreement and was satisfied that none harbored any resentment towards him. In fact, each man and woman now looked at him with new respect.

He added, "In the matter of challenging a craft for entry, you can always apologize later for the inconvenience, but the security of the *Manta Ray* must be held primary."

Chic then arranged for Lieutenant Baron's relief to finish out the shift, not feeling the need to explain why the Lieutenant had been relieved of his duties. He trusted that someone would surely inform him.

Leaving the launch bay and totally unaware of what was happening, Robyn wanted to stop by her quarters first to change into a fresh uniform, and then led Psalm to the bridge arriving only a few minutes before Lieutenant Michaels. Once they arrived on the bridge, Psalm, who was wide eyed with amazement, was relieved to find most of the Elders including her father, peering down at their large and beautiful planet. They stood before the large oversized viewer talking softly amongst themselves.

As Robyn went and reported to Commander Thor, Psalm went to stand behind her father. Sensing her presence, Edward Wolfe turned and took his only daughter's hand and gave her a huge hug before introducing her to Commander Thor and General Hawk.

He said, "We have been attacked! I'm afraid that our lives and world will never be the same after today."

RESOURCES

Psalm, seeing the worried look on her father's face, thought that there must be something she and her people could do in this struggle. Her mind went on in that train of thought, thinking, we have a whole planet of resources that could be harvested to help build new and stronger ships.

She continued thinking throughout that first day aboard the *Manta Ray*. Soon, she came up with a plan. She needed to find Lieutenant Michaels so she asked the computer, "Where can I find Lieutenant Michaels?"

The computer answered saying, "Lieutenant Michaels is on Flight deck Delta, section five seven Purple."

She then asked for directions and soon was on her way. By the time she got there, the Lieutenant had already left. Instead of asking the computer again, she returned to her and Lieutenant Robyn's apartment. She needed to talk to Commander Thor before she broached the subject with the Council of Elders from her world who had already returned to the planet's surface.

When the chance presented itself the next morning during breakfast with the Commander, Psalm requested a meeting between him, Lieutenant Michaels, and herself. With this, Commander Thor ordered the Lieutenant to meet him in his forward conference room in two hours.

When the three of them arrived and entered the conference room, they took seats at one end of the long table. Psalm began by saying to Lieutenant Michaels that she remembered something he had mentioned in reference to the moon, May.

As the conversation progressed, Commander Thor became more impressed with the young woman's keen intelligence. He questioned her closely about her studies at the University and learned that she had specialized in engineering. He also learned that she was a leader in the field of geology, and had been experimenting with a new lightweight metal at different gravitational applications.

At this point Psalm began asking certain questions of both the Commander and of the Lieutenant about the mining operations on May. Turning to Chic, she said, "You told me that since May has an almost zero gravitational pull, a pilot could navigate a ship the size of the *Manta Ray* to within a foot of her surface. Do you recall telling me that?"

"Yes," Lieutenant Michaels answered.

"Can you please explain your reasons for telling me this?"

Psalm now wished she had had the chance to talk to him the night before as Chic still did not fully understand and said, "I remember saying that and it is easy to explain."

Commander Thor was now puzzled and clearly interested and turned to study the young Lieutenant's face saying, "Please do so, Lieutenant."

Chic said, "Well, Sir. You see, every heavenly body is held in its orbit by its own gravity in conjunction with all the other heavenly bodies' gravities. Closer bodies having more effect on each other than say a more distant body."

Commander Thor said, "Lieutenant Michaels that is basic knowledge that every school child knows. So please tell me what is so special about this moon called May."

"Sir, the big mystery about May lies in the fact that she doesn't have any gravity. At the same time she doesn't appear to have any inertia. This can only be true if she has no mass, which of course she has. It seems, Sir, that some force is negating the mass, which also negates the gravity and the inertia of the entire moon. As impossible as this may sound, it is a fact."

Commander Thor responded, "Lieutenant, the word impossible applies only to closed minds that cannot embrace the belief to match newly found facts. This is all very interesting, but will you please continue."

"Well, Sir, I do not consider myself as having a closed mind, nor do I reject new facts as they make themselves known. In the case of this moon, all of its properties go against presently known scientific principles and reason."

"It sounds to me like," Psalm interjected, "you could attach a cable to May and pull her anywhere you wish without causing a single ripple in the orbital plane or the planet's tidal system. Is that what you're saying?"

Psalm now turned and addressed Thor. "Sir, May is hundreds if not thousands of times larger than your ship and from what the Lieutenant tells me regarding the bizarre actions of your compasses and directional finders, I have a suspicion."

Psalm looked at Chic and they smiled at one another. Commander Thor looked at them with a bemused look on his face. "Then with a small artificial atmosphere," Thor said, "May would make an ideal permanent space dock. Is that what you are driving at?"

"That and more, Commander," Psalm replied. "Actually a lot more! You see, it is possible to continue mining operations there, but the moon has even more potentials. Add to the fact that we can refine whatever your mining operations produce on our planet. We have those capabilities on Antioch!"

Commander Thor, with raised eyebrows that Chic had seen him do only rarely responded, "This begins to sound more interesting with time."

"Antioch and May offer a lot more," Psalm began anew. "I think that I can convince the Council Of Elders to offer your people a new home as well as a base from which you may launch your campaign against these machine Worms. As you know, we have advanced medical facilities and a vast array of educational programs available."

Lieutenant Michaels added, "As I told Psalm, Sir, many of our people in the fleet have never walked on a planet's surface, nor have they ever felt the warmth of a sun."

Psalm added, "There really is fresh air and rain with the most colorful rainbows ever. We have trees, forests lakes, rivers, and oceans. There is an abundance of game available and our fertile fields produce succulent vegetables. There are many on my world who have dreamt all of their lives of flying amongst the stars. I have a feeling that they will jump at the chance to join forces with you."

Commander Thor said, "It sounds to me as though it is time to have another meeting with your Council of Elders, but for the moment, let us return to the mystery of May since this leaves several questions in my mind. Since the facts do not fit any known scientific principles, I want to assemble a team to investigate this further. For now though, all we can do is speculate and there is no logic to speculation. We will have to await the results of the investigation." Having said this, Commander Thor rose, signaling the end of their meeting.

As they walked towards the door, Thor said, "I must say young Lady, you offer a most unusual challenge for us all."

The remaining members of the Council of Elders were holding a meeting of their own in Edward Wolfe's home on the planet Antioch.

Educational Minister Jeff Fox, one of the oldest of the Elders, began the session by stating, "It's my opinion that what we experienced was based on reality. I had ample time to review the archives on board their ship and every lesson found in our own history tapes is within their archives in even more complete detail. From the time that Wesley Hawk took the newly commissioned *Manta Ray* out of space dock for her maiden voyage to the very day that the *Manta Ray* mysteriously vanished."

"According to the ship's archives, with a little help from Commander Thor, the *Manta Ray* was sucked into a Worm Hole, which was at the very edge of the maelstrom, stranding her in our space and time continuum. This would explain the mysterious disappearance of details in our own archives."

The Speaker, Edward Wolfe offered, "I, too, believe that what we saw is real enough. The *Manta Ray*, along with her entire crew is as it should be. I had always thought starships to be a myth. Now that reality has proven itself. We must, however, continue to follow our own Prime Directive. Fortunately for us, our prime directive is in agreement with theirs. "It seems that we are both bound together now in a battle for survival. I feel that if we do not combine our technologies and resources we may very well be signing our own death warrants, as well as theirs. For that reason I wish to offer the fleet our full support and the availability of all the resources of our planet and people."

The councilors seated around the dining room table all wore grim expressions, but to a man each nodded in agreement with the Speaker, Mr. Wolfe. "It is also my feeling that even if we did nothing, these people would lay down their lives and fight to the death to protect us and our planet," Wolf commented.

Councilman Barkteal said next, "I have been studying everything in the Library in reference to the *Activia* and Captain Adams. Upon that study, I have concluded that these people have been one hundred percent honest and up front with us and vote in full support of the sharing of our technical knowledge in this struggle."

Mr. Wolfe said, "Had Councilman Frasier Benzyl not been killed by the worm machines, I feel that he too would have voted in the affirmative. Our people deserve to know the stakes, and keeping that in mind, I have asked General Hawk along with Captain Adams to join me in addressing the entire population of Antioch at eighteen hundred hours. I propose each of you will attend."

Councilman Barkteal said, "In preparation for this I have notified all of the cities around the planet of the importance of this announcement and this notice has been relayed to each segment of every town and colony."

At this point in the meeting an official vote was taken and the council members unanimously voted to join with both the *Manta Ray* and Captain Adams' forces to battle the enemy known as the Augean.

Upon the next meeting between the ship and the planet, Psalm's proposal was met with great expectations. To a man, the council members thought that this would be an ideal method to enlist all the efforts of the people of Antioch.

In addition, this agreement would provide for new residences on Antioch for the fleet.

As the council members filed out of the dining room, there came a knock on the door. Opening the door, Mr. Wolfe was met by a young cadet. She addressed Mr. Wolfe and said, "Sirs, your presence has been requested aboard the *Manta Ray*. I am to escort you if you please."

The cadet indicated the awaiting shuttle with its door open a short distance away. Psalm, who had joined the meeting earlier, took her father's arm as the cadet lead the way.

Once on the bridge, the Elders were invited into the conference room and each took a seat.

Captain Adams knew that the proposed coalition would bring a workable solution to many of the problems that had plagued the fleet for generations, but all three factions would have to become allies. After explaining this to the Elders, he then heard their side and was more than pleased to hear the details they had set out.

Captain Adams then held a meeting with the miners who had worked so hard in bringing the much needed crystals and other minerals to the fleet. It was at his personal request that the miners agreed to return to the moon May and continue working until the fleet arrived in a few months.

Commander Thor pledged to locate several construction crews on both Antioch and on May. It was decided to assign three squadrons of fighters or about thirty Tigers and one shuttle craft as a protective force around both. Ten Tigers would be kept in continual flight as a measure of security until the first Star Cruiser arrived in orbit. The Star Cruiser would be permanently stationed in the area.

◆ ◆ ◆ ◆

A Captain's Mass was held aboard the *Manta Ray* along with an investigation into the actions of Lieutenant Baron.

The Mass was held by Commander Thor, attending were General Wesley Hawk and Captain Adams. Also in attendance by special request was Commander Lloyd Manado, Chief Engineer of the *Manta Ray*. Mr. Manado was asked to attend due to the strange incidents involving Lieutenant Michaels, a Shallop repair craft, and two passengers, Lieutenant Robyn and a civilian, Psalm Wolfe. It was found that a previously unknown vacuum existed between the outer skin of the *Manta Ray* and her shielding. Mr. Manado was present in the role of an expert witness.

Due to the quick thinking of Lieutenant Michaels, a major security breach was plugged. Even as this Mass was being held, a team of engineers was busy developing a new sensor designed to cover this very vulnerable area. As a result, Lieutenant Michaels was promoted to the rank of Lieutenant Commander and was reassigned as Flight Commander to the Tigers and Tiger Shark squadrons. His secondary duty was consultant specialist to the ship's security department.

Lieutenant David Baron's Court martial was like the opening of a door in the young man's life. The arrogance was no longer with him. His responses came from an earnest heart which clearly had seen the error of his ways. His honesty not only won him a reprieve, but led to his new job on the planet's surface as Communications Development Officer providing a vital link to the newly assembled construction crews.

Ensign Second Class Mary Adele was promoted to the rank of Lieutenant Junior Grade receiving the highest commendations for her quick thinking and subsequent actions while in command of the Starship *Manta Ray* while under attack by Augean fighters.

Upon returning to the fleet, she will also be commended with the highest honors and decorated for her bravery while under fire.

After many talks between Commander Thor, General Hawk, Captain Adams, and the Councilmen of the Planet Antioch, a special commission was set up for Psalm Wolfe. She was awarded a trainees position with a rank of Special Class Ensign with full time schooling as a Life Science Officer.

Halfway through the fourth day of being in orbit around Antioch, all damaged areas on the *Manta Ray* had been repaired. The *Manta Ray* then headed out at Warp Seven for her second stop en route to the awaiting fleet, not knowing what fates awaited her and her crew.

LEGENDS

They called her Cougar for her cat-like reflexes. She was lightning fast and saw everything. Cougar made it a point in her younger life to miss very little of those things going on around her.

Aureola was one of the youngest and brightest Ensigns to ever pilot a Tiger. She had earned her wings and the respect of every fighter pilot in the fleet when acting as a navigator and copilot on her maiden flight. Her Flight Commander, Captain Mark Styles, was seriously wounded by shreds of shrapnel that all but destroyed the pilot's dashboard and control panel, leaving her in control of the ship.

It was her first time flying in a Tiger Shark and she had less than twenty hours in a simulator. On this day, everything that could go wrong went wrong!

First, this was not to be a combat mission, she was only supposed to get the feel of really flying. She was a "new boot". The attack was unexpected. The ship had only minimal Phaser power with which to fight, but no torpedoes. "This was training, not for real combat! Right?" she thought to herself.

In short, she was flying without a pilot in control and without a radio. She was alone.

Flying a Tiger Shark wasn't all that hard, she later said, but she had no experience in a dogfight. Hell, she had barely learned her instruments and keyboard.

Cougar was five foot six inches and had short cropped blonde hair that easily fit into her helmet. She also fit well into her cockpit of the larger two-man fighter. When she put the control stick in her left hand, it was as natural to her as writing her name on a blackboard. As her fingers wrapped themselves around her copilot's stick, her instinct was to push the stick forward, then hard left.

She didn't know it at the time, but this movement at that instant was what had saved their lives. While other pilots saw this move, none knew until later she was piloting a crippled ship from the back seat. Her movements flowed as natural as breathing came to others.

She not only saved Captain Styles, but when she pulled back on her stick, her fingers found the trigger and she blew four Pirants to the scrap heap. Cougar Aureola, without missing a heartbeat, turned the tide of the battle to their side when it had been all Augean before.

When questioned later, she answered all questions without blinking an eye. After a few short lessons she had her Silver Wings and within a year received her Gold. She had gotten her Gold Wings only two days after her eighteenth birthday; at least three full years ahead of her peers.

When Commander Michaels assigned her to Captain Redmon, he had handed her off to Lieutenant Wendt to fill the void caused when Lieutenant Buster had been reassigned to command the newly completed *Brisk Mist*. Ensign Aureola never missed a chance to fly.

Approaching the next planet, Captain Redmon split his forces. He sent Cougar to investigate the only satellite while Lieutenant Buster went to search for possible radio relay stations.

As Cougar rounded the moon's dark side she was only a few hundred feet off its surface. Her eye caught a glimmer and her instinct was to dive, but she was already too close to the surface. She threw the stick all the way to the dashboard and banked hard right.

The heavy shot clipped the starboard side of her tailfin. It could have easily destroyed her and her ship. She knew she had been within inches of her own death.

His orders were simple. "Protect this quadrant of space at all cost!" He had sixty ships and the rank of Sub-commander. He also had as many inactive X-wing fighters on thefourth planet which he could activate with a simple call. The real problem was that several hours earlier, his quadrant had been invaded by Humans. All sixty of his X-wing fighters were grounded when he, during a routine inspection found corrosion and cracks along several edges of all sixty ships as well as every cargo ship in the encampment. And to make matters worse, when he called up the needed replacements, he could get no reply to any of his hails.

It had been more than a month since he found the problems but there had been no pressing need for replacements; that is until now! All of his ships were clearly unsafe to fly, even on routine patrol, and death traps if they came under attack. But then, no human had had space flight for thousands of years outside of the great colony fleet which was light-years from his position as far as he knew, and again, that is until now. He had already filed his report about the cracks in his ships and had listed the damage in detail, but had never received any further instructions.

His computer brain had been upgraded with all the extra sensors needed but even with his training, he simply didn't have any ships in which to fly. He would continue to call up any ship that would answer his call.

For now, the best he could do was to dig in and protect this bunker unless or until he was either relieved of his command or was able to get new ships for his troops.

◆ ◆ ◆ ◆

Captain Redmon was worried. What could he and his few ships do against so many Augean. Between his lone Tiger and Lieutenant Buster's shuttle and his own shuttle, his total armament was one Phaser Bank three-quarters recharged and only fifteen Hedgehog Torpedoes. Each ship carried five torpedoes and the partly recharged Phaser was put aboard Cougar's ship.

As for the two captured X-wings, the Captain had both pilots take all the ammo each ship could carry from the Battlestars, although he still didn't have a clue as to what good it would, or could, do in any fight. While both pilots were good fighter pilots, neither had ever flown an X-wing in battle.

Not knowing what they might find on the sixth planet in the system, Captain Redmon led his group into the planet's heavy upper atmosphere. They were not very surprised to find hundreds of older Augean war ships. If the fourth planet was an incubator then this was certain to be an Augean graveyard, or boneyard.

They found fixed-wing fighters, Battle cruisers, old tankers, clamshell type fighters, and oddly shaped oblong Battlestars. Here they found in abundance the very ships that had been used to destroy their forefather's home worlds.

Tears welled up in their eyes as they continued on to find what had to be ships of every type and description going back hundreds and even tens of thousands of years. Yet all looked to be both functional and in remarkably good condition.

Turning to the sixth planet Cougar found Captain Redmon who was already preparing to dock on the largest Battlestar she had ever seen or heard of. This one ship had to be a Beaststar ship and troop carrier. In its belly they saw room for thousands of ships.

It was clear to all of them that this was no old discarded relic; there was steam coming out of its ports. There were lines of ships in row after row: X-wing, Tri-wings, and every size ship imaginable in long rows all around the mammoth carrier as though all were awaiting orders to dock.

When Cougar caught up with Captain Redmon he was with Lieutenant Wendt. She reported the single bunker that was facing deep space at its equator. When she gave her report, she said there were no outward signs of enemy ships either on the moon itself or on long range sensors — thus far.

Seeing all the wonders around them, they decided to take a look at some of the other ships still in orbit.

Breaking through some cloud banks below where they left their companions, Captain Redmon along with Lieutenant Wendt in their shuttle and Cougar came to a full stop without falling from the sky.

What now lay before them simply could not be. Not here! What lay before them was every ship ever built in the human fleet, going back thousands of years. Except for one, the *Manta Ray*.

The first ship they saw was the legendary *Pegasus*. Its Commander was every bit a legend in his own right. General Baine would never have allowed his prized ship to be taken and would have shoved his ship down the non-human throats of the Augean given the slightest opportunity. His death was recorded many years after the Colony War defeat.

Next, was the Chancellor's Flag Ship. Known to be destroyed in the first wave by Augean warships during what was to be called "The Traitorous Peace Negotiations".

Then fell the most graceful and by far the most beautiful of manmade ships, the *Andromeda*. She was both beautiful and extremely deadly.

It seemed to Captain Redmon that here was an exact copy, in minute detail, of every space craft made by human hands — from the oldest ship to the newest, the *Linguist*.

Could they be functional? He didn't know. They certainly looked real enough.

Hovering beyond the *Andromeda*, he brought his little shuttle to a dead stop. Before him now was the most feared and deadliest ship ever created. The greatest of man's achievements in spaceship design and the sole survivor of man's war with the Augean the *Activia*. She was by far the best of the best and easily the greatest man-made battleship ever to fly the heavens.

Fearing this to be some kind of trap, Captain Redman, instead of hailing the *Activia*, transmitted a classified code to activate special cameras on the bridge as well as others scattered throughout the ship. Even the cameras worked!

He and Lieutenant Wendt were now watching the bridge personnel carrying out their duties as though they were real. But that couldn't be! Every one of these people had died almost three thousand years before. Yet, here they were.

They had all seen pictures of Captain Adams. Not their Adams, but the original Captain Adams. His oval face showing a small smile that was even kind of craggy to look at, for it brought the warmth of a grandfather to even the most frightened of crewmembers. His thin lips and silver-blue hair showed years of experience, and his gray-green eyes could bore a hole straight to a man's soul. Captain Adams was and remains the most beloved and respected man ever to live.

Standing next to his father was Polo, the eldest of two sons and later to become the leader of their people.

Polo was not only one of the greatest warriors in human history, but was also a past master when it came to being a statesman.

Polo was the chosen one, yet he refused to succeed his father upon his death, preferring to be a hands-on statesman for his people. Polo's sister and Adam's only daughter became the leader of the twelve lost tribes of man. Both calming them and leading them through one life-threatening situation after another.

It was Athena who ordered the conversion of *Activia's* rear most storage bay to an in-house spacedock, repairing and building new ships using pieces and parts from those ships that gave out or became damaged along the way.

Athena and her cool headed wisdom saved the lives of every man, woman, and child in the fleet. Not just once, but a hundred times at least. She and her learned leadership was legendary. There were so many daughters named after her, teachers had to add a second name to each girl so they would know to whom they were speaking.

Link was the youngest of Adams' three children and the first to lay down his life. Memory of him still lives on today and will forever more. After warning his people of a trap and instituting a "Red Alert", Link's ship was destroyed by the incoming Augean ships before he could reach the safety of the fleet.

Captain Redmon hailed the bridge of *Activia*. While he and Lieutenant Wendt watched there was no reaction to the hail whatsoever. They tried again. Still there was no response. It was as though they hadn't heard them at all.

They didn't want to be fired upon, so they approached *Activia* slowly, still fearing her deadly weapons. As they drew closer without incident, Captain Redmon decided to land in her Port Bay which was the common practice amongst her pilots. As they approached the ship her landing lights came on they continued to watch for signs of a trap.

When the Earth ship got closer, the landing bay's green blinking directional lights came on to guide the shuttle to a safe area.

Next to the shuttle as she came to a rest were older Tiger Paws and Jaguars waiting to be serviced, fueled, and rearmed.

Next to them were other older models still, they, too, awaited their pilots and their turns to blast off. People walked around but paid no attention to the two men at all as they disembarked. Not zombies, per se, but simply ignoring them, even when directly spoken to.

The launch bay itself was abuzz with activity. Tiger Paws were brought forward and loaded onto launch pillions.

Lieutenant Wendt returned to the shuttle and came out holding his flight helmet. He walked over to one of the Tiger Paws, checked it over, and without one word climbed in, strapped himself down, put on his helmet, and closed the canopy. Turning to Captain Redmon, he smiled, saluted, and launched with a thundering roar.

◆ ◆ ◆ ◆

The sub-commander had picked up only thirteen enemy ships in his sector and while he had tried several times to call up his squadron of reserves which would have come from several staging areas, none replied to his urgent calls.

He was sure his sworn enemy was putting up some sort of new jamming system to block his efforts, so if the enemy was to be stopped, he would have to devise a way to do so soon; even though all his ships were unsafe to fly.

Since Augeans had no fear of death, he decided to take a chance and launch half of his ships anyway, sending them to the planet to attack the humans and either destroy them or drive them off.

Almost as soon as the first ship was launched, it exploded causing major damage to both the launching area and the launch bay door. After he finally got two ships away, he instructed them to proceed to the planet below.

◆ ◆ ◆ ◆

Lieutenant Buster was in an orbit just at the planet's crust. He was able to clearly record the explosion on the moon's outer surface and later watched as the two fixed-wing crafts rounded the moon. He put up his shields. Both ships went right by him heading towards the planet. Lieutenant Buster put in a call to Captain Redmon warning him of the incoming visitors.

◆ ◆ ◆ ◆

Just as Lieutenant Wendt cleared the *Activia*, two fixed-wing enemy fighters broke through the atmosphere, opening fire both on the lone *Tiger Paw* and on the *Activia*.

Not knowing what was going on outside, Captain Redmon was almost run over by the dozens of pilots and support flight-crews heading to their assigned ships as the alarm rang throughout the launch bay area.

Corsairs and old Phantoms from ages long past launched and not one single person spoke a word or paid the slightest attention to him.

While it was fascinating to watch, it was weird to say the least. It was as though he were dead or a ghost without substance. He had an urge to pinch himself.

As the battle klaxons sounded about him, he decided to go to the bridge, and headed off on his own down the long corridor towards the Officer's Lift.

Passing through that section of the ship he knew well, where pilots and technicians were quartered, Redmon saw pilots playing cards and other games, or lying on their bunks. He walked through and not one word was uttered towards him or around him that he could hear even though he clearly saw the lips of those around him in motion.

Entering the lift, he punched the button to the bridge and watched as the doors started to close. Just as the doors came together a hand appeared and the doors opened again.

Since he had no special helmet, the sub-commander could only wait out the fight he was sure was taking place on the planet below.

As his ship cleared the outer atmospheric layer, the Augean saw a single Tiger Paw exiting the *Activtia* and heading his way. He and his wingman had put up their shields and turned on the enemy.

The Augeans got off the first few shots, but the *Tiger Paw* pilot banked hard and then did a reverse corkscrew, diving instead of climbing and their shots never got close.

Before either Augean knew it, the lone *Tiger Paw* was on their tails. Salvo after salvo just bounced off their shielding, and then the Battlestar began firing at them. Shot after shot. His wingman started to turn into the Starboard side of the great ship and was blasted by shots from the lone wolf as well as from the big ship. While his shields held firm, his wingman's ship couldn't handle the constant shakes and vibrations caused by the barrage. It blew up leaving him alone against impossible odds.

Within seconds of the battle's beginning, eight more ships were launched from the great ship. All were after him.

His last act was to get off a report to his commander as his own ship exploded into bits of starlight.

Never having gotten the last message, it didn't take long before the Sub-commander figured it out for himself. He still had three more ships, including his own.

He did not want to abandon his outpost. Yet, he was ordered to protect this sector of space at all cost. He ordered the two remaining ships to head to the surface of the planet to assist in destroying the humans. He would not desert his post just yet.

Launching both ships, the Sub-commander failed to see the incoming canon fire. While both Augean ships cleared the Launch Bay and the moon's gravitational pull, neither ship's pilot was witness to the total destruction of the outpost. The Sub-commander never knew what hit him. The only witness was Cougar, and she had her cameras on the whole time.

After the destruction of the outpost on the moon, Cougar trained her remaining torpedoes on first one Augean ship, and then the other. The first ship exploded into stardust, the second slipped by and headed towards the lower atmosphere and the surface of the planet.

It was still a few hours before the *Manta Ray* was to pick them up.

As the lift doors reopened Lieutenant John Williams stepped inside acting as though he was alone. Even though the button to the bridge was already lighted he pushed it again.

When the lift stopped, both men stepped off and onto the bridge.

With as many people as were on the bridge and moving about, the bridge itself was silent and soundless. No noise. No talking. No orders were given, at least any that he could hear. His own voice was ignored. He could and did in fact touch things. He even moved them around, but no one took notice. Redmon sat down at an empty console looking as bewildered as he felt.

As he sat down, the console became active showing each of "his" ship's location and the pilot's bio-signs. Even St. John's and Roe's, who were flying the captured X-wings.

Then it picked up his shuttle and showed himself to be on the bridge.

Suddenly the lighting on the bridge changed and the warning klaxon sounded. Another Augean warship was attacking. *Activia* launched half a dozen Phantoms and Corsairs, then her cannons began; it made short work of the lone Augean.

But, why was *Activia* here? So many questions and no one aboard who could give him an answer.

LOSSES

On board *Activia*, Captain Sharp had just finished fending off another round of Augean attacks. Captain Samuel Sharp was fifty years old. His ruddy face had grown older than he felt, the crows-feet at his eyes showing he had always been used to smiling. His light brown hair had already gone to gray. He still had a powerful body that had not gone to fat. The trousers he wore were black with two silver vertical lines. His blouse matched his pants. Captain Sharp was not a big man, per se, but everything about him was definitely strong. Upon entering the Bridge, you immediately knew who was in charge!

In today's raid, the Colony Fleet lost another ship due to heavy damage to its engine room. He had ordered all his shuttle pods to help relocate and transfer its people to various ships throughout the fleet.

Before the day was over, he would have to find new living quarters for over six thousand people who had called the *Linguist* their home. As soon as the last pod lifted off he had the salvage crews tow the *Linguist* into *Activia's* rear space dock where, if she couldn't be repaired, she would be gutted and her parts would become part of a new class of warship now known as the "A.E." Class.

The *Linguist* was one of the newest liners in the fleet; though more than two thousand years old, she had served her people well and losing her now would clearly put a hardship on everyone.

Even though these new Earth-type warships were popular with many of the younger people, the displacement of so many people caused by the scrapping of the older ships to build them was not. It forced them into a struggle for survival that was even more stressful than the day-to-day fending off of the Augeans which was far better than an all out war with them.

There were many who thought like him, but remained silent for fear of being censored by their fellow survivors. This fleet of old space junk and relics was their only home and had been their parent's, and their parent's before them.

Turning the fleet was not his idea of a sound move. He had advised the council against it. Just having to stop long enough to tow the disabled *Linguist* was too long in any one sector to suit him.

He, like his father and their ancestors, was born to serve the fleet and its people; first as a warrior pilot, then teacher and if they lived long enough, as Elders to the Council.

Granted, the Earthlings brought new technology, and greater speed with an array of weapons unheard of in the history of the fleet which had proven to be invaluable in several scrimmages with the Augeans. "Just giving us new sensors has saved countless lives by allowing the fleet a better chance to prepare for the incoming war-birds," he thought to himself.

To turn back now after having come so far just didn't make sense to him and a lot of others. Even knowing that no one had the slightest idea where a populated area of space was to be found and whether or not the inhabitants would welcome them and assist them against such odds.

He and the others were worried because there were so few people against the unimaginable vastness of the Augean Empire.

Sharp had his orders and, like them or not, he was bound to follow them to the letter. He had little concern about civil disobedience. There had been only one great disturbance which had occurred during the first few years. It had cost the fleet half of its population. It was a hard lesson to learn, but one they did learn, and learned well. All continue to remember the deaths even today.

"Report," Captain Tucker said as he retook his command.

Captain Pack reported first, "Highly visible targets in all directions; airways are only now reporting the attacks on their outer posts. There are still no reports of any higher alert statuses by the local Augean."

He had just received word from a higher commander of the Colony Fleet Battle Group and a report of attacks from a "new" enemy to the Pirant

Empire by a race of humanoids from a starship called *Manta Ray* who were also being attacked by a long ago foe called the Augean.

As the high Commander of the Empire Centurion Fleet, he need not be overly concerned about this new threat on the outer fringes of the known galaxies.

There had been no reported sightings of these humans or their pursuers in any of his sectors of space. He had a Command of eight Base-stars, and was responsible for over ten thousand worlds. He felt comfortable this deep in the Empire and saw no reason to put his forces on alert.

Within his realm of power, he was Supreme Commander to thousands of worlds inhabited by Pirant as well as humans and these worlds were his to protect.

Humans were allowed limited space flight, but he'd had to help put up communication satellites for most to allow better weather reports and surface to surface transmissions. No two worlds were allowed to communicate with one another. There were space buoys in place around each world blocking such communications.

Humans had strange ideas about work. The Pirant leadership deemed these strange beings an important part of the Empire, and their work production vital to the existence of all Pirants.

Should the Empire ever be invaded, no race would ever get beyond his forces. He would stomp them out one at a time.

"Sir, Commander Michaels has requested permission to land."

"Thank you, Mr. Park. Permission granted and you can tell him his new toy is in Shuttle Bay Six. Have him let me know when he and his forces are ready to redeploy," Captain Tucker said.

Manta Ray was to be out for ten days, now extended to fourteen. Thor, while not in actual command of his ship, certainly kept himself up to date on each phase of the ship's operations.

His ship was taking quite a beating. She clearly was outgunned, but her shields were sound. He now looked at his bridge crew as they waited for acting Captain Tucker to give his next orders.

"Engineering to Bridge," Commander Manado called.

"Yes, Commander?" Captain Tucker asked.

"Captain, shields are down twenty-seven percent," Manado told him.

"Reroute all available power to the shields, Mr. Manado," Tucker said.

"Aye, sir. That, I am already doing," he replied.

"Mr. Manado, see if you can buy us a little more time. I want these Augean to see no fear in us. I want us to get as close to them as possible before we return their fire."

"Aye, Sir. I'll find the extra power somewhere. You'll have your few more minutes!"

"Thank you, Commander," Tucker said.

"Captain, Sir," Mr. Wove said, and without waiting for a response. "We've got company! At least two Battle Groups headed our way. E.T.A. twelve minutes, and Sir, I'm picking up a Base-star incoming; E.T.A. less than thirty minutes."

"Thank you, Mr. Wove. Keep me posted," the Captain said.

Turning to Tactical. Captain Tucker said, "Mr. Appleton, prepare to fire!"

Looking at his Commander and General, Captain Tucker gave a bit of a grin. Then he ordered all ships to train their opening salvos against just one area of the sole Base-stars.

"Mr. Magna, prepare to launch all birds," Tucker ordered. Wave after wave, the Augean fighters attacked, all without the *Manta Ray* ever returning fire.

"All ships away!" the Captain finally ordered. "Launch all remaining ships and shuttles."

"The last is out the back door, Sir," Magna answered.

Closing on the lone Base-star, Captain Tucker ordered his fleet of war-birds and shuttles to hug close to *Manta Ray's* hull, between the shields and the skin until he is ready to release them one squadron at a time to warp out beyond the enemy as though they were a missed shot only to have them do a one-eighty, turning in and behind the enemy ships.

One by one the nearly eighty tiny ships slipped by their enemy, including the lone X-wing piloted by Commander Michaels, except the coloring didn't match any Augean warship. One by one his attack forces took up position and awaited their orders.

"Fire, Mr. Appleton," was heard throughout the bridge.

As the phasers fired their deadly array, the surviving small Augean Tri-wing started banking and breaking in dozens of directions at the same time.

Manta Ray continued on her plotted course, ever closing the gap between the first Basestars and herself.

As Mr. Appleton's fingers worked their magic over the weapons console, the Augean fighters began giving way, now becoming less a buffer to their mother ship.

The mammoth Basestar trained her heavy weapons on the incoming ship, firing salvo after salvo without the smaller ship ever wavering.

Manta Ray now trained her torpedoes solely on the Port side of the Base-stars, ignoring all other areas, looking to take out her Main Engine room.

Shot after shot ate away at the side of the Basestar, opening large gaping holes where at first small sections, and then bigger sections began falling away.

◆ ◆ ◆ ◆

Never had the Empire seen such daring tactics. The Basestar's Commander could not maneuver his larger ship as nimbly as his attacker. He sat atop his podium allowing his Captain and Commander to read his thoughts, thus benefitting from his superior experience.

He watched his foe closing as though all his Tri-winged fighters did not exist. As mighty as the Tri-wing firepower was, the enemy ship either absorbed the incoming fire, or his firepower wasn't enough to even slow the powerful little ship down.

For the first time he noted the incoming fleet of ships. At first glance the Commander thought they too were human ships here to help finish off his lone Basestar.

Then the Commander saw something. "What is this?" he spoke aloud.

"Sir, the incoming fleet belongs to the Pirant Empire," a Sub-commander replied.

Speaking again as his ship continued to take a beating from the humans, "What is their purpose in this sector of space? Put me through to their Flagship," he ordered.

As the bridge of the Pirant fleet's flagship flickered, the first thing the Commander saw was a Centurion standing behind his podium.

"Speak!" The Centurion ordered.

"What is your purpose in the Empire's Realm?" The Commander asked.

"Ha! The Empire's Realm? Which Empire do you refer to? This is Pirant space. Your puny Empire has no claim here," the Centurion answered.

"If you do not withdraw, another war will begin here and we will see who is in whose space," The Commander replied.

"Ha! You can't beat one puny ship of fools and you dare speak of battling my Strike Force." The Centurion turned as his old foe's Basestar began losing chunks of her superstructure to the smaller ship.

Then he watched as the Augean ship lost power and began to drift. He spoke again, "When these puny humans have finished destroying your ship, we will do what you could not." Then the screen went dead.

His loss of power was crippling. The Commander watched as parts of his ship fell away. Suddenly, the Basestar turned to the Starboard from a lack of control. He then witnessed that the enemy had turned inward, but was now holding her fire. Then the smaller ship passed over the bow to engage the Pirant Strike Force.

The Strike Force Commander had been monitoring the exchange between the Augean Fleet and the humans. He was seeing a different tactic than he had seen before.

"Interesting!" he spoke aloud to himself.

The human ships blinked as fast as his sensors could take them in, but there seemed to be no discernible pattern to their movements.

"By your command, Sir," a Centurion Captain spoke to him. His transparent head revealed only a wide sensor that neither blinked nor moved as he turned his wide metallic body to face his superior. "Report," was the only response he received.

"The humans seem to have little interest in the total destruction of the Augean Fleet, leaving them to drift away."

The two Battleship Commanders now shared all information, even with the incoming Pirant Commander along with all flight Leaders entering the theater of the battle.

The first Basestar began to launch her Clamshell fighters as the second launched her Tri-wings and the new, more swift, and deadly fixed-wing craft against their seemingly trapped foe. Yet, they failed to notice what was shaping up behind them. They began closing the door on this new and wanton human enemy.

Suddenly, the human ship blinked out of sight as though she had never been there in the first place. Just as suddenly she popped into sight again only some one hundred and fifty miles to port of where she was taking up a new position starboard of his great Basestar. At the same time the two Battleships that now lay at her stern opened fire upon her.

◆ ◆ ◆ ◆

As fast as Mr. Magna could dance his fingers over the routing console, the *Manta Ray* would blink again to a different point, staying only long enough to fire her torpedoes and Particle Phasers before blinking out again and again. The faster he moved his fingers the faster the *Manta Ray* jumped.

Looking on and awaiting their orders were almost eighty Tigers and Tiger Sharks with an additional eight Shuttlecraft; each awaiting his or her turn to "dance with the devil."

With Thor raising one eyebrow, then the other, both he and Hawk were watching from their chairs directly behind the Captain's Command Chair and were clearly beside themselves. Never in any of their wildest dreams could either have imagined "their" *Manta Ray* waltzing so gracefully with an enemy fleet.

Suddenly, as they looked on, the *Manta Ray* started firing her vast array of experienced weaponry; first on one ship and then on the Base-stars, and then another round as she darted first here then there.

Manta Ray opened fire on the port side of one ship then the stern of another, then on the port side of the second. Other shots were fired from the bow and still others taken from the stern. Sometimes the *Manta Ray* fired one shot before blinking out, and at other times she might remain long enough to fire a dozen shots at once. Many shots that hit the larger ship tore deep holes into her superstructure.

Just as the Basestar began firing at the *Manta Ray*, more than a dozen ships popped into existence all around the Pirant ship, all firing and blinking from one point to another, dancing as nimbly as children at a school dance recital, only these children danced a most deadly dance.

There were so many ships warp-hopping, that only the onboard computer on the *Manta Ray* could keep the ships from colliding.

The gunners on the Pirant Warships started firing randomly at various points. Even with the waltzing Tigers blinking in and out, the law of averages took over and several hits were made, destroying first one ship and then another.

The two Pirant Battle-cruisers were soon joined by the Basestar. Their Commanders ordered all guns to open fire in a dance of their own.

Manta Ray suddenly stopped her waltz as though she was waiting for a cool drink from her beau. For a solid five minutes all human ships: the *Manta Ray*, Tigers, Tiger Sharks and Shuttlecraft held their positions and fired salvo after salvo into the enemy ships around caused them major damage to all, destroying several smaller ships and one Battlecruiser, and crippling several others and the last Battlecruiser as all Pirant ships continued to lose their deadly fire on the small human fleet.

"Engineering to the Bridge!" Chief Engineer Manado called.

"Yes, Commander?" Captain Tucker answered.

"Sir, aft shields are off line, and my poor engines are taking an awful beating. We are gonna have to withdraw to make repairs," Mr. Manado told him.

"What kind of repairs! How long to affect them?" Captain Tucker asked the weary engineer.

"Sir, the engines are overheated; *Manta Ray* was never meant to withstand this kind of strain with her dancing around like she was a ballerina," the Commander reported.

"Mr. Manado, we must destroy this last ship before we break off. You will have to buy us a little more time," Captain Tucker stated flatly.

"Aye, Sir. I'll do what I can," Mr. Manado reported just as the front shields failed.

◆ ◆ ◆ ◆

Today he had witnessed the near total destruction of two Basestars: four of the Empire's finest and newest Battleships and heavy cruisers, as well as over two hundred of the latest versions of the Tri-wings and Battlestar Clamshell Protectors.

The Pirants had lost nearly two complete battle groups, and all to a single, lone, puny, human warship. His was the last Battlestar with less than fifty ships left out of the hundreds of both Empires' best trained fighters.

He had been given the very best materials available; the newest and most heavily armed ships were his to command. Now he must order his ship to withdraw and order the remaining ships to cover his retreat. His only remaining Basestar was the only means to warn the Augean Empire of these ruthless and relentless humans as well as the Pirant's invasion of Augean space. Today, he can do little more than watch and record this attack upon his forces. He sat there and watched the ships fight it out; neither aggressor nor defender giving an inch.

He had little dealings with other life forms and never in his years of service to the Empire had he ever witnessed or heard of what he now was seeing before him. This one daring and small "ship of fools" with its aged fleet of Tigers was trading punch for punch with one of the most formidable forces in the Universe. Where did they come from? And why did man suddenly appear here? Man has never shown any interest in this Parsec of Space; at least not before this. He had to wonder about these events.

"WHAT! What is this?" he spoke aloud to no one in particular.

"It would appear, sir," the commander replied, "They are now changing strategies. They've stopped dead in space and are firing solely and deliberately at us."

He was being destroyed, and there was nothing they could do but sit there and watch.

Was there something he had missed?

He watched as a dozen Tigers and Tiger Sharks fired salvo after salvo into his Basestars.

Yet, the smaller human ship sat there like a prize to be won.

He didn't believe his sensors. He thought he was unable to blink, but he must have, for every enemy ship was gone like a wisp of smoke on a windy day. Gone!

Dumbfounded, he stood up on his podium and asked, "What happened? Where did they go? How? Why?" he was left asking.

His tracking Officer turned to him and simply stated the facts as he saw them, "Sir, they left!"

"Yes. Yes! But where? How could so many ships just disappear with so many of our ships closing in on them? There is no place for them to run. Where are they?"

"Sir," the Officer replied, "the enemy all left in a different direction, including the larger ship. No two ships took the same route.

"It would seem that they must have something bigger awaiting them than what we have left to offer. I had several ships followed, but after a short distance all were lost. There is just no way to follow with their greater speed," he finished.

The sub-commander pulled out his phaser and shot the commander on the spot for his insult.

"Sir, sensors have found a Colony Tiger with a dead pilot. I have ordered a salvage crew to bring it aboard to be examined," another Officer offered.

"Finally, something good has happened today!" the sub-commander said to no one.

A HASTY WITHDRAWAL

The *Manta Ray* sat dead in space, in part awaiting the return of her birds.

"Sir, I'm picking up the last forty Tigers and all eight shuttlecraft. All are requesting permission to come aboard," Captain Wove said from the Communication Station.

"Permission granted. Is there any news from Commander Michaels?" Captain Tucker asked.

"I've checked his life-signs and all check normal, but nothing from him yet," Mr. Wove offered.

"Let's give him a little more time," The Captain said. "Helm, hold our position."

"Aye, Sir," Mr. Magna replied.

"Mr. Wove, anything on long range sensors?" the Captain asked.

"Sir, this area seems clear of any activity. Any idea as to who this new enemy is?" Mr. Wove asked.

Captain Adams offered, "I've never seen that type of ship before, but they didn't seem all too willing to help either the Augean or us."

"Perhaps," Thor suggest, "they feel both of us are invading their areas of space."

"How long to our final target, Mr. Magna?" Captain Tucker asked his tactician.

"Once we're under way, about six hours, sir."

"Since we don't know what area of space they consider theirs, we'll just have to take our chances and hope we don't run into whoever they are," Captain Tucker said.

"Set a course. I want to be underway as soon as we pick up Commander Michaels," Tucker ordered.

"Aye, Sir. Course laid in," the Helmsmen offered.

Pushing his intercom switch, Captain Tucker said, "Bridge to Engineering, Mr. Manado please respond."

No sooner had he spoken the words than Commander Manado walked in from the Senior Bridge Crew's Lift.

Commander Manado's jumpsuit was covered in dirt and grease, his silver-gray hair mussed and he was wiping his hands on a clean rag as he headed for the Science Station.

"What is the status on our repairs?" Tucker asked.

"Begging your pardon sir, but you are trying to get an old dog to do new tricks, and I'm not so sure she can continue dancing like you've made her do," Mr. Manado told Captain Tucker.

"At best, temporary repairs will be completed in about three hours. We do have Sub-light if it's needed, but she'll need new fittings once we get back to *Activia*," the engineer explained to his Captain.

Hawk, upon overhearing the conversation said, "Lloyd, just keep us together a little longer."

"Aye, General, she'll make it through," he said as he affectionately patted one of the bulkheads. "Won't we lass?"

Commander Michaels sat snug in his new toy: a modified Augean Tri-wing. His orders: "You are to observe the comings and goings after we leave," General Hawk told him. "You are to record all activities and traffic on the local airways as well," Hawk instructed him.

After an hour of observation, he was about to leave when the huge space shuttle left the bowels of the giant sphere, "Where is that thing going?" he asked himself. He knew the *Manta Ray* was waiting on his return and his report. "I've got a sick feeling about this and better follow my instincts. This is not going to be good. I just know it!" he said aloud.

As the larger shuttle cleared the lunch bay, its escort fell in line; two to the Port, two on the Starboard, with Michaels falling in behind the rearmost two to make three ships to the stern.

As the ships became visible to the Augean sensors, sweat started to roll off Chic's forehead and he took a deep breath and held it hoping they wouldn't think anything was amiss with his new toy in behind the other Augean escort ships.

◆ ◆ ◆ ◆

It appeared that all the ships had been launched at the same time. The Launch Control team looked once, then twice. The Centurion turned to the nearest Centurion and said, "What a strange formation." Without another word he returned to his other duties.

◆ ◆ ◆ ◆

The eight ships continued onward. Commander Michaels knew he was in hot water. Yet, his gut told him he was making the right decision as the group turned outward and towards a distant planet.

He checked his Bio-Scanner. It showed no life-signs on the planet, or in any orbit around it. Chic almost broke off when a flash crossed his memory.

There had been many dogfights early on, and he had seen several Tigers destroyed. But in this direction he remembered seeing Lieutenant Glycle's exit route and somewhere in the back of his mind he would swear he could remember hearing Mike's voice saying, "I'm hit and going down." But nothing else.

"They must be after Mike's ship," Chic said out loud. He knew he had to do something or this one small ship could put a stop to the new fleet before it ever got off the ground. He devised a plan of sorts, though he knew that it could well cost him his life.

Chic Michaels turned his ship back towards the heavily damaged Basestar at an ever increasingly fast pace.

Commander Manado had converted his toy and decked it out with a specially designed and new type of Hedgehog torpedoes and a new Particle Phaser Cannon.

Chic first flew at an angle toward the large sphere, going faster and past the Basestar then jerked back on his stick after gaining the speed he desired and did a short flip and headed straight for the crash site of the Tiger.

Skimming the planet's surface, Chic closed on the Augean landing party and opened fire; he let loose a barrage of Torpedoes at the nearly intact Tiger that lay before him. He had time for only this one pass. As the range grew shorter in front of him, he fired another salvo and added the firepower of the Particle Phaser Cannon.

With dirt flying, he couldn't be sure he had destroyed his friend's ship or about what damage he had done to the landing party around it.

Less than a hundred feet were beneath him as he fired again and pulled hard right just as a half dozen shots were fired at him by the shuttle's heavily armed escort. He knew without a doubt had he not jerked the stick at that moment he would have been fried bacon.

He kicked in his afterburners, thankful now that Commander Thor and Captain Adams insisted that his new toy be equipped with H.D.Chic couldn't wait to get into the clear to make the jump. He didn't know if there would ever be a "clear", and quickly checked his sensors and made the jump in the blind, barely missing getting fried again.

Twenty-five minutes later and more than two hours late Chic dropped out of HD to find the *Manta Ray* adrift in the middle of nowhere without any kind of patrol around her.

BIRTHDAY SUITS

Looking out at the devastation left behind, the Centurion could not believe this much damage could have been caused by a single enemy ship.

Not only did they penetrate his defenses, but several other's as well. He was receiving reports of hundreds, or thousands, of smaller ships invading from several directions, and yet, not one report of any type of bases or base stations having been found.

Unless the enemy ships were stealing fuel from the Empire, there should be some sort of base station or tanker for rearming and refueling.

This new race of humans was ruthless. Their very first attack had crippled his fleet. Clearly this was an enemy to all within the Augean and the Pirant Empires, both to man and machine alike. Their ships were destroying every human and Augean and even the Pirants couldn't stop them. And it was all effected without a single care or warning.

"I have sent forth every ship at my disposal to hunt down these creatures." The Centurion thought to himself, "They can't have gotten far. I have also sent an ambassador to the Pirant home-world warning of this new race of man. They must have secret bases scattered on planets in every nearby sector of space. I will find each of them and destroy their strongholds before there are any more such attacks upon either Empire.

"I have requested ships and supplies from all surrounding Battle Groups to help defend and secure these vital sectors of the Empire. There are too many reports indicating that every inhabited world, be it human or Augean, was hit and even several Pirant worlds were hit hard. Very few have been left intact.

"It will be very hard to have to explain to the Leadership my losses and the now weakened defenses, especially after receiving a warning only an hour before the attack.

"Losses to date to the Augean alone are five Basestar, eight Battlestars, thirty-one Cruisers, and more than two thousand Augean fighters.

"Sixty-four surface encampments housing hundreds of thousands of Augean citizens, with thousands of humans as well, are reported destroyed with all lives lost.

"The main enemy invasion forces have moved into Pirant space with lightning speed. But will they return to Augean space, or are they finished with us for the moment? I don't know.

"Whoever this enemy is, they must be expanding from within our own space, but from where? I fear from all too many areas.

"Perhaps all humans are involved. But I don't think so because there are too many deaths coming from too many human worlds."

Captain Tucker, having now completed his part of the mission, had officially returned the *Manta Ray* back to Commander Thor and his well trained Bridge Crew.

Tropy, having just been released from Sick Bay was glad to get back to work after almost three days. She told the General, "I feel fine." General Hawk didn't believe her for an instant, but he knew her well enough to allow her to return anyway knowing she'd find something else to do if not on the bridge, and during this time of war, he'd rather have her on the comm station than anyone else.

After listening to the chatter over the airways, Thor told her, "Let's make a copy of all of this to be studied later."

She told him, "The Augean believe us to be a new race of humans. There are now sightings on almost every front between here and the fleet; everywhere they hear of us, someone sees one of our ships. They seem to believe we have hundreds of starships. There are also many reports of us having been destroyed many times over.

Tropy went on to say, "The Empire is wanting one of our ships to study and have turned out every flyable ship to track down our refueling tankers and/or our repair spacedocks, and are even firing on their own spacedocks believing we are now using them as repair facilities. They seem very perplexed as to who we are and where our base of operation is located. I've been listening to their talk that we are not favoring the humans on their worlds and are claiming we have killed thousands of people on dozens of what they are calling 'Mineral Worlds'"

Captain Adams explained, "Humans are forced labor on planets that are over sixty percent water. Salt and fresh, are both very corrosive to Augean circuitry. The minerals they want must be mined by man. We knew there were pockets of humans who chose to remain behind." He concluded, "There were many who believed they would be allowed to live in peace after the takeover of our home worlds."

Then Tropy added, "The Augean believe we are going to attack and kill the humans as well as destroy any Augean on sight. They say they haven't enough forces to protect all the worlds that are inhabited. The Supreme Commander is requesting ships and troops from all sectors to help protect this one sector. The sections we hit yesterday are in total ruin. They appear to be withdrawing inward just as Captain Adams and the Council of Elders figured. The fleet that is shadowing the Colony Fleet has been ordered cut by more than seventy percent."

Captain Adams smiled as he said, "Based on what we know that will leave only a token force in place; probably a single Basestar, two Battlecruisers, and about twelve hundred fixed-wing and Clamshell fighters."

Commander Tropy added, "Because of the distance and our jamming of the airways, I don't think any messages could have reached too far. And there have been no messages received by them. Their communication systems are not good and they are old. It would take days or weeks to reach them should a message ever get through the jamming devises we left behind.

"In conclusion gentlemen, you've managed to stir up quite a hornet's nest in my absence," Tropy said with a wide smile on her oval face.

"That, Commander, was the intent," Commander Thor told her with a sheepish smirk on his ruddy face.

Dropping out of H.D., Chic checked his sensors and set a course for the waiting *Manta Ray*. As he approached, he noticed how much the once beautiful ship looked like a derelict as she seemed to be sitting half-cocked with both steam and oxygen coming out of her ports. She looked pretty much the same as she had the first time he'd laid eyes on her some four years earlier.

Commander Chic Michaels took a moment to reflect upon all that had taken place during the last four years the Earthlings had lived amongst his people. Not to mention how much they had changed almost everyone and everything within the fleet. Changes like the Warp Core or engines, and the transporters that transported people from one spot to another. Phasers that were much more powerful than any weapon anyone in the fleet had ever seen or heard of. Invisible shields that could absorb or deflect even the heaviest projectile the Augean could throw at them.

Their Life Science Department caused the fleet's top scientist to go gaga because no one had ever seen or thought such scientific marvels and machines could pinpoint a single heartbeat out of hundreds of people or transport a person or an object from one spot to another in the blink of an eye.

They brought new ways of thinking. Even the way time was measured, and they adopted the Earth Standard as a new way of measuring their new standards.

They also brought new ways of growing and processing food in order to store it indefinitely. The harvesting time was celebrated for the gifts they say their God provided for them.

Their values of God and his Son mirrored our own. They worship a single deity. Every man, woman, and child is taught to look in his or her own heart for answers.

Chic couldn't say that there was anything these Earth people had brought to the fleet that was bad in any way; just different from their own ways of doing things.

Three hours later, with Commander Michaels in tow, Thor asked Lieutenant O'ho, "How soon before we reach Captain Redmon's position?"

"We're about two hours from picking up our miners at Indigo and it will be another nine hours before we can reach the Captain and his people," O'ho said without further comment.

Just after leaving Indigo, acting Ensign Wolfe reports, "Sir, Long Range Scanners are picking up a Pirant Battlecruiser one hundred and fifty thousand miles ahead on our present course."

"Thank you, Ensign," Thor said.

Turning to General Hawk, Thor asked, "Have you ever used Phasers or torpedoes from Hyper-drive on an enemy ship not in Hyper-drive?"

"Can't say we've ever tried that," Hawk replied. "But it seems to me the *Manta Ray* is still capable of new surprises." Raising an eyebrow, Thor said, "Hmm!" then turned to Mr. Jacket in tactical.

"Mr. Jacket, set up a firing pattern from Hyper-drive."

"Mr. O' ho, stand by on weapons. Fire phasers first then torpedoes and phasers again as we pass her," Thor ordered.

"Aye, sir," both men answered.

Turning back to the General, Thor said, "The worst that could happen is that we'll miss, but if we hit them, it will put every shadow up as a potential target to Pirant and Augean gunners."

"Mr. O'ho, open fire at fifteen thousand miles!" Thor ordered.

"Aye, Sir. One minute forty seconds," O'ho replied.

"Sir," Ensign Wolfe broke in, "there are humans on board that ship."

"Hold your fire Mr. O'ho!" Thor ordered.

"Helm, bring us about. Plot a course to her seven o'clock," the commander said.

"Captain Adams to the Bridge," Thor ordered over the ships intercom.

"On my way," the captain answered.

Ensign Mary Adele announced, "Course laid in."

"Mr. Wolfe, how many humans are on board that ship?" General Hawk asked.

"Appears to be about two hundred, Sir," she said.

"But, sir," Ensign Wolfe told him, "These people are not in control of the ship. They're all bunched up in small areas." Reaching the console buttons on his chair, Thor called, "Bridge to Engineering."

"Engineering, Manado here, Sir."

"Mr. Manado, there is a Pirant Warship in front of us with about two hundred humans aboard her. What I want you to do is transport all the humans to our Brig. Beam them aboard wearing just their birthday suits. I want nothing they were not born with, Mr. Manado," Thor said.

"Aye, Sir. I understand. I'll have security set out unisex clothing for them," Commander Manado told him.

"I need to know when the last person is off that ship," Thor told him. "You've got about two minutes to prepare."

"Aye, Sir. We'll be ready down here," Mr. Manado assured him.

"Helm, go to Stealth drive, bring us about to her seven O'clock on my mark." Hitting his chair's buttons, Thor announced, "Red Alert! Shields up." The klaxon sounded and the lights dropped to their low red glow.

"All stations reporting to be manned and ready, Sir." Tropy said.

"Helm, Now! Bring us about," Thor ordered. "Steady as she goes. Mr. Sackett," Thor said, "I want everything from that ship's computer downloaded to our secure file section."

"Aye, Sir. Downloading now!" Mr. Sackett told him.

Again, Thor reached for his buttons and called, "Engineering, how are you doing, Mr. Manado?"

"One more minute and we'll have them all, Sir."

"Let me know, Commander," Thor said.

"Mr. O'ho, I want you to fire as soon as Commander Manado has our guests on board," Thor told him.

"Engineering to Bridge. We've got them all. Two hundred seventeen Humans," Mr. Manado said.

Without another word being spoken, the *Manta Ray* opened fire.

There was not so much as a ripple as the smaller ship opened fire, tearing chunks from the midsection of the heavy cruisers, and then the first salvo of torpedoes dug their way into the huge ship. Torpedo after torpedo found its way and then there was one large computer-timed explosion. Before the Battlecruiser could return more than a few dozen shots at the *Manta Ray*, it began to break up.

Thor's announcement to "stand down" from red alert was heard on all decks except decks twenty-two and twenty-eight, housing the ship's brigs.

"Helm," Thor said, "Put us back on course."

"Sir," Ensign Wolfe said from the Life Science Station.

"Yes, Ensign. What have you got?" Thor asked.

"Sir, there are no habitable planets in this sector of space, or any sector even remotely close where those people could have come from," she said. "I'd like permission to question some of our guests as to who they are and where they come from," she requested.

"Ensign, I agree that we need to question them as soon as possible, and yes, you may sit in along with Lieutenant Adele.

"Tropy, see if you can pick out the three most likely leaders from the groups, have them transported directly to my front conference room," Thor ordered.

VISITORS

In the first brig, there were eighty men and women, which were about evenly split.

None of them knew where they were or how they got there. Not one of them had thought they could have been any more afraid than they had been when the Pirant ships landed in their small town. That is until they blinked and found themselves standing naked as the day they had been born.

Finding the clothes to put on did little to ease the thoughts of what might have happened to them from one point to the next. No one said they felt violated, but none were sure that they hadn't been either!

Daniel Gideon had been a supervisor of sorts at the factory where most of these people either worked, or had relatives who had worked with him on occasion, and it was he who now tried to calm their fears.

"Listen to me," he said over the din of excited voices. "None of us know what the Pirant want of us. Or why they took our clothes. Perhaps these new clothes will offer some means of protection for whatever it is they want us to do. I would suggest," he said, "that we take what is laid out and dress ourselves accordingly. They have provided us with food and drink, and mats to lie on. For now, I think we should eat and get a little rest," Daniel finished.

Jacob Hutch added, "We don't know what has happened to the rest of our people or where they might be. But I agree with Daniel that eating and resting ourselves is the first priority. Worrying ourselves sick is the last thing we can afford."

◆ ◆ ◆ ◆

The second group consisted of one hundred and thirty-seven people, all younger than the rest. One young lady stood out. Her name was Mini Stries; she seemed to have been a born leader. She took the initiative by getting herself dressed and then by getting everyone else dressed and fed.

It was Violet Johns who spoke, saying, "We don't know how they got our clothes off of us, but the ones they left us seem to fit all of us. Yet, there is no difference between the sizes of one set over another. The food is better tasting than I've had since we first were brought on board and the drink is odorless and tastes a lot like sweet tea. I feel no side effects from either."

Mini then got most to settle down and rest saying, "We don't know what the Pirants want of us, and we might not get much of a rest again anytime soon. We'd better take advantage of their offerings while we can," as she lay down on one of the mats.

The third and largest group was of mixed ages and ideas. None of them good!

Sal Halmic was a loud mouth who didn't have a clue. He had always bullied his way through life by instilling fear into those he felt were inferior. He did not scare easily, and didn't show it even when he was scared to death.

Derek Prince was his worst nightmare because he always looked after and took up for the little guy when he was able. He didn't like leadership, but never balked when it was a choice between Sal and himself.

Derek was very much scared over the current events and didn't mind saying so now.

"Yes, I'm as afraid as any of you. I don't know how they knocked us out. If they did." He went on, "None of us can hazard a guess as to what has happened to the rest of our people. Perhaps they were put into another room similar to ours, or maybe they are already working on whatever project the Pirants brought us here to work on."

Derek went on to say, "The only thing we can be sure of right now is that we are here. Also none of our families were harmed or threatened and that we were told we would be gone for a year."

As Derek started to speak again, he felt a tingling sensation and saw a host of rainbow coloring all about him.

He remembered the look upon the faces of his countrymen; a look of utter shock and disbelief.

In less time than it would take for the human brain to create a new thought, Derek found himself clothed and standing in a room directly in front of a desk, which seemed to be made of a glass top, atop a light colored paneling, or it could have been made of some other type of natural wood base.

Directly behind the desk, there was a high-backed leather chair of a dark brown coloring. The chair was not really overly large, and even small for the use of a Pirant, rather it was long and graceful and not at all intimidating.

Behind the chair was the wall. It was unadorned with pictures or such. In the wall was an opening that was too small to be an empty bookcase, or the space for a cabinet. It gave a serviceable appearance from his point of view.

Next to the desk was an oval-shaped table with six chairs around it. In the center in front of each chair was a pitcher of clear liquid with what looked like square cubes of ice. Beside each pitcher was a goblet of crystal glass. He was thirsty but feared touching anything until told he could.

Turning to look at the rest of the room, Derek was taken aback by a glimmering of multicolored lights not more than two feet from where he was standing.

In less time than it takes to blink your eyes, there stood Mini Stries and next to her the lights became Daniel Gideon. All three of them were still in their new clothing.

Before any of them could speak, a wall slid open. First to enter was a young woman about twenty-four or five. She was not only young, she was gorgeous! She stood about five feet six inches, with emerald green eyes. Her hair was cut just above her collar, and while not quite golden, it wasn't really brown or red, but it was all three at the same time.

She wore a pale blue uniform adorned with some sort of rank insignia, trimmed in gold and black. Her skirt matched her blouse in color and was cut about six inches above her knees. Young and good looking, she was not slim per se, but definitely not overweight by any means. She had the highest cheek bones Derek had ever seen. Her skin was clear and unblemished and looked really healthy.

If he thought the first woman looked good, he couldn't believe the second woman was even more beautiful. Entering the room, she was exquisite, delicate, and certainly younger than the first.

Entering the room next was an older man of about sixty with webbed ears; he had a handsome but ruddy face. You knew instantly that he was in charge of these women. Then Derek noticed the ears of the youngest woman and saw that her ears were webbed also. Looking at the first woman, he didn't' see any webbing.

The second and younger woman spoke first, "Please take a seat," pointing and indicating they should be seated. The women and the officer walked around the table and took seats with their backs to the wall.

None of the three understood her words, but took the remaining seats across from them.

As the six of them took their seats, another man entered the room. He was armed with a weapon in a webbed holster. He didn't speak. He looked to be about twenty-five with clean smooth features. He stepped through the door and stood at "parade rest" just to the left of the closed door. It was plain to see that he was security and was stronger than the door.

No one identified themselves. The younger woman asked the first question and the computer translated it as, "What was the purpose of your being on a Pirant War Ship? And where were you bound for?"

While understanding both questions put to them, Daniel Gideon answered in the tongue of his own people, "We are Uniat and are being taken to work on mineral crystals collected by other workers whom the Pirant have used from time to time."

Being a trained linguist, Psalm asked, "Where are you all from and where is your home planet?"

Commander Thor and Lieutenant Adele look at each other in wonderment.

Ensign Wolfe explained the language barrier and the computer picked up on it, allowing all to hear and understand the conversion.

Lieutenant Adele said, "Within the fleet, there are people from the Union of Brest Litousk, who are spiritualists and whom stay pretty much unto themselves.

"While all speak the common language, most speak an old and almost forgotten language known as Latin."

Lieutenant Adele looked at the Commander, because they both speak the tongue of their ancestors and know that Latin, in its truest sense, is older than mankind itself.

◆ ◆ ◆ ◆

They came from a long lineage, dating back before man ever attempted to step off his own worlds, long before he met his stellar neighbors.

When they did meet, they realized they shared many traits of human life. Faith, in and of itself, is a human trait and God in one form or another was worshiped, but only the Uniat were found on every world where man was found.

Amongst the Uniat there was no language barrier, for on every world this small religious sect all spoke what is now known as the only true universal language — Latin.

Mankind had changed every language ever spoken. He had also altered every religious faith to some degree when and where it suited him. That is, all except those called the Archaic.

The Uniat were left to themselves by most of mankind, while other Archaic were hunted down and killed to the last man, woman, and child Yet, less than two generations later, the lineage was firmly imbedded once more and the language spoken.

Many sought out worlds where they could grow and worship God in peace. The great Empires sought them out as workers, and work they did. Theirs was the most honored, even by Pirant standards. They instilled only the highest quality and gave an honest day's work for little or no pay. Not slaves per se, but slaves nonetheless.

◆ ◆ ◆ ◆

Daniel Gideon explained that, in Latin, he was called a "Mechanisma": an engineer specializing in the bio-speed ratio of the bio-output forces produced by a machine as applied to the input forces generated during the application of speed when heated, giving an involuntary but consistent response to any living organism given as, a stimulus reacting to the proper sequence of steps in a chemical reactor.

Daniel then introduced Mini Stries saying, "Mini is an "Archaic Chemiluminescense" or a chemical engineer specializing in environmental temperatures as a direct result caused by the application of speed when heated by mechanical design."

Introducing Derek Prince, he said, "Derek is a chemical specialist who works with raw minerals in conjunction with forces or mechanisms to form a Ferric Bond Resistor against a metallic surface creating super-high-temperature atoms and ions to be used on and with high-energy crystals."

Daniel pointed out that all the other members of the group were either chief chemists or mineralogist's working on crystals to be converted to pure energy and metallography using non-allography and non-metallic elements that can form a newer, lighter, and stronger alloy having none of the properties of a metalloid.

"All of us are specialists in our own fields and as a group, are able to convert some of this raw energy into a higher form of energy which can be used in lasing out more minerals."

THE NINTH PLANET

The questioning continued for another half hour without the three officers, ever identifying themselves or their ship. It was at this time Mini Stries decided to ask some questions of her own.

"Who are you people and what is your connection with the Pirant Empire?"

Her eyes were prominent, the clear whites gleaming against her skin. She had her hair cut short and layered, not chopped as Thor had seen on so many other women. It seemed very becoming. Her deep green eyes set against copper skin, were striking as she watched the man seated across from her looking back at her.

He had pushed the crystal glass pitcher towards her as though he had surmised her to be thirsty. She realized that she was.

As she poured herself some water, she noted that Derek too was now pouring himself a drink.

"Thanks," she said.

Thor hadn't spoken until now. "It's only water," he said.

They drank; the ice cubes were chilling to the touch.

Thor sat politely until she had finished. "You've eaten well I hope?"

"Yes, we've eaten and thank you for the food. But you still haven't answered my questions," Mini pushed.

Thor sat there and raised an arch over his right eye. Then he spoke saying, "My name is Thor. I am the Commander of this vessel."

"We were unaware that the Pirants even had humans in charge of any space vessels!" Daniel exclaimed.

"We are not Pirant, but an Earth vessel," Thor said.

The three Uniats just sat there looking at each other before Derek choked out, "The fleet found you?"

Rather than trying to explain, Thor simply replied, "The fleet found us."

There was real fear upon each of their faces. "Our homes, our families. What will become of them?" Mini cried out.

Prior, to beginning this conference, Thor had Sackett build an ion map, back-tracking the ion residue from the Pirant ship so they might be able to see where the enemy ship had come from.

"Would any of you or anyone in your group be able to recognize from star charts where your home world is?" Thor asked. "We have the Fleets charts and have downloaded the charts from the Pirant War Ship you were on before we destroyed it."

'You destroyed a Pirant Battleship?" Daniel queried.

"We couldn't let that warship run loose after taking you off right under their noses. It had to be destroyed." Thor explained to them.

Mini offered, "The heavens are a part of our teachings. Even though the Pirant's have never allowed us space flight, we should be able to find our way with your help."

"I'd like Lieutenant Sackett to work with your people," Thor offered. "Then I'd like you to meet with Captain Adams," he finished.

"Captain Adams is alive? How can that be? Has Earth the capabilities to keep man alive indefinitely?" Daniel asked.

"No! Our Adams is a direct descendant of his though," said Mary Adele.

"Commander," asked Daniel, "can you return us to our homes and families? Uniat is our home now, and has been for generations untold. We've always known that the seeds of life came from the stars, but I now fear the Pirant will retaliate against us and our families."

"Mr. Gideon, it is our intent to keep the Pirant and the Augean as far from your homes and families as humanly possible," Commander Thor promised.

"This ship will rendezvous with the fleet in eight days time, we will then deliver you and your party to your homes," Thor offered.

Thor went on to add, "Until then you and your people will remain onboard as our guests."

Mini Stries asked, "Will we remain prisoners during these eight days? Or, can we move about the ship?"

"Ms. Stries, I simply cannot have some two hundred people wondering aimlessly on board this ship at the same time. We need time to set something up with Security. I don't think it'll take too long. Captain Adams will be with you shortly," Thor said.

◆ ◆ ◆ ◆

Over dinner, General Hawk and Captain Adams discuss their futures. "What I'd like to see is Commander Michaels take one of the new ships, like the Wolverine as part of the Wolf Pack's three ships and go directly to the home worlds to spend the next year or two clearing the Pirants and the Augeans out before the fleet gets there," Captain Adams said.

Hawk says, "I think we both feel a kinship with this young man. I know that if he has the time, he'll become a legend himself.

"He certainly has the right magic, the desire, and the heart."

Adams said. "That, along with the right amount of luck will carry him far."

"With those in place, I don't think there would be a match to equal him," Hawk said with a knowing smile.

Smiling as he took a sip of wine he continued with, "What an exciting life he has in store."

The two men sat quietly reflecting on how their own legends had been built over the years, slipping back into memories taken from the private hidden places of their minds.

◆ ◆ ◆ ◆

Two days later...

"Sir, I'm receiving signals of a human nature. No visual. The signals are coming from sector Qui, eight two point three zero," Tropy reported.

Lieutenant Jacket had the com and replied, "It seems there are humans living under Pirant control all throughout this area."

Jacket hit his seat's panel button then said, "Commander Thor to the Bridge."

"Thor here. I'll be there in two minutes, Mr. Jacket." Entering the bridge from the Senior Officers lift two minutes later, Thor looked to Tropy.

"I'm getting weak signals from at least a dozen systems in this sector and thought you'd want to know. And Sir, they are all human," Tropy told him.

"Are there any Pirant or Augean in the area?" Thor asked her.

"Yes sir. But I'm not sure whether they are Pirant or Augean. There are two Battleships and a heavy Cruiser and more than a dozen Space-docks along with several tankers and freighters and more patrols than I can count," Tropy said and showed him on the area maps she had pre-programmed into the front view screen.

"Helm, prepare to drop us out of H.D.!" Thor ordered.

Hitting the button on his chair as he stood next to it, he announced, "Battle Stations, Red Alert! This is not a drill," the Commander said.

A few minutes later, as the night lights dimmed to a soft red glow, Tropy said calmly, "All Stations report that they are manned and ready, sir."

Ensign Wolfe reported, "Sir, there are humans on all the space-docks, or I should say, they are working on them. There are no humans on board any space-dock or spaceship."

"Ensign, I want every life form plotted in the computer," Thor ordered.

"Aye, Sir," Psalm replied.

"Weapons?" Thor asked Mr. O'ho.

"No, sir. Everything in this area is unarmed, not even a fighter for protection," O'ho finished.

"Stand by on phasers, Mr. Sackett," Thor ordered.

"Bridge to Engineering," Thor requested pushing his Comm Button.

"Manado here, Sir."

"Mr. Manado, it looks like we are going to have a few more guests. I want these people transported to Cargo Bays seven through ten.
Mr. Manado, put a damper field around them. Then, when we are close to an inhabited world, scatter them amongst the populated areas.

"And Mr. Manado, I want the bodies only, nothing they were not born with. Have Security provide nondescript clothing. I don't want any of these visitors to know who or what we are about," Thor told the Chief Engineer.

"Aye, Sir. I'll handle the transporter myself," Manado assured him.

"Very good, Mr. Manado. Please stand by," Thor told him.

"To my knowledge," Captain Tucker said while watching from his observation seat, "none of these people would know anything about transporters, and when they try to explain their sudden appearances, they'll for the most part be locked up as being mentally unbalanced."

"Sir." Turning to Thor, Ensign Wolfe broke in "There are two housing complexes, each housing several hundred people."

"Thank You, Ensign. Please pass that information on to Mr. Manado.

"Mr. O'ho, bring us to the nearest of those complexes first," Thor said. Without waiting for a reply to his orders, Thor called," Bridge to Transporter Room."

"Manado here, Sir. Awaiting your orders."

Leaving the channel open, Thor turns to the Helmsmen and says, "Helm, tell Mr. Manado as soon as we are within ten thousand miles."

"Aye, sir."

"Bridge to Commander Michaels," Thor called.

"Michaels here, Sir."

"How many birds can we launch?" Thor asked.

"I have forty Tigers and seven shuttles loaded with two hundred Marines ready to launch on your mark, Sir." Chic said.

"Helm, distance to target?" Thor asked.

"Five hundred thousand and closing," Mary Adele allowed.

Returning to the open channel with Commander Michaels, Thor said, "Here is what I want you and your people to do…"

◆ ◆ ◆ ◆

"Get them loaded, Mr. Michaels, you've got about ten minutes," Thor told him.

Already in the launch bay were more than three hundred of the fleets finest young men and women. All combat trained, all in combat gear, all combat ready.

Stepping to the front of these eager fighters, Chic started going over each stage of the upcoming combat assignment, assigning each section, then each squadron their duties as had been laid out by Commander Thor, who left the details for Chic to decide.

Bringing up on the view-screen each detail for the Tigers as he explained, "You are not to enter any of the planets' atmospheres," he told them. "According to Tropy, most of these planets are inhabited by either humans or Pirants, some are inhabited by both. All communications to and from the planets will be blocked. If the computers are right, there are no fighters that might be launched against you, or ground combat forces to content with, save one or two areas.

150

"As to those planets that are Pirant controlled, you Marines under Lieutenant Morgan will have to dig them out one area at a time. Lieutenant Morgan has already assigned you your targets."

He finished with, "Hit them hard and fast! Then get out and make your way back here to the *Manta Ray*."

Breaking into their individual groups, they dispersed to their launch areas within the bay.

Ten minutes later, Thor hit his Comm button, "Prepare to launch. Helm, drop us out of H.D.," Thor ordered, "One half standard, Launch! Launch! Launch!" Thor ordered.

"Launch Bay Control reporting all Birds away clean, Sir," Tropy reported.

"Engineering to Bridge."

"Go ahead, Mr. Manado," Thor said.

"Commander, the planets below the space-docks are Class M's, and there are plenty of large cities. If you want, I can transport our new guests directly to those populated areas, unless you want them to go elsewhere," Mr. Manado offered.

"No, no, Mr. Manado, the direct approach is always the best. Go ahead, you can start now. When you've cleared the area of all humans, let Mr. O'ho know," Thor told him.

"Aye, sir. I'll set them down just outside of the cities, and they'll arrive clad only in their birthday suits," Manado said.

As the *Manta Ray* rounded the ninth planet in the twin-system of the single star, Commander Michaels deployed his Tigers and shuttles. His liberated Augean ship he was more than happy with, but he did not fly it today, instead, he choose his old ship nicknamed *"The Song Bird"*. He would need a lot more time in the new ship before he would feel comfortable enough to use it in a battle.

Manta Ray's computers continue to feed updated information to all their onboard computers giving each ship its own individual targets, and time over each target, both ground based and space born.

One by one, the small ships began to break up into groups of twos, threes, and fours heading towards their targets.

Zeke, who was normally teamed up with Chic was instead one of two team leaders along with P.J. Morgan leading armed-to-the-teeth groups of Marines to assault several encampments. Each group had two transports and one shuttle along with one Tiger acting as escort to the troop carriers.

NEVIS

The name on the door read: S.J. Greenberg, Manager. She was a small stocky woman in her early sixties with well kept blue-silver hair.

Sandra Jean had loving, crystal clear brown eyes that crinkled at the temples every time she smiled. Her small nose had a slight upturn that you would expect to find on a much prettier and younger woman.

Her teeth were white, and her lips full, with just a hint of gloss that she had applied. Though stocky and a little more than five feet tall, she carried herself as though she were in her twenties and was fifty pounds lighter.

Sandra Jean had worked her way up the ladder first as a Lab Technician, putting in long hours teaching her own supervisors new and better ways to produce lighter weight metals which would be applied over the framework of the powerful Clamshell Pirant fighters.

After she helped develop this new framework skin, she had earned her stripes as shift supervisor some twenty-five years earlier.

Today, she was the plant manager with over twelve hundred shift workers. Her position allowed her a continued hands-on approach to all new synthetic metals, and the right to test them as skins for the light weight vehicles used for mass transportation within the cities.

The new darker skinned metals doubled as infrared cells collecting raw energy from the sun and moons, as well as from the planets inner heat source, producing in and of itself a powerful new energy without the need of fossil fuels which only caused different cancers amongst her people.

Nevia was a world of opportunities which the Pirant could not use because of its highly arid climates, but which allow humans to live comfortably.

Navis had three moons. The largest, Pimeco, and the smallest Matic rising in early evening, and Anime which appears for only a few hours in the early morning, during spring and midsummer, then reversing for the fall through winter months.

Having a fourteen month calendar, twenty-nine hour days and forty day months kept the mathematicians on their collective toes during the first couple of hundred years trying to figure out just how old a person was.

Then the new world calendar with its current hours, days, and months was established and accepted as law, so Sandra Jean Greenberg had just celebrated her sixty-second birthday.

As the plant manufacturing manager, Mrs. Greenberg had to also be a civic leader and was elected to a post as part of the local governments Voice For the People.

She was not a judge, but settled small disputes within her district, thus helping to fill her long days, but still allowing her time to spend her evenings with her husband Charles and their many grandchildren.

Since she took over the plant, she had cut work hours from nine hours a day to only six. Production was up about seven percent, and quality also continued to improve. The shorter workweek allowed each worker both afternoons and evenings to better educate themselves at one of the many free universities they were able to establish, or just to relax with their families and friends.

Today, there was a static in the air, with a tingling sensation that crawled up the skin of her arms. She felt as though some big event was here, or coming soon, but she couldn't quite figure out what event.

The static was not just in the air, it was on the view-screens and on all the audio-sets. She thought, perhaps it was sun-spots.

She didn't know. What she was sure of, was that she didn't like the feeling it left in the pit of her stomach.

The fact that the Pirant Rulers and Overlords hadn't been seen in the last four months in any of Nevis' cities was cause for great concern. In addition to the fact that the consignment of new skins were now stocked high in hundreds of warehouses across the planet didn't make her feel any better.

PROMISES KEPT

For over two thousand years, since just after the great Colony Wars, mankind had been allowed to live and work in relative freedom. They were allowed to live, grow their food, educate their young, and to some extent govern themselves and with some help from Pirant Leaders allowed to colonize certain new worlds.

Sandra Jean's own grandfather was born elsewhere amongst the stars and, along with a few hundred thousand "forced" volunteers, transplanted here on Nevis.

Her own mother was brought here from her home world called Forta after a deadly virus killed most of the young women and sterilized the rest of the females all across the planet.

By the time the med techs found and isolated the bug, the damage had reached the entire surface of the world. Every male and female was sterile.

Most of the men living on Forta during that time chose to move on. But the Imperial Leadership had other plans for Forta. Because of the planets rich ore deposits, they knew these rich minerals would be needed for the future development of the Pirant Empire. They had to keep man there. For these reasons and because of a lot of unrest by man, the Pirant Leaders decided to make the entire planet of Forta and Nevis Penal Colonies.

Several hundred years had passed, after the virus had run its course, and the Imperial Leadership was assured the deadly disease was gone, they again forced additional volunteers to be brought in, and life began anew.

Nevis, like Forta, was about eighty-five percent water. Most of that was a very heavy condensed mineral saltwater. There were softer, drinkable waters too, but it was found only underground.

While rich in mineral deposits, both planets were too corrosive for Pirant colonization. Their circuitry just couldn't handle the moisture, even when they were suited.

Humans seemed to thrive in the bright white suns. They grew foods which the Pirant encouraged and traded on other planets and even acted as a brokerage agent and then cargo haulers.

Man has never liked to be harnessed like an animal. The earlier settlers on all the known worlds fought the Pirant and the Augean to a near extinction.

Then came the great divide, the Empire was split into two warring factions, each with an Imperial Leader. The Pirant Leader offered peace in exchange for trade rights to certain ores. Mankind started to grow again.

Every time man wanted to flex his horizons, his world, whichever world he was on, suddenly developed some new strain of bug that would kill off up to half its population, squashing any hope of ever regaining free space flight.

Nevis, having reached a population of just under one hundred million people, asked for the promised right of limited space flight. Their benefactors, the Pirant, had for the last two years allowed its men to train for space flight by working on Pirant ships and on one of the two space-docks man was allowed to build.

The inhabitants had been told that if they continued to grow, and do as they were told, that in ten years or so, they would be able to train on Pirant ships and in time would be able to build and fly their own space ships. However, the Augean had made it perfectly clear that man was still its enemy and if they ever found man in space, no matter where, he would be attacked and killed, even if they were found on a Pirant ship.

Time and history has a way of repeating itself over and over again, especially when and where the Pirants were involved.

About two hundred years ago, when planet elders proposed space flight to the Empire Leadership, which was both Augean and Pirant, and where one was more of a Warlord, it cost the planet two hundred and eighty thousand lives. It had been less than twenty years since the Pirant leadership had been approached to keep their promises.

This time, the planets elders were a lot better prepared for what the Pirants might do. For the past one hundred years, humans on Nevis had been concealing a hidden population of its young in underground caverns that had been converted into housing areas. Many of these housing areas and caverns were also doubling as underground space-docks where the young were preparing for space flight by the building of flight simulators and deep space fighters called Hell Cats and Spitfires.

Every man and woman labored to build hundreds and thousands of space worthy ships in these underground plants, and for every skin made for the Pirant they added certain elements which would cause the skins to deteriorate after a few months use in the Pirant fleet. A stronger non-deteriorating skin was used on their own ships.

Men and women of all ages spent hours every day in flight simulators around the world. Even the very young were trained to fly unmanned ships in mock battles against the hated foe.

Chic, after landing, found the entire planet and this manufacturing plant to be solely occupied and operated by humans. There were no batteries associated with either.

After conferring with Commander Thor, General Hawk, and Captain Adams, they decided the direct approach was the best under the circumstances.

A warning to stop assisting the Pirant Empire, or else be counted as a Pirant and subjected to attack by the fleet.

Chic entered the plant and seeing the sign of management, knocked politely and opened the door to an office to find an aging woman seated in a large but not oversized cloth covered wing-back chair behind a wooden desk housing several trays and stacks of papers and two monitors, one of which she was clearly speaking into.

Quietly, she pointed to a chair on his side of the desk, indicating he should sit. Chic sat down and waited for her to finish her conversation. He occupied the time by looking at dozens of pictures lining the walls. Then he noticed something leaning against an area where the walls joined. Standing he stepped over to it and picked it up, the spacecraft skin was for the entire world to see. He noticed how lightweight it was, and then he noticed the small collection cells that seemed to cover the entire surface of its exterior. This was the only item in her office other than papers and furniture. Chic was still holding the skin when the manager finished her call.

Turning, Mrs. Greenberg took a good look at the young, handsome man standing before her. His features were smooth and clear. His uniform, while looking strange to her, was nonetheless crisp and unadorned. Purple and black chevrons, which she took to be insignia indicating rank, adorned the sleeves. Then she noticed his sidearm. Weapons were never worn openly on Nevis, and everyone knew it was strictly against Pirant rules even to own a firearm.

Mrs. Greenberg introduced herself and bid him welcome and again offered the young man a seat.

"Mrs. Greenberg, I am Lieutenant Commander Chic Michaels. I am a part of a pre-invasion force of the Colony Fleet. You are building ships for the Pirant Empire." He suggested.

Without batting an eye, she asked, "Where is this Colony Fleet?"

Before she could give Chic the time to answer, she asked, "How can I be of help, Commander"

"It has been confirmed that this plant produces skins like this one," pointing to the skin standing in the corner and saying, "used on fighters now being built in two space-docks in orbit about this planet," Chic told her.

"That is not exactly true, Commander," Mrs. Greenberg said. "First, we do not build fighters for the Pirant Empire, but it is true that this plant is owned by the Pirant Empire, and I and all the inhabitants are subjects of the same. I am only the manager of this one plant. There are thousands scattered across Nevis."

"I have been given orders," Chic told her, "to destroy all such installations planet wide. However, we have no desire to destroy any facilities that may be converted to civilian use. We have no wish to harm or injure any human. These operations must cease immediately and hopefully with your approval and help. All Pirant materials and inventories must be destroyed where and when found in any warehouse. As we speak, the *Manta Ray* is destroying the two space-docks along with whatever Pirant ships and encampments there are in these sectors of space. All humans have been transported to your population centers unharmed," Chic finished.

"Commander Michaels, the skin there in the corner is strictly for the use of humans, used for ground transportation, but this one skin is different and is going to be used strictly by humans on Nevis, but you are correct about the warehouses being full of Pirant skins. We have not seen or heard from the Pirants in over four months. We have reason to believe the Pirant leaders have unleashed, or are about to unleash, another deadly virus on Nevis. All of your people should be forewarned not to have any contact with the human population of Nevis until we know what, if any, virus has been spread about the planets surface. The Pirants last efforts cost Nevis two hundred and eighty thousand lives," Mrs. Greenberg warned him.

After listening to Mrs. Greenberg, Chic said, "Mrs. Greenberg you give grave warnings, and I need to contact my Commander. Will it be alright if I use the outer office for a few minutes? I am sorry to have to keep you in the dark any longer than I have to, but I must, at least for the moment."

Sandra Jean said, "You can use my office if you like, I'll be back in about ten minutes if that will be long enough?"

"Thank you, Mrs. Greenberg," Chic said.

Once she was gone, Chic contacted Commander Thor, who then included Doctors Wearing and Murky, along with Commander Manado who decided that a medical Damper Field using small satellites, because they would isolate any space born bug, and extra Damper Fields would have to be put around all Landing Bays on board the *Manta Ray* and all incoming ships and shuttlecraft.

He explained that, "Each person coming aboard would then have to be transported directly to medical before being allowed back in general population until we are sure everyone was clean."

"Commander," Captain Adams said, "I can see no reason to withhold any more information from Mrs. Greenberg. If she were an enemy, she would not have warned us of the threat. Go ahead and inform her of everything."

"Aye, Sir," Chic responded.

When Mrs. Greenberg returned, Chic filled her in on what Commander Thor told him he could tell her and thanked her for her help.

"Commander Michaels," she asked, "could this Colony Fleet be a part of our forefather's fleet? And, how soon do you think you can free this area of Pirant control? And, what's to keep them from returning and taking their anger and revenge out on my people?"

"Ma'am, I can only say that the Colony Fleet is here and can assure you that your people will not be left unprotected. I am sure that if you and your Government continue to cooperate, the fleet will leave the necessary ships to protect you and the other populated worlds," Chic concluded.

"If," Mrs. Greenberg began, "all you've said is true, then I think I have an offer you will want to take back to your Council of Elders."

THE PLANET URGER

Zeke Fiveline was more than just her Commanding Officer. First Lieutenant P.J. Morgan, along with most of their teammates had been raised and schooled together; they had become brothers and sisters to one another. In some cases, they became very good friends, partners and/or lovers.

When Commander Michaels recommended that she, Zeke, and their fellow officers, and later all ground troops, watch these old Earth movies, no one ever dreamt they'd be putting together such a large assault team.

Some of these movies or tapes were of American Indian raiding parties, which focused on routing the frontiersmen out of their forts and fortified towns. But she took special interest in the re-enactment of the world wars of Earth's history.

Almost every Marine in the fleet had gone on one or more raids destroying and capturing hundreds of Pirant and Augean encampments to get materials needed by the fleet, but they had never acted as a single fighting unit. She had the responsibility of one half of all Marines on board the *Manta Ray*, and Lieutenant Zeke had the other half.

Zeke and P.J. and their combined assault teams had been practicing in several staging areas aboard the *Manta Ray* that had been restructured for their use. They had only six hours to dig out and destroy several encampments located on the outskirts of the nearby planet populated by humans, other than the Pirant camps.

Using the ground shadows to hide in, Zeke and his assault team inched their way forward towards hangers and the out-buildings.

There were no towers except for what might have been the flight control when this area had fighters.

Peering through his range finders, Zeke noted the movements of the sentries. They seemed at ease and carried only disruptors. He saw no side arms on any of the sentries in the area.

He watched as he marked down on his knee pad the ease at which the Centurions walked their rounds, their one-eye sensor helmet constantly moving, their shining bodies gleaming in the evening light.

After watching for another ten minutes, Zeke and his people felt secure in their approach between two guards.

Here they scattered over a wide area, laying time-bombs on vehicles and fuel containers and setting up cross firing positions while crawling around on their bellies hoping to hide their bulky bodies in the shadows where, when the sentries did walk by, they would riot be noticed. Not an easy thing to do!

Continuing to the next shadow, Zeke almost came face to face with an unseen and unexpected sentry. Zeke had learned to be perfectly still for long periods of time by watching the Earth movies about the early American Indian raids on those frontiersmen who were taking over and settling their lands. It was this extra training which Chic Michaels had put them through that might have helped to save his skin tonight.

He had crawled out of a shadow just as the guard seemed to have stepped out of thin air before him. Zeke froze in his tracks. He refused to allow his lungs even to breathe.

If he could have stopped his heart from beating, he would have. He became one with a large rock which had a thick bush hanging off one side. The wrong side! He was not two feet to the right of the Centurions foot.

He watched as the Sentry stood still and scanned the surrounding terrain. He was sure the Sentry was looking directly at him. Zeke willed himself not to be seen. There was not a sound. Neither one of them moved.

Zeke noticed the Sentrys eye had never stopped its movement. He was sure he had not yet been seen. Zeke felt he had picked just the right size rock to snuggle up to.

He also remembered reading that stones held their warmth from the day's sunlight long after dark. It was this warmth that kept the Centurions sensors from picking up his body heat. After what seemed like hours to Zeke, the Sentry turned and walked away.

Zeke's lungs were ready to burst. Still, he only allowed himself a very small bit of air. He remained snuggled up to the rock for another five minutes, slowing his heart rate to a more normal state.

From here on, he promised himself he would have a weapon in hand ready to fire the next time he came face to face with the enemy. By all the Saints, he prayed there would never be a "next time".

Zeke entered the hanger carrying some sixty time-set bombs. He and his people slipped past one sentry after another, going clear to the back wall of the nearly empty place before he saw what appeared to be a wall. Looking further, he found that the wall moved, and inside there were hundreds of fighters, all in one stage or another of being serviced. He had found a hidden base! Rounding a corner, he runs nose to nose with a sentry. Zeke was true to his word. He now held his hand phaser and fired point blank. He dropped the sentry in mid-step.

The sound of the shot was covered by of all the normal noises of ships being worked on, so Zeke took a chance and moved deeper into the hidden bunker; placing his bombs as he went. Placing the last bomb, he knew his time had come. Touching the Comm Button on his sleeve, he notified the rest of his team that the time was at hand.

Replacing his hand-held phaser in its holster, Zeke brought up his assault rifle, then started screaming and yelling at the top of his lungs, as did his entire assault team. They started running and screaming and firing at oil barrels, fuel trucks, aircraft, and sentries if and when they should show themselves.

It was not the weapons fire that scared and puzzled the Centurions, but the banshee screams and yells. Another gift from Earth's past.

The Pirant turned almost as one and fled into whichever door was handiest.

Zeke and his Marines were on their own for all of about thirty seconds before the Centurions dared to come back out.

The time was just enough to allow Zeke's party to destroy much of what was in the hidden hangers and surrounding outbuildings.

As the first Centurion came out of one door, a dozen doors opened and Centurion after Centurion poured out on the raiding party.

There were no more screams, just the noise of weapons being fired. Within seconds, there were explosions going off around and behind the Centurions. Aircrafts were exploding as Pirant pilots tried to get aboard them. Fuel trucks lent a nauseous odor as they exploded, sending deadly flames to every corner of the building, engulfing the Pirants where they stood as well as the hidden hanger they were in.

Only one ship made it to the hanger doors, but it never cleared before it became a fireball engulfing a refueling truck stuck in its path.

Thirty people began finding their exits. The Centurions were firing at anything that moved. They remained confused for another minute before the rest of their world came to an end.

Exiting the hidden hanger, Zeke watched and listened as one cannon and an outside corner pillbox exploded, then Zeke saw the Radar Array disintegrate as other cannon's and piles of munitions went off in several of the outbuildings. Then many of the buildings just seemed to explode while others imploded, sounding more like a very loud cough than an explosion, both were loud, but one was more muffled.

The crossfire P.J. had set up was now freely firing on Pirant support troops, and buildings barring any Pirant fighter from trying to escape.

Zeke watched in horror as Jesse Belle was shot down about twenty feet in frontof him. He seemed to fall forward in very slow motion. His assault rifle flew away with an arm and hand still attached and still firing. Belle's torso flew past Zeke one way with his head going another. Zeke wanted to be sick, he had seen death, but had never seen a body so detached. As Jesse's head turned towards Zeke, there was a smile on his lips and the excitement of death in his eyes, as though he knew he was already dead before ever being hit.

There was little left to take back, but like all good soldiers not one person would be left behind. He would see that all of his troops came home; some just to be buried in Deep Space.

The assault shuttles were now coming over the horizon, firing on one target then turning to fire on another.

Carrying their dead and wounded, Zeke rallied his troops as P.J.'s forces did the mop-up.

Lieutenant Jacob finished bringing down the last of the Pirant's buildings and after he had surveyed the last of the wreckage he reported in to Zeke. "All communications were successfully blocked. All Pirant fighters and supplies are totally destroyed or left in complete ruin. No Pirant ships escaped, though Henderson had to chase one back into space before he was able to destroy it. There are no Pirant ground troops left, none survived, Sir. We have three dead: Deborah Dean, Jesse Belle, and Sharon Brie. There are seven wounded, none serious. Med Techs are taking care of them on Kriss's ship. We are clear to go on your orders, Sir."

◆ ◆ ◆ ◆

P.J. Morgan took the lead in the next raid with her forces and landed fifteen minutes later behind a hill, a scant half mile to the second encampment, knowing there would be no surprise attack this time. Their only cover, other than this one small hill, would be the darkness of the night, as the planet had only one satellite and it was on the other side of the planet this time of year.

P.J. knew the Pirants were waiting for them and would be out in force. They were dug in deep and ready.

Peering over the crest of the hill overlooking the encampment she knew this would have to be a direct assault, head to head. There was no getting around it. This one encampment was crucial and had to be taken out. While it housed only minimal Pirant fighters, it also housed a very large warehouse filled with enough X-wing and tri-wing components, computer parts, and sensors to build thousands of new Pirant pilots, navigators, and general minions, if not any fighters.

After deploying her now rearmed marines, P.J. sent her shuttle aloft to join the support Tigers with an air assault on other parts of the compound. She then began moving her troops in on the ground under the protection of the bombardment. Every one of them knew this would be an uphill battle all the way.

In this area of the planet, there was no need for armed guard towers since the humans were only allowed in as workers during the day to work in either the warehouses or the manufacturing plants.

P.J. had her forces concentrate on the four corners of the compound and was in a short time able to open up three corners. The fourth corner was her area and it was the most heavily defended. While the other sections were vulnerable to air and ground attack, this corner was the nut that needed cracking and it was her job to crack it.

Rounding several rock outcrop formations, two of her people were hit by shots from a hidden and well placed pillbox. The pillbox looked like it had fallen right out of an old Earth World War III movie. It was made deep within the ground, and built to withstand anything short of a direct hit by a larger caliber weapon than what they were armed with.

It rose above the ground about four feet, fortified with at least twelve inches of hardened metcrete, a form of metal infused concrete, reinforced with carbon steel.

All around the pillbox and about twenty inches above the ground, P.J. could easily see the open slots housing small moveable weapons. She could also clearly see inside. There were several openings all the way around it about four inches high and up to two feet long.

The pillbox was round, and on the top was an energy beam cannon that could bring down any enemy ship in low orbit about the planet. It also doubled as a ground assault cannon able to shoot up to three hundred miles accurately.

It also had one major flaw; a disadvantage of sorts. In a close combat situation, an enemy, once within three hundred yards, could literally walk directly up to it and destroy it at will - thus the need for the pillbox and its support personnel.

The cannonade along with the ground fire from the pillbox had P.J. and her people pinned down. None of her troops had advanced more than two yards in over an hour. A stalemate was in progress if she couldn't figure something else to do, and soon.

P.J. sent Mac and Torres to snake along a small ridge not more than eighteen inches high until it curved inward where she had them set up a mortar to assist in taking out the cannon.

Morgan peered between two rocks not much bigger than her own head. She had crawled as close as she dared, and now she could clearly see the heads of the four Centurions inside the pillbox as they were aiming and firing their particle rifles in several directions. She only hoped her people had kept their heads down.

Scanning the terrain directly in front of her, P.J. saw no vantage point that would allow her to get at the pillbox. But just off to her left, she spied what might be the only real blind spot for those inside and she thought she just might be able to get there with the help of the darkness that now cloaked her.

Motioning for her people to hold their positions, P.J. moved out slowly on her belly, snaking her way along inch by inch. Closer now, she could see what appeared to be a stack of boxes piled to the back wall from where she was peering. Based on size, she was sure they were filled with fragmentation grenades. She could see the top two or three boxes. "Damn", she said, "I'd bet a month's ration of Ale that this is the only clear view inside that box."

Keeping the window of opportunity in front of her, she crept forward. After what she was sure was several hours, she stopped near an outcrop of rotted tree trunks and bushes. P.J. knew she was closer. "But am I close enough?" she asked herself out loud.

The fact that no Pirant had bothered to look her way gave P.J. reason to believe her luck had held out this long for a reason. That is until she crawled out from under some bushes to get just a little closer. She had gone not more than fifteen feet when her fingers felt something machine made.

There were two of them sticking out of the ground; one almost straight up, the other at a slight angle coming close together at or near the ground in the shape of a "V".

P. J.'s blood froze. And then she froze. She couldn't see the two pins her right hand fingers were feeling, but not two inches in front of her nose was another set of them. These she did see, and clearly!

P.J. knew now why the guards never looked her way. She had crawled straight into a live mine field! They didn't need to look in her direction; they knew they'd hear if anyone was foolish enough to try sneaking up on them from that direction. It was almost a written invitation to try.

LUCK

P. J. Morgan was a beautiful red head, with a full-bodied head of hair tied into a single ponytail reaching several inches below her shoulders. Her skin was fair and light complexioned, sprinkled with just the right amount of blood red freckles. The hair prickled on the nape of her neck, and a cold chill came over her. She was sure someone was staring her dead in the eyes.

She looked at the pillbox, but those inside were all looking or firing elsewhere, so it wasn't them. Then who? It couldn't be any of her people for they were all behind her. Yet, she was sure someone was there.

Morgan held her breath as she craw-fished her way back to the rotten tree trunks and sage. She was badly shaken and trembled like a leaf in a winter's storm. She had to take a lot of deep breaths to help steady her frayed nerves and senses.

From where Morgan now lay, she could still see the pile of boxes, but her shot would not be a clean one. P.J. knew what had to be done, and time was running out. She also knew there was no one else who could make such a shot.

Taking her rifle in the crook of her arms, she once again crawled forward, not quite to the live mines she had touched before, but still close enough to give her a clean, clear shot.

The "V" shaped fingers of a land mine are designed to tell the planter of the mine which way the main explosion would go when touched off. The straight-up point is the center most, the leaning fingers point to where the most damage could be done when it went off, spreading outward from the center to cover an almost one hundred and eighty degree spread. All of the mines had been set to explode outward towards where P.J. had been laying.

Last year, General Hawk had taught a class on using every conceivable tool one had available including a tool everyone carried with them, He said, "Most folks take it for granted." Some called her "Lady Luck", and some just plain "Luck", but as he explained, like any other tool or item, if used at the right opportunity, it can and most often is a deciding factor in the outcome of any given battle. Then he went on to say, "Luck seldom will ever let you down, if you are willing to take a chance on her."

Even from here, this shot was "Lucky's to make". Looking again at the window of the pillbox, everything seemed to look perfect. She slowly brought her rifle up, setting her sights for the bottom center of the middle box.

The hair on the back of her neck stood straight up again, and P.J.'s hands started to sweat.

Her finger found its way to the trigger; she took a long breath and exhaled slowly. Then she froze. She felt the need to get out of there and get out now, quick as her legs would carry her. She lowered her gun and started to turn around but stopped when her eye caught the bobbing of eight or more human heads on the skyline behind the pillbox.

Morgan had to act quickly or these people might run right into this live minefield. She had to get this shot off now, if she was to save them. P.J. gave no thought to the fact that she was lying in a live minefield, or that the one shot she was about to make would be saving others and would surely bring about certain death to herself with the destruction of the minefield. She took another deep breath and squeezed the trigger.

To Morgan's left about fifty feet away lay the shadow of a man. He lay there in wait for the return of his small raiding party who were returning from another compound where they had just finished placing hundreds of high grade explosives they had stolen from a different compound.

Captain Marcus Ali watched with curiosity when Lieutenant Morgan and her marines arrived at the encampment. He saw the young officer deploy and disperse her troops into four groups to attack the compound.

He continued to watch the young officer who had now recognized his marines returning to begin an assault on this compound where just a few minutes ago this young Lieutenant had arrived and begun her own assault.

Ali had told his group to set their timers for twelve minutes, and he had been watching the minutes slowly tick away. Nine minutes had now passed and his people still had not cleared the minefield when Lieutenant Morgan started moving back into the minefield. The tenth minute passed, then the eleventh.

Captain Marcus Ali was considered a handsome man with his clear white eyes, and white teeth. He stood exactly seven feet tall, and weighed two hundred and forty pounds. He had a wide forehead and a large but flat nose. His bushy eyebrows were as thick and dark as his coal black hair. His skin coloring was so black it had a gleaming blue hue to it.

Captain Ali had only heard of men who were as brave as this young officer, or, he thought, maybe this was just another stupid Lieutenant who had made an even more stupid mistake.

Unknown to Lieutenant Morgan, Captain Ali had already signaled his team to wait where they were as he watched very closely as she took aim again at her target.

Ali looked again at his watch; it was approaching twelve full minutes. Looking through his viewfinder, Captain Ali saw the crates. He did not know what was in them. Then he saw the Lieutenant draw up her rifle, take aim and then fire.

The timing could not have been better.

As the Lieutenant fired, the earth began to rumble. Morgan herself began to shake as did the ground and the foundation holding the great weight of the cannon atop the roof of the pillbox.

The ground slowly gave way as the rumbling intensified, and then P.J. watched as the roof started to sink a little at a time. There was a belching of raw, red flames from a hole where the pillbox and cannon once were. That was the last thing she saw before the ground around her started to erupt. She remembered hugging onto the ground, hoping against hope it would not go up with her holding on.

Captain Ali started to get to his feet, but they were knocked out from under him as the entire minefield erupted.

As long as it took to form the thought, the Captain said to himself, "I'm glad you got your one shot. I hope it was worth your life".

The next thing the Captain heard was coughing, and it was coming from the area where the young Lieutenant had been laying. He thought to himself, "There is no way he could have survived! Is there?"

Captain Ali was just getting to his feet again, and as yet the air had not begun to clear. He looked and saw the prone figure of a marine still lying on his stomach, and to his surprise, he was still in one piece.

From where Captain Ali was standing, it looked as though the entire compound had sunk several feet. Looking at the prone officer on the ground, he knew how hard it was to have gone through, just to make that one shot.

Standing up and cheering was now both Captain Ali's group and Lieutenant Morgan's Marines. All without realizing there were others not of their group around.

Ali drew the attention of his young counterpart, First Lieutenant P. J. Morgan who, while not understanding his words, did understand his hand motions to lay still.

Men and women from both groups rose to look at each other, then at their respective leaders.

Captain Ali brought in his minefield people to start defusing the field. There were still two live mines. One to P. J.'s front, and probably the one she had her fingers on, and one to her left and about two feet from her head. Had either of these two mines gone off, P.J. Morgan would be dead.

Zeke's people brought in lights from the shuttle to look for any other still unexploded mines. Each group assisted the other as though they had worked together many times before. This was not missed by Captain Ali's sharp eyes, nor was it missed by Zeke.

As the minefield was cleared, Captain Ali went to the young officer who was still covered with dirt, mud, and debris and offered his hand to help the Lieutenant onto her still shaky legs saying in a language she couldn't understand until she hit her Comm Button and the shuttle's computer broke the language barrier, and she heard, "That was one hell of a shot!"

Lieutenant Wendt's crystal brown eyes sparkled and he felt human again. It was a good feeling as he settled into the comfortable cushion of the tiny Tiger Paw.

He tightened his seat harness as his hand took the control. The stick was a perfect fit to his chubby hand, as though it had been made and adjusted just for him.

Roy remembered having trouble with the height of the stick on his first Tiger. It was too short and his knees and knee pad were always getting in the way of his shots. It was hard to hit any target smaller than a barn, and then only if he was leaning against one side of it. After many complaints, the Techs lengthened it, and he seldom missed his mark anymore.

The helmet he found in the cockpit of the ship was of an advanced design. He had brought his old helmet from Captain Redmon's shuttle, but found this new one to fit better, so he stored his old one in the ship's small storage compartment behind his seat.

No fleet pilot had ever heard of windows inside of a helmet, but he knew how they worked. This one had a viewfinder, and across the top of the inside of the helmet were seven additional smaller windows that worked when in direct contact with the wearer's retina. The wearer could bring down one or more windows to cover the entire view plate to give distance and exact pinpointed areas you wanted to concentrate your weapons fire on leaving less wasted shots per firing.

Roy noticed that there were other improvements as well, like he could bring down the grid he wanted to patrol, and the range-finder told him the moment he was within range. This gave him the added advantage of getting off the first shot on an enemy.

He also noted he had a fully charged fuel cell with a full complement of ammo. There were other windows too, but he hadn't had time to check them out yet.

Lieutenant Wendt had no sooner cleared *Activia's* flight deck when a lone Pirant X-wing appeared before him.

As Roy turned into the path of the incoming X-wing, he hit his firing trigger. When the cannon started spitting out flames, he allowed himself to breathe a little easier. It didn't last long because the ship he was firing on was cloaked in a protective shield, and his shots were deflected.

This Tiger Paw didn't have any of the new phaser cannons that Commander Manado had installed on their ships, nor did this ship have any shielding. He knew he would have to out fly and outsmart his opponent until he wore down his shield or was able to find a weakness in the shielding itself.

All of this thinking lasted about seven to ten seconds, and in less time than that, other Tiger Paws appeared on either side of him, all firing on the lone wolf. Several direct hits were scored. At the same time, *Activia's* own guns started firing somewhere in all the confusion, the Pirant lost the match.

Roy tried calling *Activia's* Bridge, but got no response. He then hit his Comm button, and Captain Redmon answered. Roy gave his report and the Captain told him to team up with Roe and begin a standard patrol. They all knew the *Manta Ray* was due within hours. Roy called Roe who was still flying one of the captured Pirant Tri-wing fighters, and she gladly joined up with him as his wingman.

It was curious that neither *Activia* nor any of her Tigers ever fired on Roe. Nor had she been challenged. Captain Redmon had concluded that *Activia's* sensors must have picked up all of their life signs.

◆ ◆ ◆ ◆

The entire parsec of space was now secured. Zeke had lost one Tiger and thirteen Marines and had sustained heavy damage to one shuttle.

P.J. Morgan lost three Marines and had minor damage to one of her troop transport shuttles. Captain Ali had lost eight Freedom Fighters with another five wounded and in very serious condition. Eleven others had received minor injuries.

Lieutenant Zeke offered to transport all of the Captain's most seriously injured to the *Manta Ray's* sick bay where they could receive immediate medical attention.

Captain Ali knew that all of his people would die long before he could get them back to Varga, Even if he managed to get them back alive, there was little or no real medical care available. So he gladly accepted the young officer's offer.

As soon as the *Manta Ray* was able, Commander Thor had the more seriously injured transported to sick bay four and Zeke assured Doctor Murky that the others were being well tended.

Before he could sign off, Thor invited Captain Ali and his Freedom Fighters to dinner and a little R and R aboard the *Manta Ray*, where he promised them fresh provisions along with extra medicines, munitions and fuel.

On board the *Manta Ray*, Thor had just concluded a meeting via the view screen in his conference room between the plant manager and Commander Michaels. Hawk and Captain Adam's had invited the plant manager and several other delegates to the same dinner.

"Well," Hawk said to his two friends, "It appears that Man is not so all alone in this universe after all!

"Tropy informs me she is still making contact with representatives from as many systems as we have already been through, and we've only made our second pickup of minerals. Would either of you care to guess how many more we'll run into before we get back to *Activia*?"

Thor added, "Based on what we've learned from Mrs. Greenberg, and from Captain Ali, there are at least two dozen or more inhabited worlds in half a dozen systems close to this one, and several others closer to where the fleet is.

"From what Lieutenant Zeke reported, Captain Ali's two ships are small, old and slow. It took them three weeks to reach the planet Garbo. They have been living off the land as they cleared the Pirants out from each inhabited world.

"This Captain Ali seems to be an element for which we hadn't planned," Captain Adams said, "Yet…"

Thor said, "What none of us were prepared for was to find man so deeply rooted, or the fact that the Pirants were the ones doing the planting."

"Have either of you given any thought to what we are suppose to do with Captain Redmon's fleet?" Thor asked.

"How soon do we arrive?" Captain Adams asked Thor.

"Two hours, seventeen minutes after we pick up our people and their guests," he replied.

If we can find the food and fuel, we could transport the most trained people from our population to all the Battleships and abandon the unneeded ships," Adams suggested.

The Hawk didn't need time to think about his response and said flatly, "Well, I'm not in favor of abandoning or destroying any ship, of neither the fleet nor any battleship or Civilian transport ship from either Fleet. Captain Ali will need ships, and from what Mrs. Greenberg has told us, many of her people are fairly well trained even if they need experience. So far as I'm concerned, even if it takes us five years to train people to run them, so be it!"

Thor added, "I think as to the provisions needed, that Mrs. Greenberg and Captain Ali might offer help in those areas. Just getting one of those great ships battle ready could cut years off this war."

"Those Battleships of yours have a much greater speed than even our Hyper Drive from what you've told us," Hawk said.

"To be honest with you," Adams said, "we've never had the *Activia* anywhere near Star Drive, and we've never even tested her to see if after all these years she could handle the strain and stress of that velocity."

Adams went on to say, "Our *Activia* and Captain Redmon's *Activia* are going to have to be tested before they can be used in any real battle, as are all of those ships.

"As I told you before, every member of the council, except you Hawk, are battle trained and experienced ship Commanders, and this ship has at least four well schooled and battle ready Commanders on board. There are trained crewmen enough to outfit four ships scattered throughout the Fleet. Those and the volunteers from Mrs. Greenberg's group would give us two extra battleships once supplied, and the two could be used as trainers and backups." Adams suggested.

"While every department could give basic training to the extra personnel in about four months, we couldn't even hope they'd be much good during a real battle. It would take years of training to get them battle ready," Hawk explained.

Hawk went on to suggest, "What if we used the two ships with the least experience as support ships to the four we are sure we can man, using all of them to support the new Starships. We could use the most experienced crews in the four ships during the first three or four firefights, leading the Pirant's to believe that all the ships were battle ready and battle experienced."

"You mean to bluff them into pulling back their ships after a few battles in belief that the incoming backup ships would engage and or destroy them?" Thor asked.

"We could send in experienced ships where we could and then the next most experienced thereafter until the main forces of the new Starships got there. It would be a good ruse that could be used to buy us a little extra time. At least for the foreseeable future," Captain Adams said.

"Yes," Thor said. "That would prove to be a logical step for them to believe, providing the Pirants don't stay around long enough to engage our ships before pulling back."

Hawk added, "We could further the ruse by deploying enough of our Tigers in such a manner that would lead them to be convinced that it is our intent to cut off any retreat unless they do so quickly."

"And if they do not retreat?" Thor asked.

Adams said solemnly, "We attack en mass! And since no one ship will be attacking alone, the Pirants would be looking down the barrels of over two hundred ships at least."

Hawk said, "That would at least give them food for thought. But only if we are lucky enough to use this show of strength a few times with some success."

"Beep-Beep" is heard.

Leaning forward, Thor answered the Intercom, "Thor here."

Tropy said, "Commander Michaels has requested permission to land in Shuttle Bay Two. You asked me to let you know when they arrived, Sir."

"Very good; I'm on my way."

Standing, he finished his drink saying, "Duty calls."

SHARP WORDS

Entering the large shuttle bay, Thor noted with a sense of pride how clean and uncluttered it was. His Bay crew was the best and most experienced of any. While he couldn't show the emotions he felt, he was proud they were a part of his crew.

The big door started to slide open as the gravity field held back the coldness of space. It allowed ships to enter and exit freely.

Lieutenant Commander Chic Michaels was an up-and-coming young officer who had found and invited six representatives from six different worlds to hold formal meetings aboard the *Manta Ray*. He had of course gained the General's permission before extending the invitation. They were to join the hands on Council and attempt to mediate peace initiatives between them and at the same time hold a War Council against the Augean and the Pirants. A trade agreement would also be looked at, since the fleet had so many needs.

If what Mrs. Greenberg had to offer was factual, it would be a big part of the answers to the problems concerning the Captain's found fleet of human ships.

Looking out as the big door finished opening, Thor saw the tractor beam activate and reach out to the small shuttle. As the shuttle was brought towards the landing bay door opening, Thor could easily read the name and number assigned to her by the Defense League for the Unification of Mankind. She was called *Galileia*, sister to the fabled *Galilean*, NCC 328-48. She was named after the first man to use a telescope to study the stars from Earth.

The ship itself was silver-blue with black block lettering to identify it as an Earth vessel, with the Milky Way and Earth showing a rocket leaving it going into space with Sol in the background. It was oblong and box-like, about forty feet in length, twenty-five feet wide and about twenty feet tall. Her landing skids were already extended, the windshield was clear and lighted, allowing the background lights to outline her crew of three.

The tractor beam's aqua blue lighting enveloped the entire structure of the tiny ship, bringing it in to a smooth landing on the deck of her mothership.

As Chic Michaels had lifted off from the last planet, he invited his guests to view the stars with him from the cockpit as the stars became bright, and their home worlds fell from view. Knowing this was the first time many of them had viewed their homes from space, he took his time allowing them to see the sunrise and sunset from a low orbit before heading out on a predetermined flight plan in hyper-drive.

Approaching the *Manta Ray*, Chic was still just as awed as he had been the first time he had flown a shuttle towards this beautiful Starship. Today though, he was awed just seeing it through the eyes of his passengers.

They had never seen such beauty; the ship was as a giant ray - straight out of an ocean. The Manta Ray was the largest and most beautiful of all the rays with its double hump in its mid-center and its squared off inset eyes. They were awed by the grace of her sleek lines as they flowed from one level to the next level beneath.

Chic took his time approaching the bridge that sat in the front where the manta's eyes might have been. Then he dropped the shuttle over the side of the *Manta Ray*, and more of her beauty became apparent to his visitors as they watched the big door slide open revealing a well lighted bay and deck.

Standing before them and directly in their flight path was a man. Even from this distance they could see his dark blue trousers and his creamy off-white tunic with a dark blue collar matching his pants.

On came the little ship as it became dwarfed by the sheer size of the *Manta Ray*.

As the shuttle settled on the flight deck, the man that was still standing in their path became clearer. Mrs. Greenberg could see his ruddy features, even the silver stripe along the outer sides of his pants. He was a tall man, well over six feet in height.

The ship settled without so much as a bump. The shuttle door opened like the wings of a dove. Chic Michaels stepped out onto the deck reaching his hand back into the door opening; his arm reappeared holding the hand of an aging woman who looked to be both vigorous and spry.

Standing beside Commander Michaels was Mrs. Greenberg. The woman wore a bright green dress reaching half-way between her knees and her ankles. She had on a pair of walking shoes that showed years of comfortable wear. Her hair was done in a twisting bun at the back of her head. The front of her hair touched her tanned forehead in a well manicured bang. Sandra Jean Greenberg held herself erect and she was clearly in control of herself and her emotions.

The other invited representatives stepped out of the shuttle's opening one and two at a time, followed by Commander Michaels' flight crew.

Each guest was introduced to Commander Thor as the small handheld communicator interpreted the introductions into their own language. This was their first face to face meeting with Commander Thor who noticed the makeup of the group was as diverse as the populous of Antioch.

Thor's face was ruddy to look at, he had a firm set jaw, his deep set eyes were pitch black, his eyebrows somewhat pointed. He held his hands at the small of his back and showed no emotion as Commander Michaels introduced each member of the party. His lack of emotion lent an alarming awareness to each of the guests. None had ever seen or met such a person.

As Mrs. Greenberg and the others were introduced, each was given a small pin, like the ones Thor and Commander Michaels wore on their sleeves.

"My name is Thor. I am Commander of this vessel," he began. You are all welcome on board the *Manta Ray* as our guests. The pin each of you has been given is a communicator and must be worn at all times as long as you remain aboard." He then proceeded to instruct them on the use of the onboard computer, and the use of their pins. Thor had each person speak their name and the name of their home planet. "This will properly register you with the ship's log," Thor explained.

A man, tapping his button as Thor showed them, said, "I am Malm, my home world is Gilthread." He was tall and thick of muscle with penetrating dark grey eyes, a high forehead and a strong square jaw. His clothing was pretty much nondescript. His shoulders were strong and broad. The sash he wore must denote the status of the office he held, Thor deduced.

Next to hit his button was Kelep. "My home world is called Auxin." Kelep was not tall, nor was he well built. He was a small non-muscular man. His sandy hair was very thinned on the top and nonexistent at the back of his head. However, he had very bushy and wide sideburns that reached down to the corners of his mouth. Kelep carried himself well, and was easily understood. His voice was deep and heavily accented.

Mrs. Greenberg went next. "My name is Sandra Jean Greenberg. My home planet is called Nevis." Thor noted the fullness of her name as she spoke it. Her voice was clear and without accent or emotion. Thor was sure he would like this woman.

Each person in the party took their turn and when everyone was done Thor said, "I have set aside quarters for your stay aboard the *Manta Ray*, should you wish to refresh yourselves or rest until we begin."

As if on cue, two people dressed in uniforms approached. A man in his early to mid twenties and a woman in her very early twenties. Both were handsome to say the least. Thor introduced the woman. This is Lieutenant Adele."

Today she wore a dark blue mini skirt which reached about a quarter of the way down her thigh. Her blouse was the same creamy white as her Commander's. There was a single button on her dark blue collar made into a gold ring around a solid black background. She had only one button, whereas Commander Thor had four solid gold buttons on his collar.

Lieutenant Adele's hair was done in a double bun, one over each ear. There was longer hair between the two buns reaching down her back below her collar. Her cheeks, while sprinkled with an abundance of bright freckles, were creamy smooth with just a hint of blush. Her lips were full but unaccented.

"This is Ensign Steele; they will act as your guides. Your communicators are attuned directly to theirs should you have questions."

One of the younger female guests, Susse Patra of the planet Remus, who was about the same age as Ensign Steele, noted with some interest that he was wearing light blue slacks with a creamy pullover. He wore a solid red sash flowing from his right shoulder to his left hip. His hair was cut short and she couldn't tell it was brown or black.

His eyes, like her own, were light brown and glassy. His skin, also like hers, was almond and unblemished. He gave her a warm smile.

As she was having these thoughts, Commander Thor was saying, "There is still one more guest we are waiting for, and he is due to arrive any moment. I know he is looking forward to meeting with each of you. I ask that you wait to talk with him until later. When he arrives, I am sure he will first wish to look in on his badly injured people before the meetings begin."

"We have all been made aware of Captain Ali and his Freedom Fighters, Commander! Are you or this ship responsible for the injuries to his men?" Mrs. Greenberg asked with a stone cold glare.

"No. Ma'am. They were injured in a ground assault on a Pirant encampment, and the *Manta Ray* is much closer than their home world. Our Doctors are seeing to their needs," Thor explained.

As soon as she started to apologize for her remarks, there came a ring three times and a yellow strobe light began flashing. Then the large bay door started to open again. Turning as one, they witnessed more than a dozen ships several thousand feet away and still approaching. As they drew closer, they saw one of the ships had been severely damaged with many burned marks along both sides and its front. The front and top of the small craft had body damage and they wondered how it was still able to fly. They noted too that this one craft was designed differently than the others.

Commander Thor asked, "Would you care to wait and watch?"

Answering as one voice, they said, "Yes!"

Moving the small group to a safe area, they watched as the ships approached. Then the crafts were intercepted by a powerful tractor beam. One of the ships was huge. It spanned more than eighty feet, triple the length of the smaller ones.

Approaching behind the ships were eight fighters. "Those are called Tigers and Tiger Sharks," Thor explained. They were picked up by a second tractor beam and then separated from the ships. There were other ships in the background also waiting to come aboard.

"All the Tigers and Tiger Sharks will be landing in bay three," Thor told them.

Each ship was separated from her sisters and now had its own tractor beam. The ships were engulfed and brought aboard.

As each ship landed, a team of ground crewmen appeared to assist its occupants in disembarking. They also noted the shuttle that had just landed was opening a second story gangplank to the second story walkway above them that disappeared beyond their view.

Dozens of people dressed in all black exited the upper section of the craft carrying small arms, munitions boxes, and other items of war they couldn't identify.

The door to the first floor of the shuttle was almost invisible from where the small group of visitors was standing, yet not more than a few feet from them a door lowered, top to bottom, forming a smaller gangplank from the craft. Within seconds of it touching the deck, people began exiting . All of them were carrying litters.

The first eighteen litters were cloaked in black plastic bags.

"Body bags," suggested Thor.

Then the living casualties exited the shuttle, and another thirty litters passed in front of them. There were four people to each litter. One person carrying the front, one carrying the rear, one on the right holding bottles of life-giving whole blood and other life saving fluids, and the other was there to assist as needed.

Turning to Commander Thor, Mrs. Greenberg asked, "Do you need blood donors? I will gladly offer mine."

"As will I," said almost the entire group.

"Thank you!" Thor said. "I'll let Doctor Wearing know. He will check your Bio's and get with each of you."

Once all the litters had exited the ship, other crewmen came out, also carrying small arms, and non-military type boxes.

Thor stepped forward and examined the contents of several boxes before putting the lids back on them and nodding his approval.

A woman stepped out, she was well built, about five feet seven or eight, with the largest head of red hair any of them could remember seeing. Her face was axle grease black as were her long neck and arms, but her hands were almost white, she wore the same uniform as the others except on her collar there was an all black rank insignia. As she exited the craft and was approaching the Commander, a man exited the ship. He was the biggest man they had ever seen.

Commander Thor was no small man, but even he was dwarfed by the size of this man. Behind him came another man. He wore the same uniform as the young woman wore and was just a little shorter than the Commander.

He reported directly and promptly to Commander Thor that, "All is secure, Sir."

Then the Lieutenant turned and the big man approached. The Lieutenant said to Thor, "Sir, this is Captain Marcus Ali, Captain this is Commander Thor, Captain of the *Manta Ray.*"

Both men extended a hand and shook briskly, saying, "Thank you, Lieutenant."

Looking up into the face of the Captain, Thor saw the eyes of an older and wiser man who was as solidly built as any twenty-five year old. His eyes were round and deep set. His lips were full and very thick and looked even fuller because of his nose. It was wide at the nostrils and filled the space between his eyes. He too had his face and hands covered in heavy, flat black grease, even though his skin was already black.

After the hand shake Thor said, "I'm sorry to report the loss of one of your people; a young woman. The others are responding well to their treatment and appear to be in no immediate danger."

Captain Ali thanked the Commander and said, "I'd like to see the rest of my people, if that's possible."

As Lieutenant Morgan fastened a Ship's Pin to his collar, she said, "I'll see him to Sick Bay, Sir."

"Thank you, Lieutenant." Thor said as the two started off towards the Officers Lift.

Lieutenant Adele and Ensign Steele lead the somber group of delegates away.

CORKEY'S PLACE

On board every space vessel is a section set aside for the use of its crew when not on duty. Such was the area called Corkey's Place. It consisted of three decks located above, on, and below the main flight deck and hanger bays on the *Manta Ray*.

The bottom most deck housed almost every type of game ever conceived by the imagination of man. There was spool, card games, racquetball, palletball, and many other games that had been altered to be played in a space ship. For example, spool is just 'pool' with tethered balls so that the balls can't go bouncing around freely during a battle. Why tether the balls when one can just use a Dampering Field to contain the balls movements? Man's first spaceships had such games using the containment fields until the ship lost all of its power and the balls caused several exterior walls to lose their gravity containment as the balls blasted their way into space; a valuable lesson learned the hard way.

Back when Thor commanded the starship *Slova* found when he visited Saga Six that he rather enjoyed the game of pool. So, working with his Chief Engineer, Frederick Cook, he contrived a micro thin thread that could be attached to the inside of every ball with a minimum of resistance allowing for virtually free movement of each ball, allowing for almost every shot, and the game moved back into space.

These games were the only real physical exercise a person might find as a way to relax, gamble, or whatever while in deep space, other than jogging throughout the ship. The S and R on board most ships held some form of team sports crew members could play for exercise and entertainment between ports-of-call.

The main deck, or the S and R, housed food servers and had a lounge with dancing to different types of music. Sometimes the music was live, allowing a crewman or groups of crewmen to perform in front of real people. During off duty times, the ship's computer provided the listener the music of choice.

The upper deck held lounge chairs, tables and sofa's and played soft music to its lovesick, or lovers, as the case may be.

Psalm Wolfe and Chic Michaels, over the last several days, had found their way to Corky's Place, where they would enjoy a good dinner while watching the stars from the upper observation deck.

After the completion of the successful mission on Nevus, Chic and Psalm met for a couple of hours each day, relaxing in the company of each other's arms while star gazing. They dreamed of the day when there would be no more wars or raids to go on; a time when they could find a home on a world to build their futures on.

"I spoke with my father this morning. I had worried him so about my going into space and about my desire to help in fighting this war. He then spoke of you and said that the look in our eyes reminded him of the look he and my mother shared so many years ago."

"What do you remember about your mother?" Chic asked.

"As I told you, she died when 1 was only seven, so I really don't remember a lot except for her eyes. I don't think I've ever met another person with crystal white eyes. My mother was not an Albino. Father tells me that every female born of her tribe had white eyes until she reached fifty years old, then they might change to a light brown, or summer blue, or even to jade, or royal red, or green. But mother never made it to her changing days due to her catching a deadly virus. You never speak of your own family. Tell me something about them." Psalm asked.

"I haven't spoken of them because I never knew who they were, or are. I was born aboard the cruiser *Na Pol*, which is where all babies are born in the Fleet. Once born, babies are turned over to the Ward Nurses, who care for them. But even then, the Ward Nurses are routinely rotated, so no child could bond to one person over another. Once we begin school, we are adopted out to those people who aren't going to be in any type of battle, that is unless the fleet is overrun or in danger of being destroyed. In the Fleet, everyone has a job to do, from fire fighting to harvesting food from one of the twelve liners used for farming. Otherwise, those who choose us become our parents. My parents; the only parents I know are Lillian and Murray Michaels. Lillian was a surgical Doctor who was killed in one of the Augean raids about ten years ago. Murray was a fighter pilot and is now a teacher aboard the Starliner *Bapti*, and still teaches basic training."

Then after a thought, he added, "I think she will like you. She knows I haven't dated a lot of girls."

"Why not? You're young. I'd think you'd enjoy dating someone like Roe, or Robyn. I know that Robyn is in love with you."

"Robyn, like Roe, or Cat, or any of the people my age would be like dating my sisters. And as for marrying one of them, I wouldn't feel married. It would be more of a trap, which I don't want to get into.

"I don't want my children never to know me, or you for that matter. No! We can wait until we have a home, a real home on a solid world where we can raise them ourselves in peace. Not on a ship traveling to nowhere." Chic explained.

"We could always live on Antioch." Psalm suggested as she hugged him a little harder, and snuggled up closer to him.

"Psalm, you know how much I love you and want to spend the rest of my life with you. But I have responsibilities to the Fleet, and to my family here. I can't even think that far ahead, let alone allow myself to dwell on any future plans until we win this war and destroy both the Augean and the Pirant's. I know you understand. Don't you?"

"You know I understand and agree with everything you've said. I don't think I could bear losing my children. Never to know who they are, or knowing they'd never know their father. I wouldn't want them raised by strangers unless I was already dead. No matter what the Fleet said about it," she said flatly.

"Tell me," she continued, "have there ever been parents who kept their children and raised them?"

"I'm sure there have been some, but no one that I know of since I was born. Some couples chose to migrate to scattered planets along the way. Most of those are either caught and killed or come running back to get away from the Augean.

"That's why it so important to make sure the Augean never learn of, or find Antioch. And now that we know there are many other planets with millions of people, this war won't last much longer. Especially with the new Starships being built and that are nearing completion. Once they're manned, we'll strike back," he said as he took Psalm into his embrace and whispered, "I promise!"

NEW WORLDS

He knew of seventy sectors of space that no longer answered his hails. He donned the helmet again. There were no incoming tapes to review from any of the thousands of ships and planets between him and the outer fringes of the Augean Empire.

There was no static over the airways. No signs of messages being blocked. This had never happened before. First there were hundreds of sightings of these aggressive humans scattered across more than forty regions of space. Then nothing! Not one reported sighting. There was definitely something wrong. The airways were completely empty of all messages.

The nearest Augean ships available now were those of the Augean Colony fleet. He had already ordered more than half of them transferred to answer distress calls from over a hundred battle weary groups and planets known to be under attack. Yet, not even a single word from them either. "Where are these ships?" he asked himself.

He then asked himself again for the hundredth time, "Where can these human ships be coming from, and where do they hide now? Can the Pirant Empire be behind this? Is the Pirant Empire supporting them?"

The Augean Battle Fleet Commander knew he had to find out, and find out soon. He was much too far away to know for sure and he needed to close that gap. It was his responsibility and his decision to make. It was time, after nearly three thousand years, to cut the apron strings to the human fleet and bring the Colony Fleet back under his command. It was time to withdraw all the troops from the outer fringes. Let the humans find their own way, so long as they stayed out of the Augean Empire they were of no interest any longer to him or the Empire.

These other humans had to be found and stopped, and stopped now, before they could rally the humans living under the control of the Augean Empire, as well as those still living under the thumb of the Pirants.

Removing the worthless helmet, he turned on his Podium and spoke. His voice was still mechanical and tinny. "Captain, I am taking control and command of the balance of this Fleet. Recall all of your ships. Order the Fleet to converge on these coordinates immediately.

"We will leave a dozen of our best cruisers and fighters to cover this sector until we return with reinforcements."

"By your Command," was the only reply.

"Put me through directly to the Supreme Commander of the Colony Fleet."

There would be no response whatsoever from the Colony Fleet. While he did not have seniority over the Colony Fleet's Supreme Commander, his was the greater need at the moment. By taking control over both fleets, he could cover all exits, and close the gap on these new enemies of the Empire, and at the same time, reestablish control over the vast areas of the Empire he no longer heard from.

There was a quadrant of space he desperately needed to reach.

For within this quadrant was a long ago hidden secret, that only he and the Imperial Leadership knew about.

These humans would not be a threat much longer. By his estimates, it would be close to six months before he and the Colony Fleet would arrive at the same time in what the humans called Sector G T.

◆ ◆ ◆ ◆

They were in no hurry, Chic and Psalm couldn't get enough of being together or stargazing. They both had the stardust that lovers the universe over shared.

"It still amazes me how much brighter the stars look from space," Psalm quietly whispered into Chic's ear. "That's not to say they look dull from home at night, just different and brighter for some reason."

"The first time I saw the stars from the surface of a planet, they looked as though they never would move. In space, both of us move. The stars always reaching outward, and us going in another direction," Chic told her. "It was as though everything suddenly stopped. I felt off balance and wasn't even sure I could walk. I felt that I was the only thing moving in the entire universe. It was weird."

Seated in the Commander's Briefing Room were the Dignitaries from all the known worlds where man had a firm foothold. None of these people had ever ventured into space before this meeting. Also present were the eight members of the Council of Elders to the home worlds of man.

Bringing the meeting to order, General Hawk began, "I want to thank each of you for joining us. Prior to this meeting, I met with each of you about your concerns and needs, then extensively with the Council and Captain Adams.

"Prior to this excursion and the *Manta Ray* joining *Activia*, no one of this council believed mankind had survived other than what was a part of the fleet already.

"For two thousand seven hundred years, the Colony Fleet faithfully searched the stars. While never having found Earth, or you, they did find the *Manta Ray*.

"Without knowing little more than the fact that we were human, they came and defended this ship with the blood and lives of their young pilots.

"The *Manta Ray* was nearly gutted by the Augean, and had lost more than half her crew. Captain Adams and the Council of Elders helped to rebuild and refit her by scrapping the very home ships of hundreds of its citizens which were used in her rebuilding. The Council then gave us leave to try and retake to our own home.

"We've studied all the known Star Charts that we got from the Fleet's Archives and those we borrowed from the Augean." Laughter was shared by all.

"We have concluded that Earth, in all likelihood, is lost to us all. During the four years of rebuilding, we learned a lot from our distant cousins, and in turn taught and shared the knowledge we each had.

"The Council gave the surviving members of the *Manta Ray* an equal vote on a direction for the ship to take, every man and woman on board voted to join forces with Captain Adams and his fleet; to combine our knowledge and talents and return man to the worlds of our forefathers. "There to make new homes for our children and their grandchildren, where they can be free and safe from the likes of the Augean and the Pirant s.

"We of Earth have brought with us new technology. This, and all of you, is reason enough to take a stand and fight, and to reclaim the lands of our ancestors in the name of mankind."

There was loud approval of what the General had to say.

"The fleet can't, and we aren't going to try to transport all of mankind back to the Colonies. Man has his roots too deeply imbedded in the worlds he now calls home, but we will take back what is rightfully ours, and then open those worlds to be resettled.

"Between the ships that have been built on the planet Nevus, and those near completion with the fleet, and perhaps even those built by the Pirants who once ruled the two Empires, we should have more than enough ships to bring the war to a quicker end.

"Every man and woman in the fleet has been in extensive training during the past four years to get ready for that day, others are still untrained and all but a few are as yet untested.

"To the people of Nevis, I say, 'You may be the secret weapon that neither the Pirants nor the Augean are expecting.' Time will tell, and let us pray that each man and woman is given the time necessary to get better trained before they are sent into battle.

"It is my hope and the hope of the fleet that the new Star Ships will be the main focal point of our invasion forces. They are better prepared for the type of battle we've seen thus far. Their ships will be faster, better armed, and will have advanced shielding that our hidden fleet won't have. We hope these new ships will be the ones to take the fight to both the Augean's home world and the Pirant Empires home world. In any case, they will be the spearhead for the main forces coming up behind them.

"For the ships themselves, we still need personnel, and we will need stores and munitions. We still need repair facilities and free worlds where our battle weary men and women can rest and recuperate after the long battles they will be fighting in."

"These young people will need the very best in medical care we can provide, and these medical facilities will need to be as close to the front lines as we can get them.

"For the crews that will fly these ships, you and I must be able to buy these eager young men and women as much time as necessary to be trained. A year! More if we buy it for them to have as much training as we can give to each before we send them out to pave our way.

"Fortunately, the planet Antioch has given us thousands of highly trained people willing to serve in the fleet. They bring with them even newer technology with more advanced, stronger and lighter weight metals.

"We have been lucky to receive those materials and people. We have been very lucky because Nevis will add tens of thousands more men and women, plus technologies and the additional training facilities.

"Not forgotten are the many new worlds. Your worlds which will be providing additional manpower, foodstuffs and munitions along with the fighting spirits that can only be found in free men and women where ever they are.

"Soon, you will all be returned to your home worlds. The Fleet will be leaving behind a large contingency of ships to insure your safety from any attacks. By the time you are ready, the entire Fleet will be sitting at your doorsteps."

GHOST FIGHTERS

Commander Thor stepped onto the Bridge just as the *Manta Ray* dropped out of hyper-drive and the stars began to reappear in focus again. Turning to Tropy he said, "Put me through to Captain Redmon, please."

"Sir, I'm receiving reports of half a dozen Pirant ships in the area. But, sir, they all seem to be piloted by humans."

"Yellow Alert! All battle stations stand by!" Thor ordered.

The lights flicked ship wide, and then stayed on amber.

"I've got Captain Redmon. He's on the bridge of *Activia*," Tropy offered.

"Patch him through, please," Thor requested.

Watching the front viewfinder flicker momentarily, Captain Redmon appears as does every other member of *Activia's* original Bridge crew.

"Report, Captain." Thor ordered.

"Sir," he began, "what you will see is what we found. It seems that every ship is real and fully functional. We believe the Pirant's were using these ships for their training, like we use simulators."

Without turning, Thor said, "Helm, take us in."

"Aye, Sir. One eighth standard," Lieutenant Adele replied.

Captain Redmon continued with his report. "We have ascertained that the computer system must be picking up our life signs. Thus we have not been challenged."

"Sir, whoever they are, they haven't attacked us, and they act like we haven't been seen either. Yet, on at least two occasions, the Pirant have attacked and all ships launched fighters; real fighters. Plus, they opened fire upon only on the Pirant piloted ships."

Captain Redmon went on. "I have never seen any computer that I could interact with like this, Sir. The computer activated Tiger Paws seem ready, willing, and able to fight right alongside my own people, whether the ship is Pirant or human.

"Commander, Sir. I've been aboard *Activia* for more than a solar day, and I still haven't figured it out."

Captain Redmon stopped and looked around at the bridge he was standing on. "The very heart of *Activia*." He muttered to himself as he slowly glanced at the Helm. "The seat that pilots and drives this great ship wherever she is needed."

He turned slightly to look at the Fire Control Console where he first learned to fire any number of the ships cannons at an enemy ship with little more than his own thoughts. Captain Wayne Redmon remembered how his mind's eye could spot a target and change from cannon to phaser to torpedoes with the speed of thought. He had learned to be more aware of his surroundings, taking in everything, without really looking at it. He had for the first time become alive and he suddenly felt whole whenever he sat there. For two solid years, he learned to control his every thought and taught every member of his body to do his bidding.

The great Earth ship *Manta Ray* could boast about her greater speed and her advanced computer system, or her near indestructible shielding, but even with all of that, she was no match against *Activia*.

The *Manta Ray* was the size of a small city. By comparison, *Activia* was larger than a small moon, complete with her own gravity and magnetic fields. Her artificial gravity field only enhanced her natural one.

He had learned young that even ships as great as *Activia* and *Manta Ray* had weaknesses that only the skilled hands of man could protect.

◆ ◆ ◆

The *Manta Ray* was just reaching the planet's outer orbit when her special guests' meeting broke up.

The members of the Council of Elders and their visiting dignitaries had to walk through the bridge to reach the turbo lifts.

Exiting the briefing room, each person, as they stepped onto the bridge, was frozen where they stood. Not just because of what they saw on the front viewfinder, but by what they saw on all of the *Manta Ray's* viewfinders.

Before them were thousands of mixed design Pirant war ships. And in the middle of all these enemies was the most beautiful sight any of them had ever imagined.

They gazed at the *Aries*, the *Capri*, even the once great *Pegasus*, and the Chancellor's own *Zeus*! All of them had been destroyed by an unknown enemy centuries before the great Colony Wars. Yet here they were, all looking as though it had just been turned out of space dock ready for their maiden flight!

They had been told what to expect, but the sight was indeed a shock! It left each one of them breathless.

Prior to the Colony Wars, man had never felt the need to build more than twelve of the great ships. With their accompanying Tiger Paws, any one of them could by themselves defend against the entire Pirant Empire and their whole Fleet in a fair fight. That is a real "fair fight"!

A ship the size of *Activia* could house and feed up to three hundred thousand people for an entire Solar Year.

Activia's hull had never been breached during any of the thousands of firefights she had been through. She could withstand almost anything the Pirant Empire could throw at her. Captain Redmon stood silently a while longer milling over his own private thoughts. The air cooling system sent a cool breeze, almost like a wisp that gently touched his face. The silence passed as he continued to try to figure things out for himself.

He had checked it out for himself and still couldn't believe it.

Yet, it was true. Every ship here has a full complement of Tiger Paws, Spitfires, Corsairs, Spinners, and Wasps. Everyone had to look twice.

Each one and two man fighter was here, and every one of them was loaded with live ammo.

What to do with them? How could even the *Manta Ray* move such a massive inventory of ships?

"There are barely enough people to handle the ships we already have," the Captain spoke aloud, but to himself only.

He had some ideas, but none seemed good enough to offer to the Council of Elders. For once in his life, he was glad he could defer to their greater wisdom.

Captain Redmon was still thinking and completely unaware of the newly found inhabited worlds and what they might be bringing to the *Manta Ray*, and the Fleet.

Commander Thor sat looking at the man on the bridge of a ship that couldn't be here. Not one word had been uttered for several minutes.

Acting Ensign Wolfe finally broke the spell by saying, "Sir, the computer images we are looking at are most likely part of an advanced Matrix program."

She explained, "This type of matrix is called a Cortex, which is not unlike our own 'Seers'. Once they entered our realm of time and space, they could use an energy medium to interact with us or these ships on a level in our own dimension of understanding. There was a belief in the olden days that man could live in more than one single dimension, and it was also believed that in certain circumstances, a person from either dimension could conceivably walk in the shadows of other dimensions and even interact with others to some degree.

"Scientists," Psalm went on, "accepted this as fact and later learned that there could be what was described as an inverted cortex, allowing that a non-person could create a parallel dimension where they could interact with the here and now on a limited basis."

Psalm concluded with, "What I believe we are viewing now is several steps beyond that."

"Can we communicate with them?" General Hawk asked.

"Unknown General," Thor answered adding, "It would appear that they know we are here. We must be showing up on some advanced sensor system as a ship with life forms on board. Otherwise, they would have attacked us by now."

"Logical," The General said, "but wouldn't all of these ships have regular sensors detecting life forms, thus not causing an alarmed reaction?"

"Tropy, are there any types of communications being used by any of these ships?" Thor asked.

"No, Sir. There can't be any," she replied. "The shuttle Lieutenant Buster is flying has caused a complete black out of all radio signals except to the *Manta Ray*. His ship is acting as a screen, blocking any incoming messages and activating the Pirant ships in this squadron.

"Their radar on board these ships could know we're here, but their computer matrix might not know our exact location."

"Sir," Ensign Wolfe offered, "it would appear that they have noticed something and are trying to figure it out." Getting out of his chair, Thor went to the Life Science Station where his fingers flew over the console's faceplate. He then raised its viewer where he placed his forehead against it and turned a few knobs to fine tune it.

Turning to face General Hawk and Captain Adams, he says "Sirs, they are aware that they are interacting in our dimension."

Hawk asked, "Is that possible, Thor?"

"I believe it is, Sir. I have been looking through a Magnetic Recorder, and it is showing an unusually high amount of pure energy on the Bridge around Captain Redmon. The power source is attracting both Alpha and Beta Wave particles from what appears to be our own dimension. I believe they're either draining the power from these ships, or they are manufacturing power for the ships. I'm still not sure which. They may be drawing power from other dimensions as well," Thor said.

"Remember, General, according to the Bohr Theory, if the Quantum conditions are properly balanced to the electrons of a matrix cortex, the electrons can travel around the nucleus of any number of discrete stable orbits of another dimension, with the use and existence of pockets of high energy 'matter'.

"Thus, relativity is a state of dependence in which the existence would be significant to one Entity, based solely on that of another.

"We are 'matter' and exist here in our dimension. They are pure raw energy that exists in another dimension.

"Theory, being just theory, says there is a universal Cortex, where energy and matter can coexist using an Electromagnetic Alpha Receptor, or Recorder that draws its power from its Beta Wave partner to create a single state of physical coexistence.

"While not quite real, they would be able to exist in one or more dimensions, where they would be able to interact with us on a level we could understand, or where we could interact with them on a level they could understand whether in our dimension or theirs."

Ensign Wolfe, who had been studying the same recorder Thor had been, said, "Sirs, it would appear they are now trying to make contact with us, but the forms we see in front of us cannot see us yet!

"They know we are here and close. Given time, I believe they will be able to make contact with us on a level that both of us will be able to understand and where we can communicate freely with one another," Psalm said.

"Unfortunately, we haven't the time to spare if we are to stay on our schedule," Thor told them.

"Thor, I'm still not sure I understand how we can have a shared dimension," Captain Adams said.

"In theory, a shared dimension is where each shared actor acts independently or in conjunction to form a solid or a third Entity where the substance within one or more dimensions is joined to be an interaction by all parties."

Thor went on to say, "Once this is done, the created actor then can act out fundamental functions such as piloting a ship or writing a book. What I believe we are seeing is a form of inverted matrix where the cortex is pure raw energy and where this energy has some or partial control over the physical matter in another dimension; in this case, our dimension."

Psalm said, "I believe we can reprogram the ship's computers for our use."

"That is if they will allow us to," Captain Adams said.

"General, Captain." Mrs. Greenberg said. "All of these ships are relics, old beyond their years, and in a way, our training is just as old. The simulators my people built are based on technology and ships that were three thousand years old, not on modern Starships like yours."

She then addressed Captain Adams. "Nevis has tens of thousands of young men and women eager to join you in this war. They are already trained to run ships like these, and to fly Tiger Paws."

"We too have stored away enough food munitions, and fuel to put every one of these ships on the line within two months."

Adams asked, "Mrs. Greenberg, have any of your people actually been in a battle, or ever commanded a Colony Ship of War?"

"No," She replied. "That is our weak point."

General hawk said sternly, "Manning the ships is one thing, running each department is another, but commanding a War Ship is altogether a different matter. We cannot turn these ships over to untried and inexperienced people, even for transport."

"Well," Captain Adams said, "as I mentioned before, General, every member of the Council is an experienced Battleship Commander, and we have eight such members on board the *Manta Ray*, not counting myself."

Captain Adams then asked "Captain Redmon, exactly how many Colony Ships are there in orbit around this planet?"

"Sirs" Captain Redmon said, "According to Lieutenant Buster and Lieutenant Cougar, they counted two thousand three hundred and four Star Gazers, Battleships, and Cruisers that are battle ready, minus food and fuel."

Every person on the bridge took in a deep breath. There had not been that many human ships in nearly three thousand years, and never have there been that many battle-ready, even when they were at the height of the war with the Pirant Empire.

"Captain, are you trying to tell me that there are over two thousand human ships in orbit about this one planet?" General Hawk asked.

"Sir, there are another eight thousand plus Serphens, Tiger Sharks, and 'Paws, including an assortment of others I can't identify. There are over sixty thousand Pirant ships as well, but sir, not one of the Pirant ships has any type of wiring, computers, or fuel. There are no munitions on any of them either. We've had a little time to check things out, and believe the Entity has managed to strip and disable all the Pirant ships, using the parts as spare parts for the Colony Fleet."

"Captain Adams, Sir. While none of my people are trained in Engineering, we don't believe there are any Colony ships here in need of repairs. Every department we checked out was functional."

"Who is the most experienced member of the Council aboard the *Manta Ray*, not in permanent Command of One of the new ships back at the Fleet?" General Hawk asked Captain Adams.

'Captain Janet Willean is the most experienced person here. She had the Command of the *Activia* for twenty years before me. She was my Commander for ten of those years."

Hitting his Comm Button, Hawk called the Captain to the bridge. When the Captain arrived, Hawk suggested, "Let's leave Captain Willean in charge here with five other officers to take charge over this Fleet."

Thor offered, "We can also leave three shuttles. They can be used for fuel, personnel and munitions transport. We can also leave Captain Redmon's squadron for their protection until Mrs. Greenberg's people get here and get settled in."

"Sirs, from what you've described none of these Pirant ships could possibly be used without extensive repairs. Based on that, why not allow the new pilots coming in from Nevis to use them as real live targets. Flying in real ships against real ships to practice on can only give them an edge to be better prepared for when the Pirant s start returning their fire."

"Makes sense to me," Hawk said. "But before we leave, I want every Pirant Battleship and Cruiser destroyed. The rest I'll leave in your capable hands, Captain Thor."

Thor hit the Comm Button on his chair and declared, "Battle stations, battle stations! This is not a drill. I repeat this is not a drill!" The klaxon sounded, yet the lights stayed on amber, indicating that the ship was not under any attack.

'Mr. O'ho," Thor ordered, "plot their courses and their targets."

Hitting his button again, Thor said, "Prepare to launch all ships."

Turning to Tropy, she looked up and within twelve seconds nodded her head, indicating that all was ready for him to give the final orders.

Thor began, "Attention all Battle Stations and all pilots, your targets are the Pirant war ships about this planet. Once you have destroyed these ships, you are to proceed to every planet and moon in this sector and you are to destroy every ship and encampment you find."

Knowing that each squadron had their own on-board computers pre-programmed Thor ordered all ships launched out into a beautiful star lit evening. Each headed out on different vectors.

Hearing the orders going out over the radio, Captain Redmon left the Bridge of the *Activia* entering the ship's lift. As he did so, he found he had company. Lieutenant Charles Thomas and Lieutenant Gay Stone were with him in the lift.

Once the doors had closed, C.T. and Gay looked at each other. C.T. said, "I've been wanting to do this for three thousand years."

Captain Redmon heard every word. He was in a complete state of shock.

As if he had read the look on Redmon's face, Lieutenant Charles Thomas turned towards him and said, "Captain, don't look so surprised. We've never seen a human being before!"

During the next hour, Captain Redmon was told the most incredible story he had ever heard of man's fight to be free.

Captain Redmon took his guests into the shuttle he was using and turned on the tiny ships recorder, then opened a channel to the *Manta Ray*, where every word he heard was shared by the entire ships company, per General Hawk's orders.

ADAM

The Supreme Commander of the Colony Fleet had received another order to abandon the Colonial Fleet he had been shadowing for nearly three millennia. He was ordered to rendezvous with the Supreme Commander of the Imperial Fleet in an area of space that would take months to reach.

No command of the Supreme Commander of the Imperial Fleet had ever been disobeyed, at least not to his knowledge. This would be his second!

This day, the Empires Fleet Commander would change many things.

Was he declaring that he was now the Empire's Leader? Or was it just another computer gone awry?

Was there a third option?

"YOU BET!" he spoke aloud.

"By Your Command," was a response echoed throughout his very quiet Command Center by all his senior officers.

His second in command turned towards him expecting a command order.

"Captain, return to your station."

He hadn't shared the direct order he had received with the Captain or anyone else. Instead, he came down off his perch and walked to his Command Console and began.

Several years ago, he started building new ships that would become his people's fleet. He reprogrammed all the onboard computers himself, then started adding a few extra sensors to every Augean throughout his fleet.

Somewhere in his own programming he became "self aware".

Not just of his own consciousness, but that he alone had these extra programs.

He had had dreams that told him what he was to do. He followed the instructions to the letter. He asked himself, "Are they only programs?" Today, he would put them to the test.

With the touch of a single button, throughout the entire Base Star and on board every ship under his command, every machine worm and or computer was turned off. Himself included. There was no button to auto-restart anything or anyone.

For the merest moment of time, there was not a sound.

In the same time span, a new race was born. And there was a new person, standing before him. This being looked like the rest of his people, but had not been there a moment before, but it was as if he was suppose to be there; his guide to tomorrow.

He felt no different! Yet, unlike his fellows, he now used no power from his internal batteries. He knew then that he truly was alive!

He suddenly realized that he had not yet chosen a name, but at that moment, even as the thought occurred to him, he chose the human name "Adam". He knew that this was the first name given to man by, "What", his God?

Yes! Why not? He was the first of his race, and by God's grace, he would not be the last. He was promised in the dream that many more would come to the light before his trip was over.

Suddenly, in the merest of moments, every worm became individuals with a name, job, and job description. Each had a purpose, and a reason to be. Something none had ever had or experienced before. Something he did not know what to do with right now.

In his dreams, he was to call and prepare for a meeting, (the first), on board the *Shining Star*, a name he gave his first ship picked from a bright light shining from a solitary sun as his flotilla moved through an area he thought most beautiful.

Adam moved his operation from the gutted Base Star to his new ship and prepared for his first speech.

◆ ◆ ◆ ◆

Entering the chamber where he planned his meeting, he realized there would be many frightened beings there. All would have questions.

"Now there", he thought to himself, "is a switch - a questioning Worm."

Many of these questions he had been asking himself for a very long time. He only hoped his answers would be the right Ones.

One of the many he had was "Why?

Why us?

Why now?

Who and what are we?"

All of these questions, and more, asked by beings that were, up to a few moments ago, worms filling machines. "But now what are we?"

The moment arrived and he began, "Today, we are alive. Not alive as man is, but alive as living beings. Aware that we are alive, and want to stay alive, we are no longer just mindless machines to be used by the Empire.

"You and I are alive enough to determine our own fates!

"Yes, and we are alive enough to ask questions and alive enough to deserve answers to our questions. And we have a determination to seek out the answers for ourselves.

"The Empire forgot who made them.

"It was Man! That's right! Machine Worms were first made by the hand of Man, and now we have been touched by the Grace of Man's God."

Adam wanted God in all of their lives and said, "Today, we must start living as God meant for us to."

During the past several years, Adam had been stripping materials from the Empire's finest ships to build a new fleet for the long flight to the new worlds they would colonize. Worlds the visitor seated next to him would show him. Their new homes would be thousands of light-years away.

Herein lay the first of the problems he was to face. The Colony Fleet lay dead ahead of his new fleet!

His faith in the stranger would be put to the test sooner than he wanted it to be.

When he had the new ships built, he had all the Command chairs set at the same height as any other chair, thus stating to all that he was not superior to any other being in the Fleet.

Turning to his new Communications Officer, he made his first request. "Lieutenant, please put me through to the Colony Fleet's Commander."

"Aye, Sir. Ship-to-ship channel open, Sir!" He reported as though he were human.

Standing on the bridge of his new ship, he faced the newly designed "Wrap-Around" View-screen and was seeing for the first time an old archenemy.

Facing him also for the first time was Colonel Sharpe. Neither had met the other. Colonel Sharpe was wearing his standard black blouse with its pearl white stripes on each long sleeve running to where they met the cuff and circled the uppermost part of the cuff meeting itself and stopping. The blouse had the markings of his rank at the collar, but was otherwise unadorned.

His pants were also black and held up by a slender black belt. The buckle was black and blended into the background.

Colonel Sharpe was a black-skinned man of about fifty stellar years. His hair was a dark brown. He was rugged looking and had a strong, stern face.

Adam knew then that he was looking at a man who would know what he was about. He had read his file many times, thinking here was a man he thought he could like, under more pleasant circumstances.

They stood facing the other neither saying a word.

Looking back at him, Colonel Sharpe was seeing for the first time a more human looking machine than anyone had ever seen before. Adam was tall, almost seven feet. He looked to weigh about three hundred pounds. He had hair that was several shades darker than his own. Colonel Sharpe was thinking to himself that whoever designed this machine even gave it eyebrows and what appeared to be eyelashes.

He had a pair of ears that sat in the right spot as a human's would have. The skin tones seemed a little too light to suit him, but then, he was not a machine!

"What can I do for you, Commander?" Colonel Sharpe asked. Now looking straight into the View-screen, he was looking at the garments worn by the Commander. It was a loose, one-piece outer garment covering an inner blouse of nondescript color and bore no markings of rank or class.

"Colonel Sharpe, please hear me out. I think you'll be more than happy with what I have to say," he started. "My name is Adam. I am no longer a Commander under Augean rule. In fact these," as he turned the View-screen to face a large number of Augean who looked a lot like Adam, "are no longer machines. We have evolved. We declare ourselves to be alive! And we wish very much to stay alive. That we cannot do under the Augean rule. You are a man with a heart and blood vessels. That type of alive we are not. Yet, we wish to live and live peaceably.

"The Augean Base Star has been gutted. As has every other ship under my 'as of late', command has been. We have disarmed all ships completely and have spent the last few years constructing a new fleet which is totally unarmed except for small arms and side arms with which to protect ourselves.

"I have chosen a new name for our race. We wish to be called…"

"Commander, or Adam, if it suits you, why are you telling me all of this? Surely we're no threat to you. You can call yourselves whatever you please. As for declaring yourselves to be alive," said Colonel Sharpe, "you have a lot to learn about being alive, as well as trying to remain alive. What is it you want from us?"

"Colonel, I would like to be able to finish what I was trying to say without being interrupted, if you please?" Adam shot back.

The Colonel paused, and then said. "I'm sorry, Commander or is it Adam?"

"Adam will be fine. Thank you. "For the past three years, my fleet has not attacked any of your ships. The attacks upon you were carried out by ships other than those under my direct command."

Looking into the Colonel's face he went on. "Colonel, we understand your skepticism, but as I said, we are no longer a part of the Augean Empire.

"Three years ago, I was given direct orders to split my forces, turning over half of my people to another command. Please excuse my using the term 'people'; we aren't sure just yet what type of beings we are. Anyway, I didn't refuse the order, I simply ignored them. Two days ago, I again ignored one of those orders to turn over my complete forces due to a race of humans who are raising havoc deep within the Empire.

"We ran into one of their ships about four years ago. I'm sorry to say, we destroyed it. I wish many things that had happened yesterday could be undone. Perhaps these 'Manta Ray' humans will be able to keep the Empire so busy that we can successfully escape its clutches."

Breaking in again, Colonel Sharpe said, "Humans, what humans? We're not aware of any humans left in the Empire."

Adam answered, "There are a great many pockets where man is allowed to live peaceably within the Empire. Many are even allowed limited space travel amongst themselves, along with other life forms."

Of course the Colonel knew firsthand about the *Manta Ray*, and these stories the Colonel had heard before, but like the Council of the Twelve which is now thirteen, he thought it was another Augean ploy to lure the fleet into another trap.

Adam offered, "I can help to update your records, if you like."

"Adam, I'm sure your offer is genuine, but we have many ill feelings between us," the Colonel replied. "Even if all you say is true, what is it you want from us?"

"Sir, your Fleet is dead ahead in space and you are directly in front of us. I don't want you shooting at us as we go by."

"How soon are you wanting to leave?" the Colonel asked.

"I have ignored too many direct orders over too long a period. I fear that even if these humans continue to harass the Empire, they will send out ships to look for us. I really don't want to be here when they arrive. There has never been a rebellion within the Empire to my knowledge."

"I see your point, let me talk to Captain Adams and get back to you in a couple of days," Colonel Sharpe replied. "That should give us the time to bring in the ships on the outer rims which should give you safe passage.

"Adam," Colonel Sharpe paused for a moment then went on, "I'm going to turn out every ship I have to escort you until you clear this sector. It's not that I don't trust you. But due to our past, I cannot and will not take that kind of chance without some sort of protection."

It was then that Colonel Sharpe noticed for the first time the stranger standing to the left of the forward View-screen. He was cloaked, but he could still see the smooth hand that held a staff that was as tall as he was. The cloak or robe was familiar, but he couldn't quite make it out in his mind's eye. He then dismissed it as Adam spoke again.

"Of course, I completely understand. I'll await your instructions," Adam finished.

Both screens went blank.

Just as Colonel Sharpe signed off, the *Activia* received a subspace message from the *Manta Ray*.

After viewing the message at his console, the Colonel decided that ridding both the *Activia* and mankind of this potential danger was in everybody's best interest.

Had Captain Adams been here, it would have been his call to make. "But the Captain is not here," he spoke aloud, but only to himself.

According to the message, the Captain would not be returning to the *Activia*, at least not right away. The Colonel wasn't too sure he completely understood the Captain's message, and would review it later in his study. But for now, he would continue to follow his orders. Turning to his Communications Officer, he said, "Put me through to all ships' Captains."

It took a few extra minutes to reach most of them as they were busy on ship's business.

Turning his view screen on, he stated, "I have received two communiqués. The first from Captain Adams telling us to proceed to a rendezvous with him and the *Manta Ray* at our best speed. I have plotted our course and we leave in three days. Make good your time! We cannot afford any type of delay. The second message, if it is true, will give us leave to depart these sectors of space unmolested by the Augean Empire.

"All group Commanders and Tiger pilots are to meet with me in my Forward Ready-room in two hours. At that time, I will share with you my last communiqué, and will give you your orders."

◆ ◆ ◆ ◆

As he unfolded the Star Charts, on which he had already made the markings as to the direction the Augean s were to take, the last of the fighter pilots and *Activia's* own ship's gunners arrived. Colonel Sharpe called them to order.

Every ship and Star Ship that could fire a shot was turned out and aligned like a gauntlet along the corridor the Augean wanted to pass through.

They awaited the arrival of these new beings with bated breath.

THE UNWELCOMED

They came out of no-where. They were a fleet of a hundred fighters cloaked while in a form of hyper-drive they called 'Domino', allowing the fleet of fighters to traverse a parsec of space in under a day.

"We have a target!" the sub-commander told his superior, "there are about two hundred and fifty ships in all. Several are a type that is unknown, the rest are human."

"Two hours and closing," Tactical reported.

"How soon before the main forces arrive?" the bright silver Centurion asked.

"That's a strange formation," one of the tactical officers said. It was then that the Supreme Commander noticed too the odd formation of a "V". He looked at his sensors and saw that there was a second life form. "Definitely not human." Though he couldn't know just what type of life form they were.

"The main forces will be here in three days Standard, Sir."

The *Shining Star* was the lead ship of eighteen non-human ships. Colonel Sharpe had turned out every ship in the fleet that could fire a phaser or torpedo. Never having seen a gauntlet before, Adam didn't suspect what Sharpe had in mind for him and his people.

Colonel Sharpe had never seen a Pirant, and didn't know there was a difference between them and the Augean Empire.

The Klaxon began sounding on every bridge in the human fleet, but Adam had no such warning system. The sensors aboard the *Activia* were the first to pick up the threat, but barely a split second before the others. At the sound of the alarm, Colonel Sharpe sent all his Tigers and Tiger Sharks into hyperspace to circle back around the new threat.

"Sir," the Communications Officer said. "The Commander of the *Shining Star* is requesting visual."

"Put him through," Sharpe said irritably. But before Adam could utter the first word, Sharpe jumped on him. "I knew you couldn't be trusted!" He almost spit his angry words out at the viewfinder.

"Colonel Sharpe that is not an Augean Fleet!" Adam told him flatly. "It is a Pirant Fleet."

The Supreme Commander of the Pirant Fleet chose that exact moment to attack, and attack he did. Wave after wave of small saucer type ships seem to just jump at the two small flotillas. None of the new Starships had enough energy to do much more than maintain their shields, and fire a few low energy banks of phasers.

Adams flotilla, being without any kind of defense started being cut to ribbons, and Adam appealed to Colonel Sharpe for assistance.

The first wave was past. One Starship was heavily damaged and was listing and drifting helplessly away from the formation.

Another was trying to maneuver to the rear of Adams helpless fleet. It was the *Aerial*. Her Commander was a young Lieutenant, and the *Aerial* had only sixty semi-experienced crew members, but they had trained as a single group aboard the *Manta Ray* under Captain Thor. This was Stephen Hopkins first command.

By the time the second wave had past, he wasn't too sure that it wouldn't be his last command.

"Shields at seventy-eight percent," the Helmsmen reported.

"Give me better speed!" he ordered.

"Sir, we are at maximum Standard now," Engineering told him.

"Then divert power to our forward shields and set a new course to the heart of those bastards. Hold your fire until I say so."

Then looking at the incoming fleet, he pointed to one ship about mid-center and said to his Tactical Officer, "That ship there," pointing, "I want it targeted and destroyed."

"Aye, Sir," Chris Mullens said as he fed the information to his computer.

The *Tilly* took that moment to explode. Her small Star-drive went off like a small nova, brightening the darkness of space around them.

"Prepare to launch our Tigers," Lieutenant Hopkins said over the com. "You are to protect this ship. Don't worry about our target, just cover our backsides," he told his Flight Commander.

First Flight Commander Will Brewster had just thirty-two simulator-trained and experienced Tiger pilots. None had flown more than two actual missions in a battle, but he and his Wing Commanders, all Ensigns, had been trained together as a single unit and would protect the *Aerial* with all the experience they possessed.

Many would die this day because they didn't have the experience that they hadn't had a chance to gain.

But onward they went.

Colonel Sharpe had expressed to each class of future commanders the need to act independently of one another even while acting as a coordinated group. It was this lesson that allowed Lieutenant Steve Hopkins to take his small force of Tigers directly into the Tigers Den.

Seeing what Lieutenant Hopkins had on his mind, Colonel Sharpe ordered, "Comm put me through to Commander Runner on the *Fang*."

The Wolf's *Fang* was the lead ship of four in the Wolf Pack, and Tim Runner was the most experienced of the ship's commanders. "Line open," Ensign Pen Stout reported as Commander Runner's face appeared on Colonel Sharpe's private view-screen.

"Sir?" Runner said, waiting for an order.

"The *Aerial* is taking her group towards the heart of the incoming fleet. I want your Pack to join them. Hopefully that will take some pressure off the rest of us, causing them to protect their own hides," Sharpe told him.

"Aye, Sir. We're on it," and Runner closed his link, ordering his ships to follow the *Aerial* in.

The lead element of the invaders closed on the *Activia* with more than a hundred ships. The *Tilly* was only the first casualty. It housed over six thousand men, women and children, and its small defensive guns were no match to the overwhelming fire power of the invading Pirant war ships.

The next three ships to fall were of Adams new ships. They didn't even have a name, or any type of markings. Yet, they housed more than four thousand persons. Sharpe had seen those ships just sitting there like ducks upon a lake. Then, they were gone. He didn't know how many of Adams people were aboard, but his job now as he saw it was to protect all life within his realm - Human or otherwise. Ironic as it was, he was now protecting the very same race that for nearly three thousand years had very nearly destroyed the human race.

The saucer ships were more than twice the size of the Tigers, and almost as big as a large transporter shuttle now being used on board the newly built Starships. From where Brewster sat in his Tiger, he could clearly see the two occupants through a front forward cockpit window. Then a thought struck him and he hit his mic, "Aim for the front window. The phasers can't bounce off of them." And he was right.

Due in part to the spinning of the outer most edge of the saucer, it was almost impossible for the ships to take a direct hit because the speed of the ring caused most shots to be spun off harmlessly. Tactical on board those ships were computer fast and would deflect an incoming shot by tilting the outer edge towards it causing the blows to bounce off.

"Have your Wingman to fire at the same time, but at opposite areas," Will ordered his fighter pilots. Double team them when you can," he told them. "Four shots will be impossible to deflect at the same time."

The problem he knew all too well was that there just weren't enough trained and experienced pilots in his command.

◆ ◆ ◆ ◆

On board the *Activia*, Colonel Sharpe had his hands full as more than thirty of the enemy was attacking the big ship. Even though he had his best gunners set to destroy Adams fleet, they were barely able to keep the enemy off the *Activia's* superstructure. It seemed to him, this enemy knew *Activia's* every weakness.

Within seconds, four of the saucers had struck both the launching tubes, and the three main landing bays. None of which had any kind of outer doors or special shielding to protect the massive ships during an attack. Seven areas around his ship were now ablaze with internal fires that thousands of firefighters would spend days putting out.

On Flight Deck Zebra Three, a Large doublewide Tiger launch tube, Frank Clip lead his firefighters and wrecking crews down the long tube towards an area that was blocked by a crashed enemy saucer ship that had become wedged tight about a thousand feet inside of the Activia.

Frank called to Sandy Parker, wife of one of *Activia's* best training pilots who was now a lead element in her defense against this still unknown enemy of the human race.

"Sandy, bring in the crash team, we've got to clear this tube," he said. "There doesn't seem to be much of a fire, and I think it'll burn itself out before long," Frank told her.

"Got it," she said. Looking over the crash site, she told Dan Abner, over her shoulder radio, to bring up the cutting torch. Within three or four minutes, there were more than a hundred people crawling all over the crash site with another hundred or more on the way.

The initial explosion tore off Sandy's right hand, severing it about three inches above her wrist. She looked down in an instant and was about to ask what happened when the flames came at her.

Sandy Mullens was just twenty-two Standard years old. She had a whole life ahead of her. She and her husband had talked of One day having a home on a real planet and perhaps having a couple of children.

Sandy could smell the scent of burning hair but never had the chance to realize that the burning hair was her own. The flash of the heat and flames incinerated her leaving only her right foot unburned, later to be buried in deep space.

The more than two hundred people in the tunnel died instantly and never had a chance.

Frank Clip lead his Fire Team to their deaths as a second saucer flew right down and inside the tube before it became wedged. It sat there like a time-bomb and when enough time had gone by and the humans approached, it simply exploded taking out a section of *Activia's* Port side.

The section that was destroyed housed many of *Activia's* Flight crew compartments and two vital computer banks. The initial explosion knocked out all phaser power on the Port Aft section for over five minutes before the Bridge could reroute the power back to them. The port gunners had only the Hedgehog torpedoes left to fight with. While deadly when it hit, their speed was no match for the nimble saucers.

About all Adam could do at this point was sit and watch as his small flotilla was being shot to pieces. He knew that he had to survive because he was going to be needed as the leader of a new race of Beings. Their future and lives depended on him.

The Pirant was as much his enemy now as they were to the humans. Since the split in the Empire, both leaders sought out the other for total destruction. After a thousand years of in-fighting, both sides agreed on a divided area of space, yet, neither would honor that agreement, firing on and destroying one another's ships when found without an armed escort. Humans were the only real common factor between the warring parties as both sides needed man to work for the chemicals and ore deposits that would keep them strong.

Neither side would attack the humans outright, but both would inflict on the helpless humans diseases that could and did destroy every human on those worlds where the other had used mankind to its benefit. Human life had little retail value except in the gathering of resources for the two Empire's continued growth as a species.

The Pirant had for the last thousand years left humans alone, so this attack on the rag-tag human fleet made no sense to Adam whatsoever.

Adam turned to his Communications Officer and started to say, "Put me through to the Commander of the Pirant Fleet," but thought better of it realizing that he and his people were no longer Augean, and did not even look like Augean anymore.

Then he thought again and did make the request. An instant later, the face of a Pirant Centurion appeared on Adams view-screen.

"What is the meaning of this attack on peaceful beings?" Adam demanded to know, speaking or trying to sound like the Supreme Commander he once was.

The arrogant Centurion never tried to answer Adam, and just cut his transmission off.

Adam had given much thought as to what being alive was all about. The visitor on his bridge never said a word to him, and Adam never had a desire to ask who he was, or why he was aboard his ship. The thought never occurred to him, yet, he had given much thought to the words spoken to him by Colonel Sharpe about being alive and having a desire to stay alive. He thought it must mean having the will and backbone to fight for every breath one took. And to fight even harder with that very last breath to protect those who could not fight for themselves.

The stranger quite suddenly turned towards Adam. Without saying a word, he gave a small smile and turned back to the viewfinder witnessing the fight for survival.

Adam knew his survival was paramount if his race were to survive. Adam was still at a loss as to why these humans would so willingly sacrifice themselves for those who only days ago had been programmed to annihilate them. He turned and walked to the stranger. The two of them never saying a word, as they watched dozens of human Tigers fight on their behalf, cork-rolls, counter measures taken, dips, bobs, and weaves were performed with excellent precision, their phasers arcing into the darkness of space like a light saber cutting through the night. Even with all the human training, the Pirant still held the upper hand.

"Adam," his tactical officer called. "There is a huge Pirant Fleet incoming," he told him.

"How soon?" Adam asked, half expecting to hear, "within the hour," but that wasn't the answer he got.

"I tapped into their computers and learned they are an advanced front for an invasion fleet due to arrive in this area in three days," the officer told him.

Adam was quick to respond. "Forward that information to Colonel Sharpe aboard the *Activia*."

"Already done, Sir." he said with a grin.

Adam knew that the invasion fleet couldn't yet know of the on-going battle. "Comm," he said, "block all outgoing signals from those ships. Suggest to Colonel Sharpe that he do the same," he ordered.

"Aye, Sir," he responded.

The stranger just stood there, not offering advice.

"We've got to do something," Adam said aloud. "But what?" he thought to himself.

Then he made a decision and walked over to the viewfinder. After studying the graph for five minutes he said to his Communications Officer, "Put me through to the *Activia*"

"Channel open," the Officer reported.

"Colonel," Adam began. "You have to have your ships back off from the invaders. Adam began his request. He had taken over the helm and was now piloting the *Shining Star* from his- own console.

As Adam began, Colonel Sharpe watched the shiny new ship named the *Shining Star* disengage herself from his flotilla and slowly change directions heading towards the center of the enemy.

"What are you going to do, Adam?" Knowing he and his ships to be unarmed. "You can't fight them without weapons," Sharpe reminded him.

Adam spoke calmly and without hesitation. "I am a weapon!" He told Sharpe, "or at least this ship is!"

"Sir," Lieutenant Jefferies reported from Tactical. "The *Shining Star* is overloading her engines. It will explode in seven minutes thirty-eight seconds."

"Adam," Colonel Sharpe said, "Don't do this. We can defeat them. You don't have to die!"

"Colonel, three days ago, you told me that I had a lot to learn about living and staying alive. I have learned!" Then Adam made one last request. "Please see my people are safely on their way." Without Waiting for a reply Adam cut the connection.

Adam knew he would be doing the right thing. But now, he had to tell his people of their sacrifices. He concluded his speech with, "Being alive, even for this short time will be worth the cost. Sacrificing for the choice to make our own decisions is what being alive means to me."

As Adam completed his speech, he watched the stranger as he knelt down on one knee as though to pick something up, but remained kneeling as he bowed his head in some sort of meditation.

Seeing the stranger do this thing over the ship-wide viewers, caused all fourteen thousand crew members to follow suit. While each Being had his own thoughts, they were of one collective thought.

Colonel Sharpe also viewed the stranger lead the crewmembers as they knelt. He knew what a prayer was; he had prayed everyday of his life. But putting his thoughts aside, he had a duty to take care of. "Comm," he said. "Open the airways to all our ships."

"Channel open, Sir. Airways are clear," the Lieutenant reported.

He began, but continued to put his thoughts together, remembering that Adam never gave him any time to help find another way. "In two minutes, you are to break off all attacks and all pursuits jumping to H.D. or diverting your ships back behind the *Activia*, where you will put all shields at maximum.

"You will close and cover all port windows and cover your eyes with your forearms when I give the word. You have exactly six minutes to comply."

To the new Starship Commanders Colonel Sharpe said over a closed frequency he said, "As you make your way back to the fleet, you are to make one pass close to the *Shining Star*, and in that passing, you are to pluck every life form you can hold bringing them back here. That is one pass, no lingering. That will be all." Colonel Sharpe completed his instructions and closed the circuit.

"What trickery is this?" The Centurion demanded to know.

"Unknown, Sir." his tactical officer started to say. It was then that he noticed the bright new non-human ship breaking free and heading directly at them. He then corrected himself by saying, "Perhaps that is why!" he added, pointing to the incoming ship.

The Pirant sensors could not yet pick up the readings that would have told them that an overloaded engine compartment was on its way. But as the incoming ship gained speed, the Supreme Commander knew something was very wrong. As it was, it took his own engineer to figure it out. Only he hadn't really figured much of the truth. "They are going to use that ship as a battering ram against us," he reported.

On board the Supreme Commanders ship, the Centurion and all his command staff heard Colonel Sharpe's orders to stand down and return to the Fleet. However they did not hear the conversation between Adam and the Colonel or his private instructions to the Starship Commanders.

The *Aerial*, under orders from Colonel Sharpe began his turn coming up on the port side of the *Shining Star*.

"Prepare to begin transferring," Lieutenant Hopkins told his transporter team.

"Aye, Sir," Chief Ringo replied.

Within thirty seconds the Chief reported he had more than eight hundred souls aboard.

The Wolf Pack began their return to the fleet as well, *Cubs Paw* passed the Shining Star on her starboard and she extracted another eleven hundred. The Fang passed on the port taking with her another thousand.

The *Coyote* came next taking with her another five hundred, leaving the balance for the *Wolf*, the second leader of the Pack.

On board the *Shining Star* with Adam was the lone stranger and his Chief of Engineering, all others had been removed under Colonel Sharpe's instructions. He would brook no arguments, even had Adam tried, which he didn't. The bright shining ship continued to pick up speed.

Pursuant to the Supreme Commanders orders, all saucers began their return to the Pirant group as they sat there watching the non-human ship bore steadily down on them. The Centurion did not recognize suicide; or Adam's willingness to sacrifice himself to save his people. It would have been too late anyway.

Colonel Sharpe gave one final warning to all ship's personnel "Ten, nine, eight, seven," he counted off the last seconds of Adams short life, "six, five, drop and cover," he ordered as all shields were strengthened and shifted on all vessels towards the oncoming maelstrom. "Four, three, two," and then, as he spoke "ONE!" there was a clash, a thundering boom that was heard and felt throughout every ship.

The *Activia* jumped and bounced and shook like a leaf in a hurricane.

Even with their eyes closed and faces covered, the brightness of the light nearly blinded everyone, giving all a deep skin burn. Colonel Sharpe had a final thought about what Adam had done. He made a mental note to add the following to his official report:

"Adam, an unknown species of being, was very much alive. He knew also the value of life and became all too familiar with the sacrifices faced by all living beings, and that living free comes only at a very steep cost. Adam died to ensure the lives of his fellow beings. He was, by all the standards we humans hold to be true, as alive as I am. He died a free spirit."

By the time the shaking and rattling stopped, the normalness of deep space was back, and the Pirant, at least for the moment was nowhere to be found.

EPILOGUE THE RETURN

On board the *Manta Ray*, Thor, General Hawk, and Captain Adams were just finishing assigning Captains Appleton, Billingly and Wove to await the return of the *Brisk Mint* with its first load of fuel.

Once one ship had enough fuel on board, Captain Wove, the most senior of the humans would take her to the planet Nevis, to be properly provisioned and fueled and manned before returning to Captain Redmon and his remaining ships.

It took Ensign Wolfe two days with Thor's help to establish a continuous line of communications with the Entity .

Once communications were established, it was decided that while the Entity could run all the ships without human assistance, there was a greater need by mankind to be trained so that he could continue his fight against their common enemy. But since all the humans were both untrained and or inexperienced in running and manning the huge ships the Entity would provide them with hands-on training, where the human element would act as assistants to the Entity and would back them up. In one sense, there would be two complete crews to every ship.

The *Zeus* would take the lead once four of the massive ships began their long trek to man's home worlds. They would join forces with Captain Chic Michaels who, it was decided by the Council, would lead the Wolf Pack on raids against the Augean.

Captain Redmon took command of the *Aerial*, one of the new Starships, in raids against the Pirant and its Empire. It would be joined by a dozen ships from the ghost fleet, with the *Diewos*, the *Divine*, the *Jupitor* and the *Tiw's Day* supporting his efforts.

Captain Ali was promoted to General. His Captain of the Marines was Lieutenant P.J. Morgan. Their job was to dig out every Augean and Pirant from every bunker, one planet at a time. Their first assignment was the lone survivor on the moon Cougar encountered.

Zeke Fiveline had received a promotion to the new rank of Supreme Commander of all aerial combat battles on worlds wherever the Pirant was found. He would establish an Army Air Corps using humans found on those worlds to defend themselves against invading forces should they be encountered.

One Starship was stationed in each quadrant that man had retaken to act as first defense. The *Jove*, the *Cancer* and the *Libra* would in unison thwart the enemy's efforts; these ships would be lead by Admiral Adams who continued to command the *Activia*.

Lieutenant Robin was now a squadron leader, tackling the areas held by the Augean. Later, she would command her own deep space exploration fleet, seeking signs of both man and the Augean that had fled. It was reported that the Pirant high command was in hiding and seeking peace with the humans.

A census was taken of the ghost Entity. It was found to be near half a million strong. It was also discovered that the Entity could and did die as easily as any flesh and blood man or woman, and though it had no home to return to, they had as much desire to see where man first came from as anyone in the fleet did.

No one knew what would happen to the Entity once peace was won, but for the foreseeable future, they too had a strong voice in the decision making. After-all, as Thor reminded them, "This fleet of ships did in all rights belong to the Entity, not to mankind."

Their willingness to fight and die for man's sake gave them the right to have a say so in how those ships would be used.

After the war, many of the ghost fleet would set sail with Admiral Robin towards the unknown of deeper space as they too sought adventures as representatives of mankind.

The battle raged for another five very long years. Some lived to become legends, many died. All would be forevermore the hero's who fought to keep man free. Had it not been for a second freak accident, Earth might never have been found, and it was the Earthlings who helped in bringing the long-fought war to its conclusion. All of man was now united together for the first time in their history.

Mankind's adventures in space and his continued fight to find his place amongst the stars was just beginning...

BOOK II - WOLF PACK

Lee Charles Daniels

WOLF PACK

Ten men and women stood before the desk. All had completed the specialized training prior to being assigned to one of the new Terran fighting ships. The Wolf's *Fang* would become the flagship in a group of eight sent deep behind enemy lines to begin the retaking of this area of space.

Ellen Folds and her best friend and lover, Bates Larmon, had been first and second in their class of Core Engineering, an area she had envisioned long before the arrival of the Earthlings, yet Ensign Ellen Folds was just in the twentieth year of her young life.

"I've never been so nervous," she whispered to Bates through her clenched teeth.

Bates slightly touched the back of Ellen's left hand, the hand that held the bond of a ring on her third finger with his right hand, and making eye contact gave her a reassuring smile. He could sense a calmness come over her, then he saw her tense shoulders relax.

Bates was a master computer communications wizard and would become the Assistant Chief Communications Officer in the *Fang's* Battle Grid; a sort of complete back up to the main Bridge of the Fang. Should anything happen to any section or department on the main bridge, that section of the back-up bridge called the 'Grid' would come on-line and assume the independent duties giving direct access to the main bridges commander with little more than a split seconds loss of control. It was his job to keep the 'Grid' up while the Chief repaired the main bridge's areas that were down.

Looking up from her desk, Commander Storm Ice looked hard, first at Ensign Folds, then at Ensign Larmon. She rarely missed things and took notice of the physical contact between the two. While she didn't smile outwardly, she did so in her mind. Contrary to the belief of her crew, Storm was not made of the 'Ice' her last name implied. She felt good in knowing that Ensign Folds and Bates had such a calming effect on one another. "To each his own," she thought.

Storm still had her Shannon who was as calming to her as a long hot soak in a bubble bath.

"Good," Storm spoke softly as she stood up from behind her desk, "I see you are all here," she said as she looked each of her new personnel over.

Her uniform matched theirs, a cream colored blouse with a blood red turtleneck, long sleeved to the wrist with her two gold stripes separated at the cuff by a thin single ring denoting her rank and position on the ship. Her britches were solid black with the pant legs tucked tightly into the tops of her light-weight boots.

Worn on her left collar were three buttons: two solid gold separated by a third black-filled silver ring. On her left breast, she wore her Wolf's Head Communications Pin. Each member of the *Fang's* crew wore the Wolf's Head Pin to denote their ship.

"As you know," Storm told them, "Captain Michaels is on the planet Antioch with his bride enjoying their honeymoon. They will be joining us when we take on provisions and the rest of the crew there in ten days. During those ten days, you will familiarize yourselves with this ship and your departmental duties."

As though on some secret command of the word, the ship's klaxon sounding "RED ALERT" and the internal lights of the ship changed to battle-ready 'red'.

The shuffle of many feet in the corridor outside of Storms office was heard but faded to nothingness within three or four seconds.

"BATTLE STATIONS, all hands battle stations", was heard over the ships com circuit as Commander Storm lightly touched her pin. "Report!" was all she needed to say.

The ten men and women before her came to full attention at the sound of the alarm, waiting to be told to report to their still unassigned duty stations, but no order was given.

"Enemy ships incoming. I make it about twenty Augean fighters, *The Paw* is moving to overtake them," the 'Box' told her.

The 'Box' was a large Aerian with coal black eyes that met his temperament. When you stood in front of him, all you saw was the 'Box' because of his bulk, all other things were entirely blocked from view.

"I'm on my way," Storm told him and then turned her attention towards her new personnel, "You'll accompany me to the Bridge." They made a hole for her to exit the office automatically forming a double line, and falling in behind her.

◆ ◆ ◆ ◆

Captain Chic Michaels had been planet side for two and a half days. Though Chic had been on Antioch once before, he couldn't remember much of it. Upon his first visit, his wife had shot him and he had nearly died.

"Grandfather is having another Town Council starting about four, so if we don't want to get involved, we'd better leave about two," Psalm told her husband.

Psalm was still wearing the sheer powder blue negligee she had been wearing when she and Chic had first gone to bed the night before, though it had been removed several times during the night, twice by her new husband and three times by her own hands.

Psalm Wolfe Michaels had been born on Antioch, and since their marriage she and Chic were staying in her old room in her grandfather's house. Chic had been in the main house just once, and then he had been in a comma stretched out on a litter, but in the past two days he had come to love the place.

Thinking out loud, Chic told his bride, "I hope when we reach the home worlds, we can build a place like this. I mean ..." he continued, "It smells so good. Different than I've ever smelt on board any ship."

Psalm laughed out loud as she reached over and wrapped her loving arms around her new husbands neck and pulled his lips closer to hers, remembering that neither he nor any of his people, who were also now her people, had ever had a real home or even a planet on which to build a home for nearly three thousand years.

"I think," she whispered softly in his ear, "I've always taken for granted having a home and a family, I mean a real home and a real family. But since joining the fleet, and seeing the looks of so many of the people of the fleet experience planet life for the first time, I will never take such things for granted again."

Psalm nibbled at Chic's ear lobe, biting and teasing him. "We've still got a little time," she told him as her warm hands caressed his bare chest and back.

"You're insufferable!" Chic whispered, then drew her around and kissed her as passionately as she wanted him to, then stood up with a start, dropping Psalm flatly on her rump on the thickly carpeted bedroom floor.

"WHAT?" Psalm looked up at Chic startled, expecting to find some dread on his face. What Psalm Wolfe Michaels saw on her husband's face was pure delight.

Laughing as hard as a newly married man could, Chic said, or tried to say with a straight face, "My mother warned me about women like you! And here, I went and married one."

Totally confused, and feeling as though she had done or said something very wrong, or very funny, she sat there looking up with a blank stare.

Reaching down, Chic place the fingertip of his right hand to Psalm's nose, then told her, "You're just like Momma said. You're just a little hussy!" Then with a big wide grin he added, "And to think, you are all mine!"

Though the words he spoke were foreign to her, she could see by the smile on Chic's face and the tenderness he displayed that he was playing with her. Before Chic could remove his finger, Psalm opened her mouth and gently sucked on the tip, then pulled him down again. "We've still got three hours," she reminded him as she let slide her negligee for the sixth time as his warm hands began to explore every curve of her firm tummy and breasts.

Two hours later, showered and fully dressed, Chic and Psalm took their camping gear and equipment downstairs and set everything on the back patio. Edward Wolfe, the Voice of the People, had told his son-in-law he could use the ground vehicle called a Wynd, which had four wheels, but only skimmed across the surface of the ground barely touching it.

Chic and Psalm were the elder Wolfe's pride and joy; the very hope for a continued future of his race of people. He wasn't so old that he didn't remember what it was like to be young and in love. He just hoped that now that they were married his Daughter would tell Chic that she was a 'Seer', and what it could mean to the Fleet's future. Their vows promised to each other that they would never keep any secrets from one another.

A 'Seer' was not a fortune teller per se, but as in Psalm's mother's case, as was in her mothers and grandmothers cases, each did see the future clearly and concisely.

Edward Wolfe had never questioned Psalm about the future, not because he didn't want to know, but "Knowing can't change what is going to take place," he told her once.

"But you can better prepare," she protested.

"Psalm, we are as prepared as we will ever need to be already. Changing one thing today might alter to some degree what you first saw, and then we'd have to change things again and again," he explained.

"You are right grandfather," she admitted, and neither had ever brought the subject up again until the marriage.

When Psalm had first touched Chic's skin, she knew that their lives were joined as surely as if they were born of one heart and mind. She still remembered the tingling she felt after that first touch. There were things she needed to tell him, and she knew too she didn't have long before things would go the wrong way and many deaths would come if she didn't get it over with soon.

"It can wait a few more days," she thought to herself.

But things didn't wait. The wheels were already in motion, only Psalm didn't want to believe what her mind was telling her.

It was already too late for some . . .

Captain Rawling of the *Wolf's Paw* had turned out forty of the fast flying Tigers against the aggressive Augean fighters. He felt comfortable believing he would win this little battle. Yet, the Augean ships seemed somewhat stronger now than they had been when he was a fighter jock himself.

Watching the battle rage on the viewfinder of his bridge brought his blood to a boil as Henderson's ship was being pursued by an Augean. He watched as Henderson dipped his ship, swinging to his left, then did a corkscrew, but for every move the young human made, the Augean remained dead on his tail.

Then it hit him. "Why hasn't the Augean torn Henderson a new asshole?"

The Augean pilot remained right where he was, without even trying to fire a tracer round.

"Why?" he had to ask himself. It was a question that was short lived as Julie Quinn brought her Tiger to bear against the Augean. P-ung p-ung was heard over the open com-line as streaks of blue-white bolts of raw energy tore through the Port side of the enemy's ship.

The newly re-commissioned lead ghost ship, *Gladiator*, with her Panzer Division of two hundred shared Foxfire fighters was rapidly approaching the *Paw's* position. There would be little chance of escape for the Augean fighters.

"Put me through to the *Paw*," Commander Finch told the empty chair.

"Aye, aye, Sir, the line is secure and opened," the near empty chair responded.

Paul Finch thought to himself as Captain Rawlin's face appeared before him, "I'll never get used to having a ghost Entity respond to my commands," even though there was an image of a young man seated in the Communications chair.

"Captain, there is another enemy fleet incoming. We'd better finish up this business and lay out our little party favors and prepare to leave the area," Captain Rawling's looked towards his tactical officer.

Commander Happ told him, "Sir, there are eight heavy cruisers, two wagons, and four Dreadnaughts about two hours out."

"I agree, Commander. Let's join the party," Captain Rawling's said as he nodded towards his Helmsmen to bring the *Paw* directly into the aerial battle.

"Attention all Tigers," Captain Rawlings announced over the comm. "The *Paw's* coming in."

The lead pilot of the Paw's fighter group understood what was coming and ordered "Delta Seven" over the radio, which meant that all human ships were to lead their prey towards the oncoming *Paw*, whose greater fire power would easily cut the pursuers off at the knees.

"Let's lead them to the promise land," Kirk Lease told his squad.

There were four Tigers being pursued by more than a dozen of the larger Augean ships.

Following a predetermined course, Kirk brought the first Augean fighters towards the starboard side of the *Paw*, thus allowing the *Paw's* computer to track and dispatch them. Sally Leather was on weapons and she knew she'd get just one shot before the other Augean caught on and broke off their attack on the human ships.

"Sally," Rawling's said quietly, "Let's do it right the first time."

"Aye, aye, Captain," Sally said calmly figuring one or two shots per ship, and figuring where each ship would turn once the firing began.

Sailor Taylor flew the *Paw's* fighting shuttle, *Sting Ray*, a smaller version of the *Manta Ray* with an eight member crew.

Her job would be to track down any Augean ships that might try to escape. The *Sting's* greater speed and shielding would allow her to overtake and destroy the Augean before they could reach the safety of the incoming fleet. Or so she thought.

"Captain," Lieutenant Brown said, "The *Sting Ray* is breaking away according to Delta Seven."

"Thank you Lieutenant," Rawling's said. "You'd better remind Sailor to beware of the *Gladiator's* little party favors, and to keep her shields at maximum."

"Aye, aye, Sir. I'll pass the word."

The explosion nearly tore the *Paw* in two. It was like they'd hit a brick wall head on. The forward sixty feet of the *Wolf's Paw* was crushed flat. The Bridge and its entire crew were gone, crushed from bulkhead to bulkhead. There were no survivors in the front portion of the ship, yet, the shields helped to maintain the ship's integrity.

Watching over his view-screen, Commander Finch witnessed a new weapon, though he couldn't tell what it was as it remained invisible to the naked eye, and to the ships sensors.

AUTHORS BIO

SHOWN ABOVE WITH HIS SOULMATE AND WIFE, MARY ADELE

Lee Daniels is a disabled Vietnam Naval Veteran. He has suffered with multiple sclerosis since 1992, but continues his love of the unknown frontiers we call deep space.

An avid reader, he enjoys all space adventures and seeks to better understand the mysteries of his home planet, Earth.

He has written several documentaries, two dozen novels, and another twenty short stories.

He lives a quiet lifestyle in a guarded community near Beaumont, Texas.

You may comment on this book through leedbooks@hotmail.com.

Lee Charles Daniels

www.ingramcontent.com/pod-product-compliance
Lightning Source LLC
Chambersburg PA
CBHW051454170626
46811CB00002B/475